To my children, Connor and Carson,
who inspire me to fly.

BIRDS ON A WIRE

by Ellen Plotkin Mulholland

LOGOS
PUBLISHING
HOUSE

LOGOS PUBLISHING HOUSE
BERKELEY

Birds on a Wire
A Logos Publishing House book

Library of Congress Control Number: 2013913291
Mulholland, Ellen Plotkin
ISBN-10: 0989745503
ISBN-13: 978-09897455-0-5
Fiction
Printed in the United States of America

LOGOS
PUBLISHING
HOUSE

"The reason birds can fly and we can't is simply because they have perfect faith, for to have faith is to have wings."
– J.M. Barrie, "The Little White Bird"

CONTENTS

ONCE THERE WAS A BOY

TUESDAY

WEDNESDAY

THURSDAY

AFTER

ONCE THERE WAS A BOY

Wrapped inside a cocoon, the boy inhales his own stale breath, trapped within all that is himself and what could be. The bud awaiting its bloom, adrift in an embryonic journey from what was to what could be; the adolescent awaiting the man. A dichotomic weigh station. Unconscious, he hovers between two planes.

As the bed's magnetic force strengthens its hold, Matt curls within himself, unable to surface from the soft cotton layers. They own him, pull him inside their folds, accept him. The world outside falls away, the world with all its eyes, expectations. He is a bird, in an egg, in a nest. Incubating. Waiting. The crumpled sheets, flat polyester pillow he's laid his head upon since age 11, and the short boy mattress all draw him back into slumber. Not sleep exactly but a land of heaviness. This innocuous world, fortified by the gentle stir of his mother, he dozes in and out of cognition, in and out of a world where he is 11, 16 … 11, 16 … 11. He can't choose.

At once, the worlds of sleep and consciousness blur, and he's not sure which one's holding him. He turns over to check his alarm clock - 7:08. The numbers tell no lie.

"Matt!" Lee shouts from the shower behind a closed bathroom door. "Matt! You up?"

The muffled cry slithers down the hall, around the corner and inside the sixteen-year-old's blanket-encased sleepy right ear. "Up, up, I'm up," he mumbles, audible only to himself. He knows she's not expecting a response, just needs to convince herself that she's accomplished her motherly duty. It's Tuesday, the first day of finals, the final three days before summer, the summer before senior year, the year before Matt leaves, maybe, starts his own journey away from home, away from Lee. Maybe.

Lee appears in the doorway. "Up, up." Wrapped in a thinning white terry robe, her dull blonde hair dripping slightly, she moves across the room lifting scattered dirty socks, gingerly tossing them into a white wicker basket. Matt rolls up to the edge of his bed, sits Indian style, sheets bunched between his legs' meditative pool.

"Do you want eggs," she asks as she sits down beside him.

"Do you have time?"

"Oh, I wasn't going to make them, just asking, because I think there are two left on the door. I gotta dash." Lee runs her fingers through her son's blond hair feeling its Nordic thinness and noticing the tiny streaks of red forcing their way to the surface with a determined - a knowing - sense of density. "You're getting Grandpa's hair, you know."

"Yeah, I noticed that. Hope I don't turn into a complete redhead. Think by the time more red starts to come in I'll be going gray, so it won't matter?"

"I hope not. I loved your grandpa's red hair." She pauses, lets her fingers slide down his cheek. "You know, these are the years now that I never had with my folks. You get them with me. You get to see me go through menopause and get hot and sweaty and cranky. Aren't you lucky?"

Never lost, filled only with passion, covered with a film of regret. A description of Matt West? Possibly. Certainly words found within the encyclopedic narrative of his mom. Yet Lee West has never truly been lost, though she easily could have been.

The West family might seem your typical white working class types of a late twentieth century California suburb. European descent. One adult gainfully employed. One adult absent, incarcerated, or dead. Minor children in school, playing sports, obedient. Adult children in college, backpacking in Europe, working in a fast food restaurant, incarcerated, or dead. By these accounts, yes, the Wests are typical. Single working mom, father could be dead or incarcerated, but is decidedly absent, minor child in school, once played left field for the Santa Niña Indians, adult child does not exist. Matt, the only child of this young mom, endures every drop of her undying love and too much of her doting attention.

To fully understand the West lineage, one needs to move further back than just one generation. Back one more to Matt's Swedish grandfather, a professor, and still further back to his great grandfather who changed the family name from Vest before he reached America. Jan Vest, a mechanical engineer, a genius, a Tesla-could-have-been, a vodka enthusiast, who began the elbow-bending tradition of West men. Hoping for change, for a change to dry out his habits, Jan Vest made the move to America just after the turn of the century, a time when huddled masses could still huddle about Ellis Island, were still greeted no matter how tired, how wretched, how poor.

Understanding that if this move would work, would at once drain his veins, reestablish a proper blood-alcohol ratio, he must begin anew. That might mean dramatic changes.

Including his name. He didn't want people envisioning a disposable piece of accessory clothing when they looked at him. West sounded more forward thinking. After all, he was journeying to the West for a better life.

Lee's father, Johannes West, was born in the early 1930s, just in time for the Great Depression's onslaught, just in time for the party to truly begin, commencing a life of utter hardship, never knowing the meaning of calm, of abundance, of hope. With such a start, the chance of alcohol playing a minor role in this offspring seemed futile. It appeared that the West DNA had no chance of righting itself, of veering safely onto any path of truth and goodness. Hope lay in the arrival of the second American-born West generation, Lee and Janie, but their parents soon killed that (though neither girl has ever taken to the alcohol, both have found other avenues to avoid success and happiness – but this is not their story).

Hence, a final hope lay now in the third West generation born on this American soil, born in the vibrant 70s, an era of jiving hips, boogying behinds, and synthetic ensembles. A decade sitting on the revelatory heals of free-love and women's rights, laying ground for a time of Cold War and consumer orgies. A framework ripe for idealistic clashes and religious righteousness.

Change must emerge through chaos.

For Matt, the West genius has survived on a crutch, now moving through him like a crippled savant, only pausing to catch its breath upon a possible creative opportunity. If Matt is the generation to shift the destructive course of this family, he must seize his future with both hands, step inside the safety of himself, spread his wings and fly.

This boy does surely contain the potential of sheer brilliance, but due to his grandfather's obsessive desire for intoxication, he must work that much harder to unveil this Einstein-like ability to awe the world. He must work that much harder to dig out his convictions and step to the edge of the platform, fearless, ready to take flight.

Fortunately, much of his path is laid out, for Matt West has been gifted with smart, gifted with a knack for numbers, a drive for perfection. There is no doubt that he will ace his AP English exam and enter a prestigious college. However, he might never change the world like a Bill Gates or Walt Disney. He might not simply because he lacks one essential ingredient of that county fair winning recipe of DNA.

Confidence.

This boy must write his own equation if he's to change the world. He must find the right formula to reveal his own declaration; with arms open wide, Matt West must be the one to set the world aright with love, the kind of arms-open-wide love that accepts without judgment, without shame.

Lee's parents didn't make it past her 15th birthday. Heavy drinkers both and professors at the state college, they developed a habit of coming home late most Friday evenings. Late and very drunk. On those nights, Lee would lie awake in her bed, not able to sleep until she heard the slight humming of that old brown Toyota as it pulled into their gravel driveway. This she loved - the sound of the rubber tires' crunching across the rocky spread. In the end, that sound evolved into a comforting expectancy, and after the accident whenever she'd hear someone pull into the drive, she'd run to the window thinking it was them, hoping. Of course, it wasn't, couldn't ever be, but she still ran, fooling herself time and time again. Hoping.

Hope. The one thing we fool ourselves with, she'd think. *Something we use to drag ourselves through a life unfulfilled, a life that offers up possibility then tears it away.* Hope. The one thing that keeps us running to the window, clinging desperately to that single buoyant chance that perhaps everything you *knew* to be true really isn't. Perhaps everything you *hoped* to be true really is. Once she heard the engine turn off, she'd instantly fall asleep.

Lee's sister, Janie, three years older, found it easier to doze off on those expectant evenings. Janie seemed to possess an elusive patient quality unfamiliar to Lee. Both girls understood that the only time their parents moved patiently through the house occurred when they were too drunk to move their bodies quickly. It wasn't really patience but lack of muscle coordination that caused such slow, methodical movements. It was these careful, detailed, slow-motion actions that convinced Lee her parents could safely steer a car through the solitary suburban streets of Santa Niña and arrive in that gravel driveway, crunching rubber along millions of tiny pebbles.

For the most part, for seven years, approximately 350 Friday evenings, Johannes and Nancy West drove their faded brown two-door Toyota Corolla through the simple streets of Santa Niña and into the straight, 15-foot gravel-covered driveway of their three-bedroom single-story home as their two daughters lay in their single beds – one asleep, one not - listening to the engine hum then idle then shut off. As Lee allowed herself to drift off to sleep – starting from the age of eight when Janie had turned 11 and old enough to babysit (this deemed so by her parents' selfish alcoholic logic) – she imagined her parents exiting the car, walking over to the backdoor, fumbling for their house-key, unlocking and opening it and stumbling into the kitchen, shutting and locking the wooden door behind them. It was only at this point – usually around 1AM, never much later as they didn't like to stay until closing and be labeled drunks like the others – that Janie would awaken and listen as her parents moved down the hall, passing the girls' rooms and closed doors, then as an afterthought or due to miscalculated opportunistic timing, turning to pause at each one, listening and gently opening each door one at a time to peer in on them, those two sleeping angels, their quiet, docile, hopeful angels.

At this point, Lee would be asleep, never bearing witness to these tender moments, missing out on seven years, 350 Friday nights of quiet visits by these two people who loved her so much but not enough to in time stop something that would eventually kill them.

Janie, however, embraced these moments, and later as an adult replayed them over and over in her mind, seeing her parents, side by side, silhouetted by the dull hall light within the crack of the opening of her bedroom door peering in on her lovingly, gently, patiently. Their inebriation, however, impeding control, not allowing them to actually speak and say the words Janie knew they thought, *Good night, Sweetheart, we love you.* So she'd say them to herself then return in silence, *Good night, Mom. Good Night, Dad. I love you, too.*

They'd close the door gently, lovingly, patiently, continue down the hall, stumbling occasionally but never falling.

Saturday mornings, Lee and Janie would rise, clean the house – mop, dust, wash the dishes, take out the trash – and cook up scrambled eggs, toast, bacon and brewed coffee. By 11, Johannes and Nancy would find their way into the kitchen, kiss both girls on the head, thank them for cleaning and cooking, and sit down for a family breakfast. No one talked much at these Saturday morning meals.

Lee remembers them as ritualistic, kind of like a Sunday morning prayer service. Or maybe this was Lee's fabrication because in her mind that's where she believed they all needed to be those mornings, in a sacred place, praying, praying for hope because hope was not something that came naturally to Lee. She believed she needed to pray for it.

That's what she did each Saturday morning as her parents sipped their bitter coffee, nibbled on their overcooked eggs, stared out the curtained window and read the newsless weekend paper; Lee prayed over her bacon that God would grant her just one slice of hope.

Lee never remembered that last Saturday morning ritual. She would spend the next five years trying to pull out a memory of something her dad might have said that morning or something her mom might have gazed upon in her characteristically thoughtful manner, but she recalled only generic moments.

So on the following Friday night when her clock ticked past 1, past 1:15 and past 1:30, 15-year-old Lee started to search in her mind for the last Saturday morning because this was the night she'd been expecting. Seven years, 350 Friday nights later, this was the one she knew would come.

Then the knock and soon the doorbell and her sister's footsteps, a door opening, a strange man's voice, and Janie's gasps and gagging sobs. Lee knew this was it. Her parents weren't coming home. She would never again sit across the table from her father as he sipped his bitter coffee while the Saturday morning sun played quietly off the red strands of his thinning hair and his wife pushed around the cold yellow rubbery eggs on her butterfly-covered china plate and their older daughter wiped the creamy melamine countertop and Lee sat praying over her bacon for hope.

A little more than nine months later, Lee would bring home her own bundle of hope, wrapped in a tiny yellow flannel blanket with a lime green cap and a pair of eyes that stared out in wonder of this new world and the part he would play, and who he would love. And who would love him back.

TUESDAY

Once baby birds make their way from the egg, parents find no rest. These dependent fluffy beings rely solely on the adult birds to bring them food, warmth, and attention. The young are referred to as "nestlings" because they cannot leave the nest. They are "brooded" – in the care of an adult 24/7.

1

THE THREE MUSKETEERS

Sitting on the curb like birds on a wire, the three boys ponder their limited futures in Santa Niña, an ordinary town not far from Los Angeles but far enough and too far at the same time. Jesse crouches against the gutter, pokes the compacted silt with a 6-inch twig he found yesterday outside Ruby's bedroom window. Matt tosses pebbles into the road playing a game against himself, seeing which stone will survive the longest without being run over by a car. Miguel breaks the silence. He leans back on his left elbow circling the pavement with his right index finger and begins to lecture his buddies about their limited future.

"Ya know, she says if you pass Trig, you have it made. Leaves the door wide open for college, something like that. Says, 'here's a ticket outta Santa Niña, grab it and run.' Chicken shit, I say. Numbers ain't takin' me on no train ride to the American Dream. Anyway, who says that dream ain't here, right here in glorious, smoggy, hot, flat, borin' Santa Niña? Huh? Jess, you takin' Trig?"

Jesse flicks a thick patch of gutter silt up in the air, watches it crash to the ground, splinter into three unequal parts. "I dunno. Shit, it's hard to believe we're the Class o' 92. Damn, man, it's the 90s. Next year, we graduate, huh? Then, off. Off to, to, somewhere, I guess. I dunno. Trig? I suppose I'll need some kinda math skills in art school."

Miguel nods, rubs the razor-thin layer of fuzz that wraps his round head like a soft black kitten. He refuses to grease his fine Mexican mane back like his cousins; so one day, he just takes out his mom's hair trimmer and buzzes the whole thing flat, nicking himself just once above the left ear, leaving a millimeter of bald patch that will most likely never fill in.

He rolls his precious soccer ball underneath his legs as he wipes his fingers clean on the undersides of his Levi's. "Miss Thomas, what does she know about tickets to Dreamsville, anyway? Shiiit. I mean, look at her. Where is she livin', and what is she doin'? She's stuck right here in Santa Niña same as the rest of us. Oh, so, she graduated from some college in LA. Big whoop! She didn't get far. I ain't believin' nuthin' Miss Pony-Tail Thomas says about no ticket outta town. Yeah, she's in our boat and I ain't sharin' my paddle with her!"

Jesse laughs. "Pony tail! What's up with that thing anyway? I think she thinks it's sexy. Floppin' back and forth while she's got her back to us, jottin' mumbo jumbo goofy equations up on that dusty board."

"What the hey? What are you jammerin' about?" Miguel barks. "You hot on her or what? You sure seem to have that boppin' pony tail action memorized!"

"You brought it up, Big Head!" Jesse flicks a tiny pebble toward Miguel who instinctively lunges for his friend in a gentle but forceful wrestling move.

Takes him in a headlock then fakes a kiss towards him, "Ooh, Miss Pony Tail, flick your tail at me!"

He releases Jesse who quickly jabs his friend in the thigh. "Lay off, Girlie!"

Jesse pulls out his pick and cleans up his short afro.

"Oh, sorry, sweetie, did I get your jheri curl all twisted and outta style?" Only Miguel can tease Jesse in such a way.

In fact, he does it so often, Jesse's stopped coming back with any clever retorts, like 'you're just jealous of my fine African locks' or 'you jealous of the curl, little girl!'

They have just about six more minutes before the bell and their second final of the day. Art for Jesse, Psychology for Matt, and a dance final in PE for Miguel (something he's actually anticipating not dreading).

Matt ignores the adolescent ribbing and attempts to return the conversation to its topic. "So, Mig, you takin' Trig next year?"

"Nah, I dunno. I gotta work at the station. Don't know how I'll keep up." He smoothes down the creases of his jeans, stands and starts juggling the ball from one knee to the other.

"I could help you with the homework. Come on, take the course with me. I signed up. Maybe we can all get into her third period and bribe her with Three Musketeer bars." The boys laugh in unison. Three Musketeers. The moniker their secretly favorite teacher dubbed the trio freshman year at Santa Niña High, affectionately known by the locals as SNiHi. After just four days in her first period, she had them down.

By the fourth day, they had each earned a detention for passing notes. It was actually Miguel who was passing a note to Ruby for Jesse, but each of the three claimed it was his fault, so Miss Pony-Tail Thomas kept them all after school. She said she didn't care who was the guilty party, if they all wanted to take the rap, take it.

"So," she pointed at Matt. "You're the smart one. The one that actually takes notes and does the homework. And you two, you two are the goofball, girl-crazy pals who some cop won't ever get to rat on the other. Three Musketeers, eh? One for all, all for one."

"How 'bout you, Lover Boy? Ruby's takin' it, for sure. Huh? Jess, you signin' up?" Matt knows his friends too well. Been buddies ever since they were in diapers. Neither pal could ever keep up with such a high level math class, but Matt can't afford not to take it. More importantly, he can't imagine finishing up senior year without any shared classes with these two knuckleheads.

Jesse only needs five classes, and he won't take any AP except for Art. Miguel barely scraped by this year with a 2.0, and coach Vince had to twist some arms to help his star striker pass two of his classes. Whether Matt wanted to or not, his counselor would place him in all honors classes next year ('alone with all the nerds?' he'd complain to her), so Trig was the only chance to see his buds. Not that it mattered a great deal, really, he'd tell himself. Soon they'd be off in three different directions. College. The future. A blessing and a curse, in Matt's eyes. All they ever talk about is getting out of this town, but when it comes right down to it, all they really want is to have the benefits of the adult world without the worries, without the struggles. All of their families have seen their share of each.

"Probably," Jesse breaks into Matt's daydream. "Ruby'll help me with it, I suppose. Let's just all take it and share the load. Whenever one of us has to work or has a game, the others'll let us copy."

The three laugh, knowing the only paper anyone'll be copying from will be Matt's. Jesse used to copy Matt's addition facts in first grade. This is not to say either Jesse or Miguel can't flex the ole gray matter. It's simply that their interests, their priorities, lie elsewhere.

All three boys sailed through elementary school in the same classes. When there was need for a split, the boys would be chosen from the lower grade to work with the older students.

By fourth grade, though, Miguel had discovered the soccer ball, and Jesse had re-discovered a certain Ruby Newton. This left Matt to research the "group" reports, Jesse to add the artistic flair to the posters, and Miguel to amuse the class with his animated presentations (and sometimes acrobatic; just once with a biographical performance of Argentinian soccer phenom Diego Maradona). They quickly realized their individual talents and, more notably, how well they completed each other. They were indeed the Three Musketeers.

Matt, completely book smart, a true nerd, would've been a *bona fide* one had it not been for Miguel getting him to join Little League and play ball. And, Miguel? The jock, of course. The one either of the other two call on if someone's picking on them. Once, in Mr. Carney's third grade class, Miguel had to beat up Carlos Sanchez because Jesse kissed his girlfriend Leslie Taylor. And so, that leaves Jesse, the lover boy, the artist. From the time he could crawl and crawled right on over to Ruby Newton's blanket at an Orange Growers' Picnic and kissed her right on the mouth, he was labeled 'lover boy', and it stuck.

Now in the final hours of their junior year, the boys feel a tightening grip on those destined paths. It seemed only minutes ago they were seven or eight, racing each other down the venous roadways of the east end, daring the other to cut across some old man's lawn or through some mean lady's daisies. Life was simple, and what lay before them was rose-colored hope and a rainbow of adventure. Today, that landscape reels in and out of focus, vacillating between fear and hope.

Matt knows in reality he can't exactly carry his own load senior year *and* his buddies'. He envies Miguel's family loyalties, yet he worries his friend might have to tackle a few credits next summer and miss the whole cap and gown affair.

Jesse will make it. Mrs. Waters isn't about to let her number one son mess up a high school diploma. As much as she says art school is a waste of time, he knows that she and her husband plan to support their talented boy's every move.

Coach Vince will pull Miguel along, get him a tutor or something. But there's no way his high school grades will help him earn a soccer scholarship, not even to State.

Soon, just three little months sit between their youth and launch out of Santa Niña. Just a few days of junior year and another ten weeks of summer. Then senior year begins, and the dreamlike excitement of college applications turns to dreaded reality. If Matt finishes this year with straight A's (only a calculus final stands in his way), he will have a 3.97 GPA. Colleges don't care about senior year. Heck, grades don't even come out before the applications are due in November. There's still the chance for a scholarship. Still a chance one of the two dozen pennants tacked to his bedroom wall will remain. A chance that his mom'll smile and get to say, *See, Boy, I told ya that you were going to college.*

Matt pauses his musings and flashes an optimistic smile at his friends. "See, now you're talking. Okay, settled then. Just pass this class, and we'll take Trig next year. Come on, it's our senior year, we gotta end it together. On a good note."

Miguel stands, stretches, swats at Jesse's afro then fakes another jab toward his chest. "I s'pose no one'll know what hit 'em when all three of us walk the stage on our way to college."

Matt flips a stone out into the street, knocking one of Miguel's out of the way, just before a pick-up rolls in its path.

The school bell interrupts this prelude to summer break and the three slowly stand and begin their return inside the two-story structure.

Small towns like Santa Niña dot the American landscape like a child's coloring page. What makes one stand out from the other is not necessarily its location but its inhabitants. For this Southern California landlocked community, its people reflect every one of the American dreams available. It's a geographic potpourri with rolling mountains to the north, fertile farm lands to the south, a rising urban skyline in the downtown, blocks of residential neighborhoods, and an obsolete rusty railroad track that divides east and west sides into the haves and have-nots.

It boasts its own minor league baseball team, a five-block wide country club, four high schools (two public, one Catholic, one alternative) and classic cross-town rivalries in football and basketball. Like a pathogenic one-celled organism, Santa Niña has always existed and thrived on its own monotonous momentum.

If you grow up here, your parents either own some small mom and pop business, a restaurant or nail salon maybe, or they work there. A handful commute to city hall every morning hashing out small deals like big men. Unlike Mrs. Waters, few teachers actually live in town. Most commute from nearby Wellands – 'it's well because they all own the land' people joke. This neighboring community claims half the population size of Santa Niña and in no way mirrors its ethnic diversity.

If America were indeed a melting pot, Santa Niña would be the leftovers, a mosaic of broken bits of glass, a hodgepodge of culture and society where its social elite vacation on the Pacific Coast or in the nearby mountains by Pine Crest Lake. Middle Class European descendants, the ladder climbers, debate the number of signs in Spanish and argue for an official English language. On the weekends, anyone can easily spot the working class families with their birthday party jumping machines – large billowy castles or Spiderman heads – that spill over petite front lawns and slanting driveways. The social pyramid is in play, but most kids pay no attention to it at all.

Still, like most small towns, it's more a place people come *from* than move *to*. It's one of those American cities you read about in some hotshot celebrity's bio or obit:

READ ALL ABOUT IT! - After growing up in rural Santa Niña, Joe Starr found a way out. He packed a bag and hitched a ride on a local freight, swearing never to return to his childhood home. One day, though, he would return, and establish a community theater for underprivileged youth ... blah, blah, blah...

So, on the minds of most high school upper-classmen sits the question: *where will I go after graduation?*

Of course, nearly half of them won't move anywhere, except perhaps across town from their parents, settling into one of the dozen apartment complexes that crowd the southern part of the city. And why not? There's a pool, instant community, familiarity, and the opportunity to continue to squeeze cash from the folks.

Yet for Matt, the possibility of not leaving Santa Niña is simply not a possibility. So he spends the majority of his time not just dreaming but researching – most weekend afternoons Matt is holed up in the Tenth Street library, various college catalogues sprawled on the wooden table before him, his nose in an atlas, his other hand thumbing through career guides. All the while he holds two thoughts in mind – distance and money. What could be the most lucrative career, and is it too far from home?

His single mom hasn't been able to save a penny towards college. Not because she doesn't value it or want him to leave. She simply can't. Yet Matt's bedroom wall hosts a carpet of colorful team pennants from almost a hundred different colleges. Every birthday, Christmas, Easter, Memorial Day (any holiday embedded on a stationery store calendar), Matt comes home to his room, and there on the wall he finds pinned another pennant from his mom. Her way of saying, "You're going to college, Boy."

So Matt's lack of confidence owes nothing to his mother's routine support. Matt must take true credit for this burying and layering. Still, nothing can be uncovered if you don't even know it's hiding.

2

THE SHACK

"What's up, amigos? The Juice, or what?" Miguel squawks at his sluggish friends. He dribbles the black and white ball a few feet before stashing it in the Japanese Boxwood he's deemed *his spot*. His 'street locker'. He needs to push aside one of his beat-up skateboards to make room for the bi-colored sphere. He does not consider that anyone would ever think to steal the property of Miguel Alma de Ramón. This is how he sees it and convinces himself everything will always be there when he returns.

And it always is.

The afternoon sun beats down on the boys as they unwind from the long Tuesday at school. It's finals week, just a few days of junior year to go and a summer of freedom ahead.

The three friends begin the 15-minute walk from the high school down Orange Grove Road. Different in flesh, but similar in shadow, from far away, one might mistaken the three for triplets, three brothers cast from different mothers. A closer look tells a different story. The boys are an ethnic mixed salad, a sampling of what is America. More than a variation in skin tones from a portrait painter's sampler palette, their graduating hues move up the color chart; beginning with Eric's pale freckled complexion to the deeper tan of Miguel's Latin skin, and finally settling into the rich African mocha of Jesse. Their builds, typical teenage boy; standing nearly shoulder to shoulder, neither one more than 6 feet, strong broad shoulders sit solidly above their slender hips and long legs.

The difference in each falls more in their gait. While athletic Miguel settles into an almost dancer-like stride from the hips, the more sedentary artist Jesse moves from his shoulders. Matt's walk reflects his own inner confusion, sometimes a bounce, sometimes a lumber, often with his head down, hands in both pockets. Anyone in town can easily spot the friends; siblings in the shadows, distinct personalities up close.

The first to break the travelling silence, Miguel spots a turkey vulture circling over head. "Don't those things eat dead meat?" he asks.

The other two glance skyward, shielding their eyes from the afternoon sun. Jesse nods. "Yeah, they smell decaying flesh and circle above to make sure there ain't no other predators about. Then they swoop down and tear into the bloody meat. That's why they don't got feathers on their beak, so it don't get gunk in it when they're shovin' their face inside the carcass."

"Damn! Birds is disgusting," Miguel returns shaking off the shudder that runs through his body. "Think if you were a bird, you'd be a vulture, Jess?"

"No way, man, I'd be an owl, a Great Horned Owl. You know, majestic, proud."

"Hey, Daydream, what about you? You'd be some cerebral Northern European smarty pants bird. Eh?" Miguel teases Matt who still holds his hand to the sun watching the vulture lower in its circling pattern.

"Matt?" Jesse breaks into his friend's thoughts. "Whaddya thinkin'?"

"Not thinking, just watching. What'd you ask, Mig?"

Miguel rubs his right hand around his shaven head, resting his large brown palm on the hard bone that protrudes in back. "Just wondering what bird you'd be. If you were a bird, ya know. Ever thinka stuff like that when you're daydreamin' and thinkin'?"

Matt looks down from the sky, blinks away the phantom dots from the sun's glare and shoves his hands back into his jean pockets. "Yeah, sure. I guess. I think about stuff like that. Yeah. A bird, though? Well, hmm." Matt continues his stride, moving in rhythm with his pals, in step with their step, his thoughts lie elsewhere. He coughs, clears his throat, considers Miguel's random question. "I guess, maybe, well, maybe one of those swallows that leaves but returns to nest in the same place it was born. I think they travel in packs, like wolves, lots of family close by." He removes his right hand and bends down to pick up a round black stone. He juggles it in his hand then holds it up to the sky, eyeing it like some jeweler with a prized gem. Tossing it up in the air, he catches it then drops it to the ground.

"What are you, Mig? A hawk? Stealin other birds' partners and scoopin' up unsuspectin' mice from the fields?" Matt lets out a rare laugh as he nervously glances over at his athletic friend.

"Ooh, I like that. Is that me? The alpha bird!" he laughs loudly then louder. The other two can't help but join in the hilarity. "Yeah, I'm a hawk. Jess, you be the horny owl. Matt's the family guy. We ain't none of us vultures, though. I ain't eatin' some decaying flesh off of some other guy's kill. I kill my own. Eat my own. I feed my family. I take care of my own. Sabe?"

"Sabe, Amigo," Jesse offers. "We got it. You're the top bird, we're the pretty little ones that follow you around for protection." At this, they all laugh. The truth can be funny.

When the three reach Grove Court, they make a left and travel another ten yards until they arrive at The Orange Shack. Housed within a perimeter of chain-link fence, the dingy juice bar come taco stand has been a Santa Niña fixture for 60 years. Started by the Grove's owners, The Castillo family, back in the 1930s, its décor hasn't really changed. The Shack is pretty much that, a fifteen-by-twenty-foot square stucco building with an orange and white painted shingle roof. The Grove's owners built the fence around the venue to keep kids from stealing oranges off the adjacent trees that embellish the backdrop.

The surrounding grounds pale in beauty to the lush green trees that decorate the landscape most of the year. About seven round white plastic tables with attached benches sprinkle the dirt carpet, while sturdy white and orange umbrellas provide patrons necessary shade. Typically a hangout for teens after school, the Shack closes its outdoor counter window at 7 on weekdays, except for Fridays when it takes in the after sport crowd. The employees usually leave around 11 not re-opening until Monday at noon.

Some local businessmen take in a taco and Orange Swirl for a quick lunch during the week, but they know to be gone by 2 when the truants begin to show, followed closely behind by the after school crowd. Paper trays of fries and nachos soon appear atop the tables, along with narrow bottles of Orange-Ade and plastic cups of the famous Shack Swirls.

Saturday nights are a whole other story. Rumors abound of the used condom wrappers that litter the grounds Sunday mornings. Most kids, however, will tell you that the Shack is not the site of teen fornication. It's just not private enough. Pine Crest Lake is the place for those who want to go all the way. The Shack is just practice for heavy petting and juicy stories to tell your buddies the next day.

For this reason, locals have dubbed the Shack, the Juice.

And any girl who gets caught at the Juice should have known better.

A gaggle of sophomore girls giggle and preen as they down Orange Swirls and re-apply their cherry lip gloss. One slightly chubby brunette spies Miguel. She adjusts the spaghetti straps of her faded floral sundress that hides her heavy hips and amateurishly attempts coy eye contact with the handsome soccer star.

Miguel pays no attention to these "babies" as he makes his way toward the back table where Lucy Peña and Karen Gibbons sit sipping Orange-Ade from a bottle. "Hola, ladies. The fun's arrived. Let the party begin."

Karen tries to ignore him, but Lucy can't stifle her own flirtatious giggles. Miguel sits beside the vivacious Latina and pulls over her drink, holding his eye on her lips, he lifts the straw to move it then returns it to the center and takes a small sip. He licks his lips. "Yum. Nice and sweet, just like I like it."

He returns the bottle to Lucy who sucks in her lower lip before Karen lets out an "Oh, God, really Lucy. You're fallin' for that?"

Jesse and Matt join them with a tray of fries and a couple of Orange-Ades. "You seen Ruby, Karen?" Jesse asks.

"Yeah, saw her in second period doodling some jiggly J's all over her English notes," Karen returns. Jesse's never figured out why, but Karen doesn't care too much for him. Whenever opportunity offers, Karen jabs him with some undercut of a comment.

Maybe it's the whole location thing. The Gibbons reside on the other side of town, the east side, just two blocks south of the Pinewood Country Club. Because her twin brother Nate wanted to play football for SNiHi (due to its being state champs three years running), Karen had to give up attendance at Grove High. This also meant she would take the bus for the first two years until they both earned their drivers' licenses. A local business bought Nate the Camaro after he went all-state his sophomore year. Since Karen's folks said they wouldn't pay for two car insurance policies on the teens, she would have to wait on her own car. So her handsome brother ends up escorting her and her friends about. Nate doesn't mind rolling around town with a carload of pretty girls, and the girls don't mind being seen with the all-star running back and his shiny used Camaro. They don't mind at all.

At first, Jesse thought Karen didn't think he was good enough for her best friend, but then he sensed a different intent. Jesse didn't match the muscle of her studly brother, and Karen once told Ruby that she thought Jesse was 'too soft' for her. Jesse knows this because Ruby told him. She even laughed about it. Later she confessed to Jesse that she liked 'soft', and he shouldn't worry. He didn't, but he still couldn't shake his concern of Karen and her intentions to break them up.

Miguel grabs the Orange-Ade from Jesse's hands. "What's your trip, Karen. Just tell him where she is. Damn, girl, you's such a..."

Jesse quells his friend's ire. "Chill, man. It's cool. Karen's just havin' fun." Miguel eyes her coolly across the table, stretches his long arms, and taps his fingers along the underside of the plastic umbrella. In the kingdom of boyfriends and girlfriends, Jesse realizes the necessary importance of placating the best friend. He has no intention of adding to Karen's crazy list of Why Ruby Shouldn't Date Jesse.

"She'll be here soon, Romeo. She's tutoring the football team, remember, getting those lugheads ready for finals."

"Ain't your bro one o' those *lugheads*?" Miguel chimes in.

"Yeah, well, no. He's hella smarter than all of them, but he's not a fool to turn down Coach's free tutoring sessions with the cheerleaders." Another jealous point for Karen. Since she tore her ACL in cheer camp sophomore year, she's been off the squad and has had to work that much harder to maintain her popularity sans short skirts and tight sweaters. Karen isn't the prettiest, but she's sure a lot smarter than her jock brother. Jesse worries that she's that much smarter than him, too.

At that moment, the hum of a rusty red Camaro breaks through, heading down the dusty drive toward the Shack. Jesse turns in time to see Ruby's pretty smile as she exits Nate's car with about four other girls.

"Aint' you got no room for your bro's, bro?" Miguel jokes with the running back.

Nate Gibbons stretches one long muscular left leg out of the driver's side, followed by its twin then pulls himself up, turning to Miguel. "Only room for the ladies, man, only room for the ladies." He flashes his toothy grin and the girls giggle on cue.

Jesse senses a fire moving up his spine which soon settles into the backs of his eyes. He's conflicted with the spark Ruby ignites in his schoolboy loins and the hatred Nate enflames in the jealous veins pumping across his bony chest. Miguel detects the demon rising within his friend and tries to break the tension with a change of subject.

"Ruby, ya know you shouldn't be seen with that rusty old beast...I mean *in* that rusty old beast," he laughs. Proud of his novice humor, Miguel turns to Jesse and slaps his pal on the back and whispers, "Don't worry, bud, he ain't nuthin'. We got this."

Swallowing a soggy lump of Orange-Ade and pride, Jesse decides to play along. "Eh, Mig, don't be so hard on the star's wheels. We ain't got any. Maybe one day he'll see fit to chauffeur *us* about." He smiles Nate's way.

Nate rubs off a bit of dust from the left front fender with his knee. "Ha, yeah, that's a good one Picasso." He moves toward the group. "Let's see, roll around the town with pretty girls," he glances over at Ruby, "or pick up a group of cheapass skaters and would-be jocks? Yeah, I think I'll stick with the pretty girls."

Miguel pumps his chest and pushes Jesse aside moving in toward Nate. Ruby steps in, "Don't take the bait, Mig. Come on, he's been hit on the field too many times. He don't think straight. Let it go." She grabs hold of Jesse's hand and uses their bodies to guide Miguel away from the table.

Jesse rests his hand on Miguel's shoulder and whispers, "Thanks, bud, but he's an ass. Jus let it be." He looks back over his shoulder at Karen who's smirking as she stares up at her big brother. "Let it go. This time."

Miguel shakes off his fury and retrieves a bird-bitten orange from the ground. He tosses it in the air a few times, catches it then hurls it deep into the orchard. "Damn Thunderhead!" he mutters. "We shoulda never let him cross the tracks. Stuck-up muscle man needs to stay on his side o' town. And he can take his bitchy little twig of a sister with him."

"Drop it, Mig. Yeah, he's an ass. Whatever."

The three bend open the loose wires along the middle of one section of fence and climb through into the orchard. Miguel first, then Jesse who holds back the stiff material for Ruby.

"Why thank you, Lancelot," she smiles.

Jesse gently lays the fence back in place and joins the other two inside the grove of sweet smelling orange trees. "Ya think Nate's good enough to go pro?"

"Nah, his ego's stronger than his skills," Miguel returns. "He's just a big fish in a little smelly SNiHi pond. He's gonna end up in his dad's cement business, you'll see."

"I dunno," Ruby interrupts. "I heard the coach talk to him

about some scouts coming out to training this summer. I think there's some big plans for him. Karen says her dad's been writing to colleges up in Michigan and Illinois. He's buckin' for a scholarship."

"Shit, girl, not every high school star turns pro. Look how many college teams there are compared to the pros. It's like an oil funnel; you catch all the drips from the engine then drop it all into that big white bucket then that gets dumped into some old landfill or somethin'. That's where your musclehead chauffeur is goin', to some football landfill." Miguel pulls a leaf off a low-hanging branch and laughs.

"Don't swear at my girl," Jesse breaks in.

Ruby grabs onto his left arm and runs her fingers along his thin biceps. He tries to flex. She laughs and holds him tighter. They travel further inside the Grove then stop near a pile of cracked buckets and torn canvas tarp. Jesse takes hold of Ruby's soft hand and swings it slightly. He looks over at Miguel.

"You cool, Miggy?" Miguel fakes a punch at the closest tree.

"Yeah, I'm cool. That sack o' muscles just pisses me off, man. Damn, I just wanna kill the mutha - !"

"Uh, that doesn't sound cool," Ruby breaks in. She squeezes Jesse's hand and nods over at Miguel who is now running his hand along a branch of leaves watching as several fall from the tree and float to the ground.

"I'm cool, I'm cool," Miguel returns as he gently kicks at the fallen leaves. Two crows sit on a tree top. *Caw. Caw.* "Caw, caw! Scat, dirty birds. Shoo!" Miguel shouts from below. "You know, I hear crows circle death, like an omen or sumthin'. You hear that?"

Jesse laughs. Ruby squeezes his hand tighter.

Miguel sets his hands in his back pockets and returns his gaze skyward toward the opening in the tree tops. "I'm as a cool as a summer breeze." He closes his eyes, inhales deeply through his nostrils, and exhales.

"You still doin' those meditation classes with Coach Vince?" Ruby asks.

Miguel opens his eyes and squats down to the ground, rubbing his fuzzy skull. "Yeah, some. But it only works when I remember to think of it. When I get pissed, when someone like that sack o' muscles trips my switch, I dunno, a fire just sparks in me, and all I want to do is kill someone."

"Damn, Mig, that's kinda intense," Jesse leans back on a tree.

Miguel snorts. "Yeah, it is, huh. That's me. Live Wire Miguel. Set the World on Fire Miguel. That's me. What can I say."

"You've come far, though, Miguel. You have. I think that wire, that spark, is diffusing a bit. Don't you?" Ruby moves from Jesse and bends down next to Miguel.

He looks up at her as Jesse watches. "Yeah, I have. Thanks, Rube."

Ruby stands up and moves back to Jesse. She takes his hand. "You guys are lucky to have each other. I mean, friends help you through rough stuff. It's a real good thing." She smiles at Jesse.

"I suppose," he smiles back. "But girlfriends are nice to have around, too." Jesse plants a small kiss on Ruby's soft lips. She returns it. For a minute, for Jesse, it's just the two of them. Miguel, Nate, Karen, they're all miles away. Just his girl and the sweet scent of oranges own his senses. He caresses Ruby's fingers as he concentrates on cooling his own excitement.

A warm afternoon wind lightly blows through the Grove, tickling the tiny green leaves on the tops of the orange trees, disturbing several piles of raked dry leaves on the Grove's floor. Another family of crows darts out from a distant hideout, soar above the trees and circle their way back down atop a telephone line that stretches along the diameter of the Grove then splinters likes spokes to the perimeter. About three or so of these thick birds sit upon one wire, observing the scene below. One moves its claws down the line, cawing, edging for a better vantage to spy a ladybug, spider, or mouse. Plenty of these predator-prey insects claim refuge within the sweetly scented dense orchard of trees. Local growers recently debated the effectiveness of pesticides on their crops. However, one cannot discount the benefits of nature's own natural defenses. The ladybugs eat the aphids, the spiders eat the ladybugs, and the birds eat the spiders. Unfortunately, the birds, such as these crows, also enjoy nibbling on the tangy orange peels.

To address this latter issue, workers hang tin can lids throughout to reflect the sunlight and deter these tiny top predators. It seems to do the job of discouraging the birds from hanging out much longer than necessary after eating an insect or two. Some brazen crows, however, or other larger feathered creatures, aren't daunted by something shiny. In fact, the sparkle often attracts the birds more than it distracts them.

Ruby releases Jesse's hand, "Dang, I left my backpack in the sack o' muscles' car. He better not take off with it. I still have my own studying to do. I gotta head back over there. You cool, Miguel?"

"I'm cool," he says and stands and stretches.

She smiles, kisses Jesse's cheek then squeezes Miguel's shoulder. "You're a good friend, Miguel, but don't let Nathan get to you. He just talks, like on the field. That coach has those players so pumped up with their egos, it's like running down hill. They've built up such speed during the season that they can't stop the train at will. Jesse's right, he ain't worth it." She turns, "Oh, wow." Ruby suddenly realizes how far into the

Grove they've wandered. "Geez, I've never been this deep in before. I hope I can find my way out." She giggles. "I might need to leave some bread crumbs."

"I'll walk you back," Jesse gallantly offers.

"No, babe, I got this. I'm just kiddin'. I can find my way by the sweet scent of garlic fries and Axe," the three smirk at the aromatic teen mixture. Ruby kisses Jesse again, this time on his right ear lobe, and turns back toward the Shack.

Jesse follows her shapely silhouette as Ruby winds her way through the fragrant orange trees. He imagines himself the majestic Great Horned Owl soaring high above the Grove and following his sweetheart along her path like Red Riding Hood on her way to Grandma's. Of course, he knows who's the big bad wolf in this play. The thought strikes a chord deep inside Jesse, and he turns back to Miguel after having lost sight of his girl who he trusts will make a safe return to the Shack.

Jesse kicks the dirt, remembering why they travelled inside the Grove in the first place. "That Nate. He's too high up on his perch. He needs to fall a little."

Miguel has returned to knocking leaves from a nearby tree and is tearing them into tiny pieces, blowing them upward then watching them fall to the ground. "Yeah, his sister ain't one for trustin' either."

"Wait, where's Matt?" the sudden awareness of just two amigos finally dawns on Jesse. "Let's head back. He ain't no match for muscle."

"I doubt thick neck would take a swipe at Matt. Wouldn't go well for his rep, ya know. Nate Gibbons decking Matt West is the ultimate *pick on someone your own size* bit, don't ya think?" Miguel laughs. Still, sensing his pal's guilt, he agrees to turn back to the Shack. "Did you hear her call him Nathan?"

"Ay, you kids, you ain't s'posed be in here. Out! Out! *Largo de aqui!*" A grove worker shouts at the pair.

"*Calma, hombre*, we goin', we goin'," Miguel returns.

The man pulls his dusty cap from his head and twists it in his hands. He whacks it against his knee letting a cloud of dust fly into the air. He spits, places the cap back on his head, grabs his bucket and walks further into the Grove.

Jesse and Miguel resume their journey out toward the Shack, following the aroma of fries and Axe.

When they arrive, most of the tables sit empty but for half-drunk bottles of Orange-Ade and a few stray fries and puddles of Ketchup. Matt leans against the Shack wall near the bathrooms, finding shade under the shingled overhang. "Hey, where'd you guys go? One minute I'm in the bathroom, the next Nate Gibbons is talkin' smack about Jesse, and you two are nowhere."

"Hey, sorry, man, I had to walk off hothead here. That thick-necked Gibbons pushed one too many Mexican buttons," Jesse laughs and lightly punches his Latino pal in the shoulder. "Didn't you hear the crap he was layin' on us? Weren't you sittin' there when he drove up with Ruby?"

"Nah, I was talkin' to Ricky over at the counter. I was, uh, thinking maybe I could get a little part-time job here or somethin', help pay for college apps and all, you know." Matt moves toward his friends who are sitting around a cracked table that's lost its decorative umbrella. The sun has begun to set behind the Grove and the June air has cooled to a tolerable 85. "Let's head out. It's about 5, I think, and I need to vacuum before my mom gets home and does it herself. We gotta start studying for finals and all, too. You can tell me the story on the way home."

Jesse turns toward the parking lot, or what is a cleared circle of dirt for cars. He notices no rusty red Camaro. Thinking Ruby is in the bathroom, he asks Matt if he saw her come out of the

Grove.

"Yeah, she was talking to Karen when I came back to the table. She mentioned something about letting Karen copy her English notes. I think Nate gave them a ride to the library." Matt picks at the cracked plastic table top. "She said to tell you to call her. I guess she didn't realize how late it was."

"You saw her get in his car?" Jesse can't even say Nate's name. The fury resurges inside him. This time it emanates from the pit of his belly. "Are you sure?"

"Yeah, pretty sure," Matt looks over at the empty lot, trying to evoke an imaginary replay screen. Then he turns back to his friend, "Yeah, positive. You worried? About that big lug? Don't waste your time, Jess. He's a jerk. Too dumb for Ruby. She's just takin' advantage of the wheels. Karen's her best friend. It's probably just a matter of convenience."

Jesse stands, arches his back and twists his neck, listening to the crackle of small bones. He shoves his thin fingers inside his jean pockets and purses his thick lips. "Damn, OK. Don't know why I worry. He's just so damn cocky. That Karen, she, she gets on my nerves."

Intently observing a red fire ant crawl purposefully across the dirt on a determined mission to the sticky pool of orange nectar sitting at the base of the broken umbrella stand, Miguel reaches his left foot out and stamps the insect. "Don't worry, man. We got your back. Matt's right. Ruby's too smart to fall for a Dumbo like Nate, and I'm bettin' he's smart enough not to mess with my best friend's girl." He cracks his knuckles and pounds the table top once. "Let's bounce, boys. I can smell Mama's frijoles boilin'. Gotta get home and get me some fuel for this belly." He drum rattles his flat gut, grins, jumps up and leads the journey back home across the tracks.

Matt refolds the Shack application and secures it in his back pocket. He looks up at the counter and sends a thank you wave to Ricky. Turning to take in the whole scene, Matt imagines himself wiping down sticky table tops while his classmates lounge and gossip. Could he really handle serving people he goes to school with? he wonders. Sure, he can. Ricky'll show him the ropes. Besides, he'll be a senior. Seniors are untouchable.

If anyone does try to mess with him, there's always Miguel. He slaps his friend on the back. "What would we do without you, Miggy?" Matt laughs.

"You'd be lost, boys, totally lost," he jumps slightly and fakes a kick at some imaginary soccer ball. Jesse pretends to return it. "Lost, and probably spending a lot of time in the emergency room."

The three laugh and continue the back and forth dribbling and passing of one imaginary soccer ball that can never go out of play.

3

THE HAWK

Locating the ball and board within the shrub, Miguel hops on his wheels and cradles the soccer ball in the nook of his right elbow as he rolls home up Pine then down Eighth. Pumping the pavement with his left foot, he gathers speed and engages his hips to swerve and loop along the quiet evening neighborhood streets of the Numbers. A black crow caws and glides above his head. Miguel takes the invitation and pushes harder, gathering more momentum, zooming ahead of the ignorant bird that takes a sudden dive right in a hunt for its evening meal.

He rumbles into the smooth drive just in time to help his mother carry in groceries from the car. Miguel doesn't refer to the car so kindly. *The Beast*, he calls the dented silver 1982 Suzuki that Al sold his family for 200 bucks after the owner fled the country due to immigration issues. The man had brought *The Beast* into Al for new front tires and a radiator leak. Al told Miguel that if he paid for the parts, he could have it.

Since then (about a year and a half ago), Manuel has brought The Beast in three more times. Each time, Al charges only for parts and provides Miguel lessons in auto mechanics to boot. Al's plan is to have Miguel ready to pass his mechanics license by the time he earns his diploma. "Not a bad thinga to fall back on, little man," he reminds Miguel who says he'd rather cart illegals across the San Diego desert than fix rich folks' cars the rest of his life.

Al laughs. "Yes, I wasa young and naïve once too, mya friend."

"Mijo, grab those bags by the back door. Aye, my back. You're so good to your mama, Mijo." Miguel's mother takes hold of his cheeks and kisses him square on the lips. He blushes, rolls his eyes and drops the two brown paper grocery sacks on the cold tile countertop by the fridge.

"Ah, Ma, come on, you have to stop. What if someone sees? I'm not seven anymore Mama. *Sabe*?"

"I know, Mijo, I forget. You're a man, yes, like your papa. Hey, you can take him now, you know?" She jabs Miguel in his side and they both share a conspiratorial giggle.

"I coulda taken him long ago, Mama. He's a pussy -"

"Eh!" The slap arrives hard on his round head, never his face. "Watch your mouth, Mijo, or I'll get that sissy father of yours to deal with you. *Dios mio*." She mumbles further in her native Spanish tongue then starts unpacking the groceries, chastising herself about forgetting to buy melon or something. Miguel wanders into the family room and switches on the TV.

He settles on the worn brown corduroy couch and surfs channels until he finds a Dodger game. The 1990s don't offer the plethora of cable stations that would be available in ten years, which benefits Miguel's instinctively lazy intentions from having to surf more than 20 channels to locate the closest professional ball team. While Santa Niña boasts a Minor League team, the LA Dodgers tend to find a loyal following in towns within a 100-mile radius. Such is true for Miguel's hometown. Rooting for LA teams allows residents to play out their fantasy that they live close to Hollywood. Blue and white

Dodger caps adorn every other boy's head while the occasional argument erupts between sporadic Angels fans.

Tossing the remote next to him, Miguel folds his arms behind his head. He considers the events at the Shack this afternoon, big-headed Nate Gibbons, his wheels, the girls, Jesse. Something's not right. He senses the fire burning, smoldering low in his gut.

He rubs his left hand around and around his skull, feeling the bones that protrude and dive within his structure. He laughs, thinks to himself: *Nate's got a big head, but that don't mean a bigger brain.*

Miguel flips the channels with his other hand not releasing the grip that rests on his head like a winter hat. He closes his eyes, weary from a day at school listening to teachers, taking tests and navigating the halls of his youth. Not the most popular junior at SNiHi, Miguel does command the attention of most underclass girls and quite a few of his coed peers. He was even invited to the Senior Prom by Jennifer Garcia, but he had to make up a lame excuse because there was no way he could afford the $80 ticket, split the limo and rent a tux on the measly sixty bucks he brings home each week from Al's.

He told her he had to spend time with his dying grandmother, family stuff. And, of course, any respectable Latina would not dare push herself above *la familia*. Jennifer said she understood, smiled, and planted a right juicy one on the unsuspecting full lips of Miguel. He did not resist; in fact he took the suggestive move as an open invitation. The next weekend after his Saturday afternoon win against the Wellands Sure Shots, spying Jennifer in the stands, Miguel proffered his own invitation to the Shack later that evening. One thing led to another, an unattended bathroom created the necessary haven for two impassioned teens, and Miguel learned that evening that he had just been seduced by an older woman. Much older.

Jennifer had repeated the third grade and had just celebrated her 19th birthday two days prior. This was pure icing on the cake of Miguel's Condom Conquests (his term, which referred to the stack of flattened Trojan boxes in his underwear drawer).

Matt took issue with his buddy's tally marks. "They're not conquests, Mig, they're girls. People. Someone's daughter."

"Yeah, yeah, but I'm safe, hombre. Papa always says 'no glove, no love'. So, I got the glove, show me the love, pretty mama."

Matt shakes his head knowing nothing he says could ever change the mind of his horny friend.

Miguel suddenly remembers the strange feeling that bubbled inside him when Matt told them earlier today that Ruby had left the Shack with Nate and Karen. Another gurgle rumbles in his belly.

"Hey, Mama, we got any chips?"

Miguel's mother either ignores or truly does not hear her son's request, busy shelving and organizing the few purchases her housecleaning wages allow. She bends down and pulls open the Lucite vegetable bin at the bottom of their single door Frigidaire. Pushing aside neglected oranges, she rolls them around looking for signs of mold. Spotting some white fuzz on one, she sighs, heaves up her round body lifting the entire bin with it and carts the container and its contents to the sink. Carefully, she pulls out each piece of fruit and places it in the porcelain sink. She reaches for her scrubber, turns the faucet to lukewarm and gently massages each orange until it glistens like a newly plucked jewel from the tree. She sets the four items in the drain rack and begins work on the bin. Squirting some blue detergent inside, she scours the ridged sides and bottom, rinses and sets the newly christened container on the rack above the fruit.

Taken to a cleaning mood, Francesca hums "La Nave Del Olvido", occasionally allowing a lyric or two to float past her lips and into the air, *Espera un poco, un poquito más* ...

Finding nothing else to clean or disinfect, Francesca returns to unpacking the groceries and re-organizing and sorting her pantries. She shakes a box of Corn Flakes, estimating maybe half a cup, no more, and considers tossing it out, but then she looks further into the cupboard, seeing no other cereal and knowing her son's voracious appetite, she sets the cardboard container back inside the pantry and shuts the door. *Espera, aún me quedan alegrías para darte...*

Although Manuel adds a few pennies more with his stockroom earnings at a local grocery warehouse, the Alma de Ramóns can't afford to throw out even a half-cup of corn flakes.

If someone wanted an exact definition of working class American immigrants, they would not need look much further than 511 Eighth Street. Dozens of two-bedroom craftsman bungalows sprinkle the curbs of the Numbers on the west side of town, sharing front yards and backyards due to absent or mangled fences. A clothesline begins at 322 and extends across the property line of 324. White sheets whip in the wind alongside striped boxers, cloth diapers, and a teenage girl's glitter top. A toddler's big wheel lies tilted after running through its neighbor's marigolds and into a wicker swing that sways in the shade of a quiet back porch. A passing breeze gently rocks a few empty beer cans that sit beside dirty lollypop sticks. A circle of black ants make good the rest of the sugary flavorings.

It's clear which homes wish they could land themselves across the tracks. Their manicured 10-foot square front lawns rest within tightly secured chain-link fences and sport decoy home security signs clearly visible, daring potential intruders to question their authenticity. These wannabes often sit beside more modest abodes whose sherbet paint layers peel pathetically over one another, playing a DIY game of hide and seek. A frothy mint reveals a lemon chiffon, or a dusty rose hides shyly behind a vibrant lavender. Bright colors vainly attempt to mask their occupants' ebbing anxieties.

While east end drivers might mistaken these tiny homes for weigh stations to a better life, most Santa Niña residents know better. They know the truth. The American Dream can begin and end on the numeric streets of this desert valley town. The Numbers, as the locals scathingly refer to them. Really, it's not such a bad thing. It's a home, sometimes a car, most definitely a family, food in the fridge, employment (minimum wage, often two jobs per adult), church on Sundays, beer and family and friends on Saturdays. The Numbers. El barrio. This was Manuel's dream. He would stay. His wife would work for *las brujas*.

The Alma de Ramón and Peña families both arrived from Mexico at the end of the 1960s, shortly after Ted Kennedy's Immigration Act passed. Manuel Alma de Ramón and high school sweetheart Francesca Peña, both 16, planned to marry in California and start their American family, their American Dream. Finding Los Angeles too expensive, the families secured jobs in the orange groves of Santa Niña. Pooling incomes and savings, the two clans managed to purchase a single-story two-bedroom home on Eighth Street. These longtime friends shared the two bedrooms between the six of them, and soon Francesca was pregnant with her first child. The baby girl (Lina) died shortly after birth due to breathing complications.

Sure that Francesca had infected the baby while breathing in toxic pesticides from the orchards, the Peñas begged everyone to return to Mexico. Manuel refused, saying no work awaited them. He managed to find employment with a large supermarket chain stocking shelves in the warehouse.

Francesca didn't like the late hours (he worked 10PM to 6AM). Manuel assured her it was only temporary and that soon he would start taking classes at the city college and earn a certificate in automotive maintenance, but the long hours turned into overtime and Manuel's intentions faded as the family struggled from paycheck to paycheck. By the time Miguel arrived in 1974, the elder family members had returned to Sonora and the capital city of Hermosillo where the men found jobs at the Ford plant and the women returned to working in the posh hotels that catered to wealthy American businessmen.

Manuel and Francesca took over the house payments at 511 Eighth Street, which meant Francesca (five months pregnant) needed to find a way to contribute to the family's small income. She easily found work with a group of sisters she had met at Our Lady of the Rosary Cathedral on Grove Street. Louisa, Trina, and Juanita. *Las tres brujas*, Manuel called them.

"Stop, Manny. They are nice ladies and they give me good work. Because of them - *las brujas!* - we can stay in America, we can raise our *hijo, dulce hijo. Dulce Miguel. La luz de mi corazon.*"

"I know, I know. It's a joke, *mi bella. Una broma*," Manuel would reply, knowing in his heart that she was right. If they returned to Mexico, life would change. No. Life would revert, revert to a stagnant pool. He would not achieve his American Dream. He would not achieve his Mexican Dream.

Ha! That's a joke, Manuel thought. There is nothing to dream for him there. He had bought into the fairytale of this new land, he had seen the carrot of possibility dangle before his desperate immigrant eyes and grasped for it, reached for it, lunged for it.

Still, he told himself that he would realize this dream of comfort, of plenty, of possibility. Manuel Miguel Alma de Ramón would show them all. A life can move forward. A pond can evolve into a running brook. Yes, it can. Yes, it must.

As is typical of the immigrant youths born in a new land, gratitude lies dormant in their young souls, waiting to emerge in adulthood, choosing the right moment to appear as on a stage before an adoring crowd. To wit – Miguel Santiago Alma de Ramón has lived his entire 17 years in Santa Niña, California, vaguely oblivious to his parents' and grandparents' sacrifices to get him here.

He sits inside their west end home, feet upon a second-hand wood-veneer coffee table, arm resting comfortably on a thrift-store couch and tongue joyfully taking in the flavorful salt of several tangy chips purchased by the hard-earned laboring of his housecleaning mother and stockroom clerk father. First-generation Mexican-American. Miguel knows this, and he would never miss a moment to help his family (the reason he works at Al's changing oil and tires after school on Wednesdays and Fridays and after church on Sundays); yet at this moment of his journey, Miguel finds his thoughts caught within envy and resentment. He cannot smell the apple pies from his Eighth Street domicile, cannot see the varying shades of peeling gray paint underneath the eaves and alongside the smooth window frames of the multi-storied homes, cannot hear the hum of lawn mowers and leaf blowers operated by his Latino brethren, cannot see their sweat dripping down their brown brows, cannot hear their own hearts' lament of what is and what is not.

Miguel's teen angst rests beneath bitter layers. But Miguel is not stupid. He takes this anger and serves it up like fire on a platter out on the soccer field. Each kick, each steal, each swipe at a goal knocks down one more east end home, squashes one more apple pie, destroys one more neatly trimmed rose bush. Envy sparks a fire deep within Miguel's soul, fuel for his future, kindling for his dreams. Not the American Dream or the Mexican Dream. Miguel Santiago Alma de Ramón's Dream.

Three Golden Boots rest proudly on the Alma de Ramón mantle. 1989. 1990. 1991. His mother has already moved them an inch or two to the left to make room for one more. She does this not with a parental expectation but with a mother's belief in her son. A fine line, perhaps, but a line nonetheless. However, every time Manuel passes the fireplace, he moves them back that inch or two, playing a game of chess with his wife, with his son's future.

"To expect success is to be disappointed. To achieve success with humility is to be inspired," the elder tells the younger. Then he turns to his beloved wife. "To believe in our future is to be inspired. To expect and plan for such a future lacks humility in Him," and he points a finger upward.

"I understand *mi amor*, I believe in the grace of God Almighty. I do. But I also believe in the grace of my son's almighty left foot!" and she hugs Miguel who can't help but hug back his adoring mama.

"Aye, *Dios mio*, you are going to make his head blow up like a Goodyear Blimp." Manuel pulls his wife away from their son and gives Miguel a gentle kick in the pants.

Miguel would do anything to realize his mother's hopes for him. He would. Yet every hour spent draining dirty oil from an impatient owner's German motor is another hour off the field. There lies his resentment. There rests his anger, quietly swirling down hundreds of blue plastic funnels into the vast emptiness of an infinite row of white barrels. Emptying but not filling. Destined to an unfulfilled future. Miguel watches, mesmerized, as the oil runs quickly out of the engine, then slowly dripping, then dropping and dropping and nothing and dropping and nothing and nothing and droppppinggg...

The painstaking anticipation of the final drop of dirty, used, polluted grease stirs within him a whirlpool fraught with envy. Miguel, lost in the waiting, becomes the oil moving like a slug through a mud patch, inching his way to this plausible destination, fueled only by an internal desire, void of his own motor, helpless, hopeless, dependent on nature, on this earth's gravity, the laws of physics, of viscosity. Momentum has carved the path, but it is gravity that guides the lubricant's destiny into the barrel.

Miguel's parents make up one half of his momentum; Miguel's dream to get out of this dusty town completes it. A slave now to the laws of physics, Miguel can only hope, pray, anticipate without expecting that he will fulfill his destiny. He will be the player on the field inside the TV that others root for, for whom others cheer. They will wear his number in reverence. They will shout his name with idolatry. They will place his likeness on a pedestal. They will say *there is a boy who became a man who defied the laws of physics and created his own path with a surprising internal momentum that brought him to his destiny.* Despite the uphill climb, notwithstanding the laws of gravity, this boy, this man would move out and upward toward a final unforeseen destination.

Often, just a few years back when Manuel found himself stuck on the overnight stocking shift, a shift he'd not anticipated to be part of for ten years, he would return home in the evening, quietly entering his own home like a cat burglar, hoping not to disturb the occupants, trying desperately to unlock, open, and shut his own door without allowing one click to echo down the hallway or around a corner, under a doorway, awakening his beloved or his heir. Despite his intentions, his naïve expectations, that the stockroom would be a temporary situation, Manuel celebrates his 18th year with Bag Town this October. Of course, he is the floor manager now, and he no longer clocks in and out while the sun is down.

However, Manuel enjoys no family dinner during the week; he misses out on all those conversations with his son about practice or an upcoming game or a cherry new Mercedes in the shop; he does not catch-up with his beloved about their family south of the border or a suspicious red stain on one of her client's living room rugs; he cannot help clear the table or wash the dishes. By the time such activities are complete, Manuel arrives home. His noon shift ends at 8, and he returns to his casa on the 8:22 51 Bus by 8:50. As his family prepares for bed, Manuel cracks open the first of what will usually be 5 or 6 Budweisers, settles with the remote in front of their 15-inch Philips TV, tunes into a predictable sit-com and tunes out his unfulfilled dreams.

Eventually, Manuel joins his beloved in bed around 2, relishes several hours of warmth, rarely anything more than spooning or cuddling before Francesca must begin her own preparation for ten hours of mopping, dusting, and vacuuming at a variety of east end homes.

This is his American Dream realized. No one told Manuel Alma de Ramón that his dream had stopping points, that his dream began in one generation and might not find completion for generations to come. Sometimes, in between beer pulls or during more lucid moments in his worn recliner, Manuel sighs satisfaction. This differs from his sighs of resignation or desperation or bitterness. Satisfaction sighs indicate he accepts, owns and takes comfort in the movement he has made for his grandchildren and unforeseen great-grandchildren, that a realized dream exists.

"If you want to reach the top shelf, you must use a ladder; if you don't own a ladder, you must build one." Manuel revels in sharing such pearls of wisdom with Miguel. And, unlike some indifferent immigrant sons, Miguel listens to his father. He listens and often he understands.

"Your dream must fill your heart, my son. But you must work to be a man, not simply a slave to this dream. There must be more," Manuel shares in his native tongue. "Life is a basket of many, not a single goal in a net. There is family, there is friendships, there is life. There are generations ahead of you, future Miguels who sit in wait for the ladder to reach them. The dream should not be the goal; the dream must be the journey."

Manuel is building a ladder. The question remains – can Miguel endure in the building, or will his narrow goals cause him to topple to the ground?

Such an anticipation and expectation hangs around Miguel's brown neck like an Albatross. But he tugs at this wait, eager to rip it from his neck so that he may soar higher. When Miguel looks deep inside himself, he sees a predatory bird, a bird that fights for what is his right, like a hawk that spreads its strong and steady wings over the landscape and narrows its vision down upon each section of dirt, each shadow and crevice, and dives down gathering speed like a missile, frightening innocent creatures who circle the same unlucky rodent or snake for its own family needs. Miguel cares nothing for their dreams. If his are to be realized, he will need to soar higher.

Miguel understands his father's dream – what he could not achieve, he wants for his son; but Miguel is also committed to realizing his own dream. He will do this for his father, for his mother, for his children yet unborn. Still, one other question burns a hole in this young boy's heart: *Can he complete the ladder with his wild left foot, or will he need to abandon his dream for his father's?* Will he simply become his father, living a life unfulfilled, stuck in the third rung of an endless climb?

El sueno. El sueño del padre es la carga del hijo. The father's dream is the son's burden.

4

THE COLORS OF LOVE

West end homes of Santa Niña resting close enough to the abandoned railroad tracks sit in silent envy of their east end neighbors. Homes close enough to tease at what could be, like the popular girls dressed for the prom who flaunt their tulle and satin at the quiet wallflowers, the girls in hand-me-down polyester and rayon who no one asks to dance, who no one thinks want to dance, can dance. These homes, on the other side, sit under the same brand of paint, the same number of coats, the same hours of sweat. The difference in application rests only in the hand that applies it – one, the hand of the homeowner, the other, the hand of a day laborer. The same hand of a man who happens to live on the west side, the rough side.

Sometimes, however, that hand that owns a home on one side and paints the homes on the other side can stand in line at a grocery or bank or post office undetected, undercover. Sometimes, not even the keenest eye can distinguish an east end homeowner from a west end homeowner. Sometimes that man just fits in. Sometimes a man is more than his zip code lets on. Sometimes, when a man's skin is light enough, his crosstown neighbors don't notice any difference at all.

Such is the truth of Harold Waters, a light-skinned African

American bank manager who happens to own a home with railroad tracks running down his street, a homeowner who can sit on his porch on a Sunday afternoon reading the paper and smell the apple pies baking in the other zip code homes, a kind and gentle man who knows his bootstraps are worn from tugging and whose hands are calloused from pulling and, despite all this, whose heart remains filled with love and compassion for the apple pie bakers, the day laborers, the bank customers with private keys and those with the complementary blue vinyl checkbooks. Harold Waters is the other American Dream, the one that lets you pass go and collect $100. And that's OK with Harold.

Harold grew up in the same First Street home where he now raises his two children and stands by his wife Amelia as she kneads dough for her third grade students' Father's Day gifts that they will form and bake and decorate for their apple pie-baking parents. Amelia and Harold have done well, and they know it. Things could have been very different. But they weren't. They're lucky.

Harold hadn't always wanted to work in a bank. He wanted to be an artist. Ever since he had seen his father lovingly apply a new coat of robin's egg blue to their modest two-bedroom bungalow; ever since he marveled as his mother handed his father an iced tea, dabbed a few specks of paint off his forehead, and cooed in his ear, "You are the Michelangelo of Santa Niña, Baby, and this is the Sistine Chapel. You're an artist, Marty, a true artist."

Martin Waters raised his three boys hoping they'd all follow him into his house painting business. He had the sign *Waters & Sons* primed and sitting in his basement ever since the day Harold joined the family as Wayne's little brother. *Waters & Sons* was realized when Wayne turned 15 and joined his father on weekends painting the homes of the apple pie bakers. Two years later, Harold put on his own latex gloves and joked alongside his dad and brother as they lathered another east end house with the acceptable gray or white, the undeclared uniform of neighboring homes who don't dare try to stand out in the frosting colors that peel off of the smaller wallflower abodes across the tracks. Homes like the Waters'.

When Harold's baby brother Winston was born, Harold and Wayne were Tadpoles and Polliwogs in Miss Julia Ray's preschool. Cecile would tease her husband, saying things like, "You are going to need to paint a mansion to feed these mouths" or "We'll need to stuff their Christmas stockings with brushes and oil cloths so they are well set to work when they enter high school".

Martin would laugh and tease back, "Oh this is a good brood, Cecile. These are fine boys. We are going to be *Waters & Sons*, and we will make you proud. You'll see. We are going to win contracts for every mansion around that silly old country club. You'll see, Baby. We will make you proud."

And they would hold each other and watch their three boys wrestle and tug one another out on their patch of patchy grass under the blazing Santa Niña sun while a ghost line of a railroad track ran down their street like a taunting wall reminding them of where they stood.

Martin Waters died four years ago. Fell off a ladder painting the gray trim of a grand home across the street from the Pinewood Country Club. Cracked his skull and bled to death; the fall itself knocked him out so he never felt any pain. That pain was reserved for his family - Harold, Winston, and Cecile. Harold had stopped working for his father by then. He had finished his BS and MBA and was paying off student loans with his prestigious job at The First Santa Niña Bank on West Tenth Street in the downtown concrete orchard. (Too small to be called a jungle, the locals like to joke about the real orchard that produces succulent oranges and the concrete one about a mile across the town, across the tracks, sitting in the shadows of the Santa Niña Mountains.)

Harold left the painting business for business. When Amelia announced she was pregnant, Harold knew he needed to up his income. He also wanted a job that allowed him to be home on the weekends. Harold had always been good with numbers, and he only needed 10 more credits to finish his BS. By the time Jesse arrived, Harold had made his father cry twice – once on the night he told him he was quitting *Waters & Sons* and a second time when he walked across Cal State Santa Niña's stage, black cap on head and a bright white Waters' smile across his face. Of course, the day Martin Waters' first grandchild arrived was cause for more waterfalls. Martin Waters was a sentimental man, and each time he had cried in that past year, the tears were bittersweet – tears of hope for his son's decision to leave the family business, tears of joy for his son's achievements, and tears of possibilities for his grandson's future. Martin Waters never cried tears of regret or sorrow or self-pity. He had far too much to be grateful for and far too much to hope for.

For a man who devotes his entire life – well, 41 of 61 years is nearly one's entire life – to painting the slats and window frames and eaves of grand homes boasting mortgages greater than the net worth of one's own family's history must count himself lucky or he might wallow in self-pity or drown in a pool of green envy, a pool of tart apple or key lime green envy.

Martin Waters was not an envious man. He considered such feelings shallow and beneath him. He knew how easily he could have lived a lonely path, without his sons, his lovely Cecile. Each day he awoke, pulled on his painter's pants, and checked his truck's tool boxes, he counted himself lucky.

Martin Waters saw it all. His homes were more than jobs, they were living, breathing beings; wood and brick configurations of energy and life. He was never prouder than the days he stood ladder by ladder next to Wayne and Harold and Winston. Together, the three boys were the sons of *Waters & Sons* for nine years. The best nine years of Martin Waters' life.

That's what he'd tell people. But on the dark August night of 1973, two months before Amelia's jubilant announcement, the Waters family would receive the first bad news suited to tears of regret, sorrow, and, yes, pity. *Waters & Sons*, a business as such for nearly ten years, would become *Waters & Son* in a matter of three months. The first son taken by a tragic car accident on that dark August night. The second by a long-held dream. Despite his older brother's sudden death, Harold followed through three months later in telling his father he could no longer climb ladders, mix latex, or haggle with customers.

"That's OK, son," Martin assured his middle boy then added with a chuckle, "You gonna climb some corporate ladders." Harold smiled and nodded. "You have a dream, Harold. I know a little something about dreams. You got a little bun in the oven that you need to provide for. Winston and I can handle the load. We can hire some kids from SNiHi if need be. I'm not changing my sign, though, if that's what you're wondering."

Harold had wondered that, briefly. Wouldn't take but a swipe of honeybee yellow to cover up that little *s*. That little *s* that turned a single offspring into several. Just the thought, and the memory of his dear brother Wayne brought a tear and then some to Harold's eyes.

"Daddy, I wouldn't ever ask you to take away that little *s*. That's more than a letter, it's a family. It's Wayne. It's me and Winston." He swallowed, trying to pull that lump of saliva down a throat that narrowed further each second. He raised his hand to his father's shoulder and smiled. But he didn't know what else to say. At 22, a child on the way, Harold felt like seven again. He felt like seven when Wayne was nine and Winston just a toddler in diapers. He felt like seven, but his father looked much older. And that narrowed Harold's throat even more.

"It's OK, son. We won't cover up that little s. We don't need to," he sighed and reached his hand up to squeeze his son's. "So we won't."

Despite such tragedy, Martin Waters was a lucky man. He wouldn't cry tears of sorrow, or regret, or pity. He would, however, hold his lovely Cecile in bed every night as she cried herself to sleep and whispered her own secret and private messages to her first born son, messages meant for Wayne, not meant for Martin's ears. So he would just hold her and rock her while he closed his own eyes to hold in the sorrow, and he would pray to Heaven, to whomever was looking over this family. He wouldn't pray for answers, he would simply pray for strength.

Not for himself. For Cecile. Martin felt sure that such tragedy early in their lives only meant more lay in waiting. So he prayed to God to give strength to his lovely Cecile for the time when he could not be there to hold her in his arms and rock her in her bed. And soon, Cecile grew strong again.

Seven months passed. Seven months of holding his wife and rocking her as she sent her private messages to Heaven. Then Cecile found her strength again. It lay inside the deep brown eyes of one tiny and fragile Jesse Wayne Waters.

"My little angel," Cecile calls him. "You brought my baby Wayne back to earth in that joyous heart of yours, little one, I know you did. My little angel."

Homeowners who can smell the apple pies know just how lucky they are. Martin Waters was a very lucky man.

Just moments before Martin fell those 22 feet from his metal ladder, he had been whistling and humming "Joy to the World" with Winston. Across town, Harold was helping old Mr. Forester open his safety deposit box. Cecile and Amelia were picking up fixings for Sunday's pot roast. Jesse was racing bikes home with Miguel and Matt along the ghost of an old rail road track that runs down First Street. None of them heard Winston's anguished screams, "Daddy, Daddy, no! Daddy! Help, someone, help!" as he raced down his own metal ladder that clung to the paint-peeling home of Mr. and Mrs. James Post.

Just hours before Martin took that errant step up (or was it down) that metal ladder, he had been trying to convince the Posts that Yes, Silver Mosaic was just as luxurious looking as French Gray.

Now the patriarch of the Waters' family lay bleeding to death on the cold concrete sidewalk outside a grand east end home while his youngest son sobs and weeps and wails, gesticulating over his father's body. Inside, a ceramic dish violently crashes to the kitchen floor sending chunks of steaming apple splattering across the linoleum and bits of perfectly browned pastry flying onto the eggshell white walls.

Martin Waters' life ended doing something he loved. He would say he had no regrets. Cecile knew this. Winston and Harold knew this. Wayne, immortalized in death at 24, would be there to meet his father in Heaven and shake his hand and tell him, "Daddy, we are all so proud of you. I am so sorry I let you down." And Martin Waters would feel no sorrow, regret, or pity. He would simply feel the love of a father for his son and hold strong to the faith in this world to care for his gentle family left behind too soon.

The last image that flashed through Martin Waters' mind was surprisingly not his lovely Cecile (though she did pass through). The last image was that of his sons Wayne, Harold and Winston wrestling on the patchy grass outside their First Street home. A funny thing, too, he could smell an apple pie fresh out of the oven just across those rusty old useless railroad tracks.

When Jesse Wayne Waters motions to lift a colored pen from his dented Superman tin box, he closes his eyes. He doesn't want his own expectation of how something should look dictate how it will look. "That's not art. That's just drawing," he tells his little sister Vanessa. "If you want to be an artist like Grandpa Martin, you have to let chance be your partner in creation. If Grandpa could have, he would have let chance decide those homeowners' colors. Then we wouldn't have to pass by all those gloomy gray blobs that take up space on the east side."

"But Grandpa painted those blobs," Vanessa interrupts. "You can't say that about Grandpa. He's dead. You hafta speak kindly of the dead. Mama says."

"Oh, no disrespect to Grandpa. I mean, yeah, well, it's just that Grandpa would never paint a house gray. Look at our house, dusty rose, like a cherished flower in Grandma's garden. And look at Uncle Winston's. Sea foam Green. West side's where the color's at, Vanessa. West Side's got style."

Vanessa loves lying across the brown shag carpeted floor watching her big brother create a new work of art. She didn't always get them. Sometimes she would hold a finished piece up and say, "Wow, that's something, Jesse."

Then he'd pull the paper out of her hand, turn it right side up and say, "Yeah, something, even when you hold it the right way." Vanessa would blush. Well, Jesse would think she was blushing as she'd bow her head and dig her toe into the floor. Black girls hide their embarrassment like a chameleon in the forest.

Jesse has been painting and drawing ever since he could grab the paint brush out of his grandfather's warm hand and run through his grandmother's thorny rosebushes changing her red American Beauties into speckled white or brown American Beauties. Martin would tackle Jesse and take away his tool, while Harold would take advantage of his defenselessness and tickle him until he giggled so much he'd fart. Then the three generations of Waters' fellows would roll on the grass laughing in hysterics.

Soon enough, Martin had purchased a little painter's kit, complete with two sizes of brushes, three pots of primary paints, an apron and kid-sized latex gloves. Amelia would bring home broken chairs and three-legged tables she'd find on the sidewalks left out for junk collectors. Jesse would spend hours 'decorating' each masterpiece, every now and again asking Grandpa Martin for advice on color or technique.

"Do ya think this table here, Grandpa, requires a soft yellow or a strong blue?"

"Well, what do you think the table would want? Do you think that table looks a little yellow? A little quiet and maybe a tad cowardly? Or do you think he's a bit blue, a bit sad? Maybe he'd like listening to the blues. Why don't you just close your eyes and point to a can. Here, I'll just turn you around a bit. Now, point."

And so began Jesse's borrowed technique for helping his objects and masterpieces tell him what color to choose.

Perhaps it's this Zen style of painting that inspires Jesse's romantic exploits with the girls. Mostly just with Ruby Newton. Ever since that impulsive lip-locking escapade thirteen years ago, Jesse has been head-over-heels. Sure, there have been a few spontaneous kisses since, but right now with just days to go before summer vacation rolls in, Jesse can think of no other girl he wants to look at for the rest of his life.

In Jesse's mind, it's all Ruby.

He's never really shared his futuristic imaginings with his girlfriend. After three years of steady dating, why would he think he needs to?

Most everyone can recall their first kiss, their first *time*. Jesse Waters can. And he does, over and over. This fuzzy recollection presents itself in pieces; after all, a toddling 3-year-old doesn't hold the greatest control over a memory. Still, every time Ruby Newton sashays past him in history class in her oh-so-short cheerleading skirt, or idles up to him in her tight blue jeans and loose white blouse, Jesse is knocked back with a strange sensation, a sudden shiver that travels wickedly up his spine, around his collar bone, tap dances around his mocha brown cheeks, swirls atop the crown of his head and back down his spine and settles into the crevice between his legs, tingling within his male loins with such determination that he must lean forward and take a deep breath, cast his adolescent eyes upon the lifeless history text and stale graphics in order to quell the carnal force that commands such attention.

Spontaneous erections are not entirely so spontaneous for Jesse. He is quite aware of when, how and why they arise. It's not as if he can't control them, more as if he doesn't want to. Why slow such an amazingly alive feeling when the only other thing to insist upon his consideration would be a boring history lecture by Mr. Mallicksen?

The first time Jesse and Ruby *did it* was inside the home of his best friend Matt West. There was nothing spontaneous about it either. The event took weeks of careful planning. When would Lee be gone? For how long? Was there a chance she would suddenly decide to return home? How could Matt warn them if she did? How would Matt know? Finally, Jesse decided that some things needed to be left to chance. So he asked Ruby if she wanted to spend some time with him. Alone. At Matt's.

She did.

Ruby and Jesse arrived at the back door to Matt's house around 3:30. They had easily made the first bus from school at 3:05 that carried them a few blocks then they walked the remaining 400 feet from the stop and down the gravel drive. Jesse pulled out Matt's key and inserted it inside the lock. It clicked. He turned. The two entered the quiet kitchen.

"Man, this house is just how I imagined it," Ruby said with a smile. "Clean, charming, bright. Kinda like your buddy."

The two laughed as they set their backpacks down on the kitchen table. "Want some juice," Jesse offered as he opened the fridge.

"Sure." Ruby walked over to a small white board that sat above a silver end table in one corner of the kitchen. A corded phone hung on the wall. "Gee, they sure got a lot goin' on on this calendar for just two people. Looks like ours. Only we got two more kids and a dad."

Jesse clinked his glass with Ruby. "Cheers!"

Ruby laughed. "Cheers you big goof."

The two sipped the sweet orange juice. The afternoon sunlight cascaded in through the lace curtain settling its waning rays upon the dull wooden kitchen table. Ruby set down her glass. "I guess you've been here like a hundred times, huh?"

"Hundred and one," Jesse smiled. "At least. It's a nice feel here, don't ya think?"

"Homey, yeah. Kinda creepy quiet, too, though."

"That's just cuz it's just you and me. And, I don't know

about you, but I'm kinda nervous." Jesse set down his glass then reconsidered. He lifted the two nearly empty juice glasses, walked over to the sink, washed them out, set them on the drying rack, found a towel, dried each one, and returned them to the cupboard.

Ruby ventured out into the living room. Jesse glanced up at the clock. "Matt said he'd call and hang up after one ring if he found out his mom was comin' home early."

"And how would he find that out?" Ruby sat down on the plush lavender and green plaid loveseat.

"He said he was gonna call her from the library around quarter to five and ask her what was for dinner. He says he does that sometimes." Jesse sat in the black leather recliner by the window. He peered into the darkened glass that curved over the large television. Inside, he observed the slightly distorted reflection of his girlfriend, her cropped black hair clipped back by the tiny red SNiHi bow, the never-ending slide of her slender long legs beneath the high school boy-approved short skirt, the pristine white canvas tennies adorning her petite Ruby feet, her girlishly slim fingers interlaced around her knee. For Jesse, Ruby was pure delight. He loved everything about her. The way she sat. Her laugh that began in a gasp preceded by puffs of vacuous air and maybe a hiccup or two. Her bright white smile that spread wide across the dark complexion of her African skin, her smooth, chocolaty African skin.

"Hmm." Ruby ran her fingers along the armrest. "So, uh, does Matt sleep in his mom's old room, or does he sleep in his aunt's?"

Subtle, Jesse thought.

"Wanna see? It's his mom's old room. Weird, huh?"

The two nervous teens ambled down the hall and stopped at the closed door where they were greeted by a painted sign.

"Uh, is that a 'come in' or 'do not enter'? Your boy's odd." Ruby slipped her fingers inside Jesse's hand, feeling for the first time his moist palm, she held it firmer. *He is nervous*, she thought. *Good, I must mean somethin'.*

"It's from a Robert Frost poem," Jesse remarked. "His grandpa used to teach Frost at State. Matt's always quotin' him and stuff. He found this one and thought it was a good door sign. It's called 'Come In'." Jesse smiled at Ruby and pushed the door open.

Inside was indeed dark. Matt kept his curtains pulled shut since his bedroom looked out onto the front yard. He didn't want any peepers peering inside his room, even when he wasn't there. This played to Matt's private nature. Not everyone believes in curtains. Matt West does. Some things people don't need to see, aren't meant to see.

Ruby walked over to his closet, pulled aside the sliding door and examined the neatly hung shirts and pants. "Geez, if my mom saw this, she'd hire the boy to teach me how to organize *my* room." She touched a white cotton shirt. "He even hangs his tees? Do you do that? Hang your tee shirts?"

"Nah. I got half of Vanessa's dresses hangin' inside my closet on account that I don't much hang anything in there." Jesse smiled and sat down on the narrow twin bed. "Rube." He patted the mattress.

Ruby Newton closed the sliding closet door, pressed her hands down along her pleated felt cheerleading skirt, turned and looked at her gentle boyfriend, understanding this was the moment that would pull them undeniably across the threshold from child to adult. This moment would change everything. She knew it. She feared it. Small pangs of jealousy when one would happen to pass a glance on another would increase tenfold into burning spasms of covetous rage. This concerned Ruby.

But not enough to stop her from pulling off her cheer

uniform and losing her virginity.

After that spring day in sophomore year, Jesse Waters and Ruby Newton found numerous other occasions to practice being adults. Jesse no longer has to wipe off sweaty palms. Ruby no more hesitates at what the private moments might bring. The all-consuming, passionate, sexual energy that burns uncontrollably inside each of them is enough to abandon all good sense. Of course, they practice safe sex. Always.

In Jesse's garage behind the water heater. Under the bleachers on deserted Sunday evenings. In Mrs. Griffiths' bedroom after 10 when the kids are asleep and Ruby has two more hours of babysitting to go. And once more in Matt's bedroom just last month when Lee decided to have a girls' weekend in Palm Springs and trust Matt to take care of himself for 24 hours. Matt took care of himself by spending three hours Saturday morning at the library.

Now more used to the West household, this time when Ruby and Jesse finished, they even washed and dried the dishes, took out the trash, and arranged some yellow daisies in a vase on the kitchen table.

One thing, though, when Jesse went to clean up and take out the trash, he discovered a clear gelatinous mess on Matt's bed sheet. Pulling the used condom out of the whicker trash can, Jesse poked his finger inside and observed a small hint of his flesh through a tear in the latex. Assuring himself that most of the junk surely deposited itself on the bed, Jesse bundled up the sheets, wrapped the condom in a tissue and stuffed it in his pocket.

"Let's do some laundry, too, Rube, while we're playin' Suzy Homemakers," Jesse shouted as Ruby finished her daisy display.

"Sure, that's nice of you, Jess. Matt'll appreciate that." She joined him in the back laundry closet. "So will Lee." Ruby wrapped her hands around her boyfriend's narrow waist. "You are just the sweetest, Jesse Waters. Just the sweetest."

At the moment, Jesse wasn't so sure he agreed.

WEDNESDAY

When the Nestlings' feathers begin to appear, the baby birds no longer solely depend upon their parents for warmth. The new feathers let the brood know they are ready to fly. After several weeks of caring for these 'teenage' birds, parents may stop their feeding. In some cases, they may even chase away the fledglings. It is not unusual for the young to be startled from home by a predator or sudden noise.

5

CONCEPTION

Miguel possesses a strange attraction for feathered creatures. He admires — in fact, envies — their ability to fly, to take off in seconds and soar high above the madness that exists down below. On this day before the last day of junior year, this day before the looming Calculus final, Miguel gazes dreamily out the second story math class window, imagining his own wings, strong, coffee brown feathery appendages stretching perhaps ten feet, no, twenty. Why not; it's his fantasy. If he could, he tells himself, he would open the window, step out onto the narrow ledge and spread his wings. Then he would simply push off and let the wind carry him higher and higher, far away from the chatter of his classmates, the distant lecture incessantly pouring from Miss Pony-Tail's mouth, her soft, sweet mouth, beyond the scratching of white dusty chalk across the dry green board. If he could, he would. Just step out, push off, let go.

"Would you agree, Miguel? Miguel? Mr. Alma de Ramón?"

"Yo, Miggy, she's talking to you," Jesse's firm index finger pierces his right bicep, penetrating his daydream. In a hushed tone, his friend adds, "Say, yes, I agree."

"Yeah, sure, that's it." Miguel flashes his slightly crooked grin and sends a chin-nod over to his pal. "Thanks."

Miss Thomas accepts the response, satisfied she has brought SNiHi's daydreaming soccer star back inside the classroom. She returns to the board, erases one symbol and replaces it with another. A murmur fans its way across the room, the other students now satisfied with the markings.

"What's up, Daydream Believer?" Jesse chides his friend.

"Huh? I dunno? Just thinkin'," Miguel looks back out the smudged window. "If you could fly, where do you think you'd go?"

"What the –?" Jesse shoots back. "If I could fly? Bring your birdbrain back in this room, Miggy, or you ain't passin' the final tomorrow. Come on, remember our plan? We all take Trig next year. The three of us."

Matt had convinced his pals to sign up for Miss Thomas' pre-final tutorial. Just thirty minutes after school. Nearly all of the Calculus students have shown up, but many find it hard to focus on limits when their stomachs are growling for tacos.

Miguel turns forward, stares into the fine strands of his friend's blond head. He pokes Matt with his pencil.

Matt turns, glares, mouthing *stop it.* He swings back toward the front; his pencil again meeting his notebook, gliding across the blue lines, leaving behind a military row of numbers and symbols.

Miguel knows Matt will bring home ace notes tonight; he plans on reading them over and committing them to memory. He has never fully grasped mathematical concepts, but the kid can memorize anything. Jesse calls it a photographic memory. Jesse doesn't have it. He finds that ironic. (*I'm the damn artist, he's a swift-footed soccer nut, and he has the effin photographic memory? What good can an amazing talent like that serve a dribbling goofhead?*)

No bell rings, so Miss Thomas looks out at her star students and says, "Class dismissed. Good luck," then as perhaps an afterthought, "Eat breakfast."

The students begin loading heavy textbooks into their backpacks, double-checking their notebooks for loose papers, zipping up pencil cases, and exiting the room single file like passengers disembarking an airplane. The Three Musketeers, typically the last to leave, take their time, falling to the back queue of departing pupils. Matt swings his faded blue backpack over his right shoulder, nearly swiping Jesse across his head as he bends to retrieve an abandoned mechanical pencil from the cold green linoleum floor.

"Watch it, dude, the hair, man, the hair," Jesse scolds, pulling his pick from his back pocket and setting his tight curls straight.

"Yeah, *ese*, don't want to muss up the fro before Ruby sees it. She might dump him for failure to line up his curl."

Matt titters at Miguel's teasing as the three make their way to the front of the room. Miss Thomas sits at her desk, placing red pen marks inside the square boxes of her gradebook, picking up a lead pencil and eraser to exchange a D for a C or a Missing for a Late. She glances up at the trio.

"Tomorrow's it, fellas. Study hard, Miguel."

"What, why me? You think Matt's the smart one cuz he's white. You forget it's the brown boys that keep him afloat. You got it all twisted curvy Miss Pon, uh, Miss Thomas."

Their favorite teacher smiles, "Of course I do, Miguel. What I meant was, study hard so that the other two knuckleheads can cheat off you tomorrow."

The boys smile and head out through the doorway; at least Matt and Jesse do. Miguel strikes an awkward glance toward his friends then turns back toward his teacher. "I will. You'll see. When you sit down tomorrow afternoon to grade the final, it's Miguel Alma de Ramón's paper that'll rise to the top, like a hawk in flight. Alma de Ramóns don't hover around no dead meat. We work for what's ours while the other jealous scavengers pick at the leftovers."

Caught by her student's declaration, Miss Thomas can only smile back warmly. "That would be wonderful, Miguel. I'd love for your paper to sit at the top of the pile. Good luck to all of you tomorrow."

His teacher's quiet and unexpected support brings a hush over the usually chatty Miguel. Not knowing where to look, he stares at her slender, manicured hand that fingers an ordinary retractable red ink pen. She taps it on the table, a nervous habit, says goodbye, and Miguel quietly exits the room, joining his pals in the corridor.

Out in the hall, Miguel kicks a crumpled love note, banking it off the silent metal lockers. Lagging behind the others, Matt stops, turns, and walks back inside Room 210. "Miss Thomas, you know, we're gonna take Trig next year. All of us. Think we can handle it? All of us? You know. I mean, do you think maybe we all should, um, maybe we should just stop with Calculus this year?" After his first statement, Matt can't hold his stare with Miss Thomas. He moves his gaze to a tiny black ant crawling across the paint-peeling landscape of the desktop. Feeling the silence, he looks back up.

"Sure, Matt. You boys can do anything, but *you* need Trig, Miguel doesn't."

Matt nods, moves his feet toward the door.

"But Matt." He stops and turns. "Miguel needs you. And Jesse. You don't go breaking up the Three Musketeers just because D'Artagnan can't keep track of how many girlfriends he's kissed, right? All for one..."

"And one for all," Matt smiles. Yeah, you can't split up a team. He's been carrying Miguel for the past three years in math, heck, for pretty much their whole school career. One more can't hurt.

As he turns to re-exit, his teacher interrupts, "Oh, and, uh, Matt, just remember what you believe about friendship, remember what you've believed since you first met these guys. Just because they're hormonal teenagers doesn't mean they don't care about their friends."

"Uh, yeah," Matt responds, not clear where that came from.

"I mean, you guys really are the Three Musketeers, you know," she smiles. "I honestly think your friendship can survive anything." Miss Thomas stands and walks around the desk, standing so close to her pupil as to make him feel uncomfortable enough to back off just one step. "No matter what, Matt, no matter, no matter what happens next, next year, next week, whatever, you guys are buddies. I've seen a lot of kids pass through this door, and I think I know real friendship when I see it. It's like a family. It's more than finishing sentences, giving someone your homework to copy, or stuff like that. I think you know what I mean."

He doesn't, but he thinks his teacher is trying to say something else. "Yeah, I guess. We'll be friends for life. Sure. Maybe. Maybe not. We're friends right now, that's all I know. Life can change in a minute. Ask my mom." Matt pauses, drops his head, takes in a breath. "But I get it, Miss Thomas. I'll just take the math I need. I can't control their paths. They can't control mine."

Miss Thomas smiles. "So true, Matt. That's so true. You need to tread down your own path. Now's the time. You can do it. You're far stronger than you realize."

"I guess."

"You are. Miguel will be fine. Jesse will be fine. They need to find their paths, too."

"Okay, well, I'll just, we'll just see then. But, uh, I gotta go. Gotta get to the library and study for some stupid math final."

The two share a laugh. "Of course. We wouldn't want you to miss a problem."

Miss Thomas' smile lights up her whole face, and Matt thinks for just one moment that he could fall in love with her, that maybe he has fallen in love with her. But no, it's different. It's more an adoration, an admiration, a respect. He wants to hug her, to tell her that her words mean something, that she's not just Miss Pony-tail Thomas, that she's a person who's made a difference for him, for probably a lot of kids.

He tells her none of this.

Matt says goodbye and falls in line with his friends in the hall as they make their descent down the stairs to their lockers.

Miguel withdraws his beloved skateboard from within the tall metal box and secures it under his arm. The three head out the building's main doors and into the bright Southern California sunshine and oppressing desert heat. Unable to hold his feet steady, Miguel kicks a small stone, dribbling it along the sidewalk until they reach the corner. He places the skateboard under his right foot and steadies himself.

"I gotta go to Al's. I'll try to leave by 6. We gonna study?"

Matt and Jesse laugh. "Yeah, we're gonna study Miggy, and you can photograph our notes."

"Why you hate on me, Jesse. I can't help it if I have such an amazing memory. You jealous." Miguel fakes a swipe at Jesse's curls.

Matt breaks in. "Jess, you wanna go to the library? I'm gonna look over my Spanish notes, too."

"Maybe later," Jesse smiles as he spots Ruby moving towards him.

Miguel wolf-whistles and steps off the curb, dodging buses and novice teenage drivers as he skates across town to Al's, teasing a race with two crows that circle the school then veer down the road, cawing and diving.

"Hey, baby," Jesse coos as he kisses Ruby lightly on the cheek. "Wanna come home with me for a lemonade and we can study? Or somethin'?"

"Hey, Matt," Ruby greets her boy's best friend. "You know, babe, I'm gonna go with Karen to the library and read over our notes for the Spanish final. Let's just take a break tonight so we can focus on school. Tomorrow's our last day, you know, so we got all summer to hang."

Jesse digs his right toe into a crack in the sidewalk, "I guess. Okay." Wounded, rejected, he looks over at Matt who is staring off into the crowd of students waiting for the 51 home. Then he reconsiders his friend's request, "Matt, maybe I will tag along and study some. We could all go."

Ruby pulls her books closer to her chest, "Jesse, babe, I gotta focus. You're just gonna distract me and all. You know, I'll be tryin' to practice conjugating, and you'll be kickin' my leg and, and, Jesse…"

"I get it. Yeah. Well, I guess I'll just head home. Matt, you gonna come by before dinner to go over math notes?"

Matt's gaze fixates on the crowd of students.

"Yo, Matt, hey, hello, earth to Matt."

"Matty, boy," Ruby taps him on the shoulder.

Matt turns toward the pair, "Huh? What? I, uh, what did ya say?"

Ruby spots Lexie Cortes stepping onto the white and blue city bus. Her boyfriend, tall, skinny Ricky Traeger guiding her by the small of the back.

Ruby smiles. "I think our boy's got his eye on someone, someone untouchable." Ruby cocks her head toward the bus.

"Oh, I see how it is. You find something more interesting over their, Red?" Jesse moves into Ruby and stretches his left arm tightly around her shoulder.

"What? Whaddya mean? I was just starin' at nothing,

nothing really," Matt denies the not so unreasonable accusation as a distinct scarlet hue spreads spottily across his pale complexion.

"Oh, OK. Yeah, those city buses, they's damn interestin'," Jesse and Ruby laugh.

"What? No, I, uh, I wasn't lookin' at anyone in particular." Matt's vacant, innocent expression transforms quickly. His eyes squint as he bites the inside of his right lip and turns the questioning in on his friend. "Who'd you think I was staring at anyway?"

"Oh, we know who you was starin' at Matthew West," Ruby teases. "That'd be one long-legged cutie. But you better lay off there, cuz she's taken."

"Yeah, and no offense, but I don't think you're anyway a match for Mr. Stilts and his basketball muscles. Heck, not even Miguel'd take on that stretch of talent."

Matt laughs nervously. Relieved. "Hey, I'm gonna see you guys later then. I better grab that 51." Matt darts away before the two can respond.

"Someone's in love," Ruby sings. She shimmies her shoulders this way and that as she follows Matt's loping stride.

"Ain't you catchin' the bus, too, with Karen?" Jesse asks.

"What? Oh, no, her brother's givin' us a ride. He'll be out in a minute. Karen's getting her books from her locker. I better see what's taking her. Bye, baby," Ruby kisses Jesse softly on the cheek then whispers in his ear, "Call me tonight."

Jesse shivers. He is a useless mess when she does that. "Okay," he manages, and she disappears inside the stiff stucco building before he can recover.

Jesse turns back toward the bus stop just as Matt steps up and the doors shut behind him. *Vrrzzh!* snorts the consuming vehicle. The filled-to-capacity metal box exhales a gust of dark smoke from its rooftop muffler and screeches away from the curb heading down the long wide stretch of Blackbird Way.

Santa Niña residents laugh at the city's ill humor, naming its widest and longest road after the very pesky birds that can ruin an entire crop of oranges in less than three days. Santa Niña began its official history shortly after California joined the union back in 1850. Rumor has it that a family of Mexican immigrants, making it rich off a pan of silver in the Santa Niña hills, used their new money to build a ranch and plant an orange grove.

By the time the trees could bear fruit, the family had doubled its wealth from a bed and breakfast on the south end of the ranch. The eldest daughter, Rebecca, ran the Inn, while her parents tended the Grove. They had two other children, both girls, and it's the youngest, Salina, from whom the town owes its name.

In 1854, Salina Castillo came down with what was probably the measles. Confined to bed with a 104-degree fever, the family kept her in the servants' quarters so she wouldn't infect the guests. After seven days, Salina fell into a fever-induced coma. Señor Castillo called in the priest to perform Salina's last rites. However, unable to bare losing her precious baby, Señora Castillo begged the Father to find them medicine. After all, the family had enough money to pay for a doctor and all the medicine that was necessary to bring their dear Salina back to life. The Father sent a message to the next town via railway, but no word came back. He told the parents that they must accept God's wish; Salina could not be saved.

Señora Castillo walked out into her orange grove where she picked six of the brightest, healthiest fruits. She squeezed them and brought the juice to her ailing daughter. Salina was unconscious, she could not drink the nectar, so the Señora drank the sweet juice and said her own prayer for her niña. She then lay down beside her daughter, kissed her feverish forehead, and held her tenderly within her arms.

Two days later, Salina's fever broke and she opened her eyes. "Mamá," she uttered. "*Mamá, qué dulce las naranjas. Gracias, mamá.*"

And so the town bears the name of Salina, the Holy Girl, Santa Niña, the girl who came back from the dead.

Legend holds that the Orchard seeks replacement of young Salina, repayment of a life for a life. This rumor has aided many parents in keeping their young children from venturing too far inside the orange grove. Most kids heed the warning, though it usually loses effect by the time they reach their teens.

"Shit," Jesse remembers tossing his art pad in his locker after lunch. *Not feelin' the doodle,* as Mig says.

He bounces up the steps, hoping to surprise Ruby with one more kiss, but it's Jesse who gets the surprise.

As he turns the corner of the first floor senior locker hallway, he spots Ruby's back. Why isn't she at her locker upstairs? Peering down the darkened hall, Jesse's sure his girl is leaning into a senior locker. But whose? Karen's locker is upstairs, too. The juniors won't claim the coveted first-floor Senior lockers until August when the custodial staff has attempted to reclaim their shine. SNiHi's student government will stencil-stamp the 92 on the fronts for the new Senior Class.

He moves closer to see who's commanding her attention and spots the red and black letterman's jacket. He relaxes. It's just Nate, Karen's brother. Then he tenses. They don't exactly appear to be talking; well, not unless you talk with your lips locked.

Shit! Jesse thinks, *They're, shit, they're kissing!* At this, Jesse's brain freezes, and so does he. He stops halfway down the hall. Unable to unlock his glower from the back of Ruby's head, he can't release his stare when she wraps her left hand around Nate's thick neck and pulls herself into his body closer and closer.

Jesse's heart pounds. He forgets about his art pad. He forgets about finals. He forgets how to walk, how to breathe. The cold senior hallway closes in on him. His chest tightens. The gray metal lockers mock him, staring one-eyed at him through their black dials, whispering *sucker, sucker, haha, sucker,* through their fluted vents.

Finally locating the muscles in his legs, Jesse turns 180 degrees and walks rapidly down the hall back toward the exit. As he pushes open the heavy silver double doors, the piercing sun blinds him, and he trips over something solid, falling face down onto the pavement, his backpack flying over the back of his head and onto the front steps.

"Hey, you OK?" comes the voice of what he's tripped over.

Jesse looks up. He takes the extended hand that reaches down to him and feels its strength hoist him forward. He pushes the sun's glare back with his right hand. "Miss Thomas?" Not sure why he asks it as a question since he recognized her feet when he was on the ground, her tiny scuff-marked brown pumps, her slender, slightly boney ankles.

"You, OK, Jesse?"

Recalling why he landed on the pavement, why he darted through the silver doors without thinking, without looking, without wondering at all about anyone else, he brushes off his jeans and steps down to retrieve his backpack from the concrete steps.

"Yeah, I'm OK. I was, uh, trying to catch the bus, and, uh, I wasn't looking, and ..." He stops staring into the distance and adjusts his vision in line with his math teacher, noticing for the first time her tousled locks and missing ponytail. "Shit, Miss Thomas, I'm sorry. I just didn't see you. I mean, geez, sorry. I uh -..."

"It's OK, Jesse. I was just picking up my elastic band. I'd dropped it trying to fix my hair. Silly thin pieces of hair always falling out of that dang thing. You pushed open the door, and I guess I wasn't expecting anyone to come out of the building. I probably should've been paying better attention."

He spots the black band on the ground, bends to pick it up, and places it in the small palm of her delicate hand. "Shit, I was, uh, I mean, shoot, I was just ..."

"Jesse, you don't need to explain. It was an accident. That's all. We're OK. I'm OK. You?"

"Yeah, it's good. I'm fine." Turning, he looks behind her at the heavy door, waiting for two guilty people to push through it, imagining he'll bend down and that big lug of a football star will trip right over him.

"You sure? Jesse?"

"Huh? Yeah." He adjusts his backpack, repositions himself, and stares vacantly out onto the deserted street. All the buses and all the kids having matched up and moved on. "Well, I guess I better go. Gotta study for some lame math final, ya know." He manages a grin.

"There's a lot of that going around," she laughs at her own private joke. "But I hear that test isn't gonna be so tough. Might be there's a lot on limits." Miss Thomas flashes a rare smile, full teeth. Jesse observes the crookedness and small canines that stick out just so. Still, it's bright.

"I'll remember that. See ya later, Miss Thomas," he lumbers down the steps, his legs feeling unusually heavy. Pausing at the bottom, he turns and looks up. "Oh, and I'm really sorry about knocking you down and all. You didn't deserve that."

Sensing a teachable moment, she can't resist. "It's OK, Jesse. We all make mistakes. I know, I'm a teacher, I try to fix them. Thing is, though, it's always easier to correct someone else's mistakes than your own. You know what I mean?"

"Uh, not really," he replies, still distracted by the hallway sighting.

"That's OK. You'll get it when you need to." She smiles again, this time without the teeth.

Noticing her ponytail back where it belongs, the jilted junior turns and heads down Blackbird Way, forcing himself to walk forward, not look back. He moves at a steady gait until he reaches First Street. There he instinctively makes the right turn, continuing his long empty journey home.

"Damn her," he grumbles, "Damn him, damn all of them!"

Back at school, Nate Gibbons gallantly opens the squeaky door to his rusty red Camaro for one Ruby Newton who steps into the car just like she's done dozens of times before.

As soon as Miguel's skateboard rolls inside the garage, Al starts his tirade. "Look, kid, when you gonna remember. 3:15. You start at 3:15."

Out of breath from pumping hard the last block, Miguel withholds his own ire. "Man, Al, I know. It's just that, it's finals this week. You know. Tomorrow's our last day. Next week, I can come whenever you want. Name the time. I'm here. Right on the dot. I got no school bells holdin' me back next week." Miguel rolls his board back and forth with his right toe as he steadies and slows his breathing. Exaggerating his labored breaths for his boss. A dirty towel hits him in the head.

"Ay, relax, amigo. I'ma jokin'," Al points to the Sports Illustrated swimsuit calendar clock on the wall. Little hand passing the slender hip of Kathy Ireland, big hand not far behind.

"Shit, Al, you big…"

"Watcha you mouth, kid. Customers." Al jerks his head over to the garage main floor.

"Ain't no customers. You just got an old Benz sittin' over there all lonely."

"Like I a said, customers. Come on, my sweeta little German beauty, tella Papa all you problems." Al moves gently toward the silver sedan like a swinger in a single's bar. His hips sway this way and that, he whistles some old tune, and he smoothly rubs the soft oil-stained cloth over the front left fender, cooing softly.

Despite Al's corny attempts at humor and his inherent need to sweet-talk his cars, Miguel finds the greasy mechanic endearing. More than that, Miguel admires Al almost like a father, or an uncle. No Alma de Ramón blood courses through the shop owner's own limbs. Al Farmicello is one-hundred percent Italian. He will tell Miguel that's what unites them, old Spanish romantic genes mixed for centuries between southern European families.

"But, Al," Miguel will protest, "I'm not Spanish, I'm Mexican. Different continent all together."

"No a worries, my greasy friend. You speaka the Spanish, right?" Al will reply.

"*Si*," Miguel mocks, finding little relevance in this.

"So, you speaka the Spanish in Mexico, they speaka the Spanish in Spain; Spain's in Europe. I'm Italian. Italy's in Europe. That's it. We a family. Cousins from centuries long ago. Look," Al will bring his arm up to Miguel's. "See, same color. Now, come over here." He'll drag Miguel up to the small oily auto shop mirror on the wall. "See, rounda faces, blacka eyes, darka hair. Brothers. Course I'ma more handsome than you. No?"

They laugh. Al will rub Miguel's head, throw a grease-stained towel at him and shout, "Now, little brother, get to work!"

Something in this little mechanic's shop at the corner of

Eighth and Pine that tugs at Miguel's heart. Sometimes it tugs too much. He doesn't want to like Al, doesn't want to like his shop. He wants to hate it, wants to hate Al, so he'll have no reason not to make it out of this smelly little town.

Miguel wipes off the dusty lids of the oil jugs, straightens their pyramid structure outside the office door and picks up the red handle of the splintering whicker broom that leans beneath the SI calendar clock. He snickers, *late, that Al. Why do I fall for his lame lines? Everytime.*

The tinny double bell chimes, letting the inside know a customer has pulled up out front. Miguel looks around for Al. Not seeing his greasy head or hearing his melodic whistling, Miguel makes his way out front.

He pauses. Behind the Firestone tire sign, he can already spy enough of the dented red fender to know who has just pulled into the shop. He peers inside the vehicle and spots several passengers. He swallows, blinks.

"Yo, I gotta problem with my break pedal. Think you can find someone who knows a little something about cars come out and take a look?" Miguel twists the dirty rag around his fist. *Bite your tongue, Miggy, bite your tongue.* He can't let anything interfere with this job. Not even a thick-necked lughead like Nate Gibbons.

"What's goin' on? Too much weight on the pedal can make the lever stick. You puttin' too much weight on, Gibbons?"

"Funny. Where's your boss? Come on, I'm in a hurry."

Miguel peers inside the car, spotting the back of Karen Gibbon's curled brown tresses and her little red bow at the side of her head. He looks deeper into the car to see who she's talking to. Yep, Ruby and Lucy sit in the back seat gabbing away.

"You pawning yourself out as a taxi or what?"

"I don't need to do no pawnin'; these girls line up to slide inside my engine." Nate folds his arms and kicks his front tire then spits on the ground. "Get the big man, little man."

Miguel decides the less said now, the better. He turns 'round and pushes open the office door. "Al, some lugnut needs your help. Seems he ground his break pedal into the floor. Probably too fat."

Al stands, glances out the window. "So, youra friendly football star pays old Al a visit, eh? Mr. All-State. Too a busy to offer me any publicity. Lugnut wouldn't pose for a picture for my ad. Say he have to clear with coach and father. *Hmph.* Now he needs my a help. Sure, sure, soon they always do."

Seems Nate spreads good cheer wherever he goes. Miguel smiles and follows his boss out front.

"So, eh, Mr. Gibbons, how are a you today? What seems to be your a problem? How can we help?" Miguel nearly gags at Al's over-acting graciousness. He strolls over to the passenger side and motions to Ruby. She rolls down her window.

"Hey, Miggy, what's happenin'!" A crow swoops over the station, its incessant cawing counters the upbeat cheerleader's greeting.

"Nuthin. Just workin' for the man," he smiles toward Al. Miguel finds no reason to be unpleasant with Ruby. After all, this is 1991, cell phones are still a science fiction fantasy to most. News does not travel fast. In fact, it travels only slightly quicker than an Old West telegram. It will be at least three more hours till Jesse will share his afternoon adventure that ended with tripping over their favorite math teacher.

"Oh, you mean your uncle? *Tio Al*?" Ruby teases, having heard enough stories from Jesse to know all about Al's *F* in geography.

"Yea, *Tio Al*, that's him alright," Miguel smiles back then moves over to his boss to hear about the heavy-footed football star's dilemma.

Nate continues sharing the symptoms with Al like a patient at the doctor's, "… then it just jammed. I mean, I barely got it in the station. It's like somethin's under the car pullin' me back, like the break is just, I dunno, like it's set." He leans in, peering over the mechanic's head which is lodged underneath the dash fingering the slender spaces around the gas and break pedals.

Al hoists his pants then himself and pops the hood. He moves around to the front of the car where Miguel joins him. Al moves in closer to him and whispers, "Listen, this kid's a idiot. I'ma gonna pretend to fiddle here with radiator cap. You crawl underneath and pull out branch or dead squirrel or whatever is wrapped around axle."

Miguel cocks his head at Al but does as he's told. After all, it's easier for the teen to bend and scoot himself beneath the low-riding Chevy than it is for some pudgy middle-aged Italian mechanic with a bad back.

Twisting the radiator cap back and forth, Al raises his voice, "Miguel, now you a pull, I turn. Got it? Gotta enough light?"

Miguel has plenty of light as he pulls the twigs lodged deep in the axle fixings of the town's all-state running back's rusty red Camaro. "Damn!"

"Miguel? You OK, little brother? What you got? Squirrel? Kitten?"

Miguel shimmies himself out from under the car. By this time, all three girls have exited and joined Nate on the cement at the front of the Chevy. "Ooh, gross!" shouts one of the girls.

Al and Miguel laugh. "Is that axle grease? Is it a leak, man?" Nate shoots out questions with complete confusion.

"No, man, ain't no axle grease," laughs Miguel as he wipes the gooey yellow liquid running down his arm. "That's yolk, man. Guess the yolk's on you!"

"What the - ?" Nate still has no clue. "What's the twisted

mess of wires then?"

"That, my a speedy footballa star," returns Al, "is bird's nest. You run over bird's nest and it a wrapped around you axle. That'sa the pulling you feel."

"So my car's good? Damn! Halleluiah!"

Karen gently slaps her brother on the shoulder. "That's good, cuz any more car fees is dippin' into my college funds, big brother."

Miguel bends back down under the car. "It wasn't just the bird's nest that you were pullin' down Pine Street, though." The auto apprentice holds up a small brown-feathered bird. Its head hangs awkwardly onto its wing as Miguel brings it toward his chest. "She was protecting her babies. The nest probably fell on the road from an Oak tree, and she was tryin' to save her eggs. Then along comes some arrogant Camaro and squash, twist, grind, mama and her home and her eggs are all wrapped around your axle."

"I told you I felt a bump," shouts Ruby. She turns to Miguel. "I looked back, thinking I'd see a bloody dog or something, but there was nuthin' there."

"That's cuz it was all underneath you." Miguel cradles the dead mother Robin and carries her inside along with her home.

"Shit. Man, I was worried my car was gonna need some hella expensive repair. Damn. That's good." Satisfied with the outcome, Nate turns to get back in his car.

"Uh, hold on, Mr. All-State. We gotta a settle you bill." Al places his hand on the driver's door.

"Bill? What the -, what bill? For what? Pullin' a dead bird from underneath my car? Don't take no rocket scientist to do that. I coulda done it myself." He moves toward Al.

"Yes, but you didn't. Miguel a did." The five-foot-five mechanic holds his ground in the shadow of Nate Gibbons. "Let's a see, what's a going rate for retrieving interfering debris from beneath a 1982 Chevy Camaro? I'da say twenty bucks shoulda do it. What you say, Señor Gibbons?"

Nate steps back toward the car. "Yeah, my dad'll send you a check."

"No, these a kinda services require payment up front."

"Come on, Nate, pay him. We gotta get to the library. Ruby, you got any cash?"

Ruby and Lucy dig inside their backpacks. By the time the three girls pull together eleven dollars and change, Nate has handed over a twenty to Al. "Keep-a the change-a," he snickers and climbs back in his Camaro, starts up the engine and pulls sharply out of the station and north onto Pine.

Miguel returns from depositing the mother bird and her nest onto the back workbench. "Hey, where'd they go?"

Al hands Miguel the crumpled green bill. "Mr. All-State said ' athanks for you troubles'."

"Huh?" Miguel reaches out for the bill, expecting Al to pull it back and rip out one of his snarky remarks. Instead, Miguel finds himself pushing the twenty inside his jean pocket. "Really? Lughead actually thanked us? Hmm, I guess you never know."

"No, you a never know, my young apprentice. You really don'ta ever know." Al rests his hand atop Miguel's right shoulder as the two make their way back inside the shop.

Once inside, Miguel picks up the splintered red-handled broom and continues his chores while Al ambles over to the Benz, humming and twirling a socket wrench, ready to work on his baby.

Miguel glances back out the shop's garage door, out onto Pine Street, replaying one scene over and over in his head. He feels certain he saw Ruby with her hands on that big lug's shoulder when they pulled in the drive. He squints, expecting the memory to reappear before him so he can further examine exactly whose hands rested on Mr. All-State, but nothing. *What a time for that photographic memory to fade.*

Trying to distract himself from the fire kindling inside his belly, Miguel sweeps up a small pile of dirt, bits of wire, scraps of paper and a dull penny. He bends down, lifts the penny out of the grimy mess, and places it inside his pocket next to the twenty.

"A penny saved, a penny earned," he can almost hear his father say. And that brings a small smile to his lips. Miguel continues sweeping.

The library stacks appear more crowded than usual. Matt saunters through the rows of ancient clothbound tomes, smiling casually at familiar and not-so familiar faces. The library staff recognize the lanky blond immediately, nearly a fixture himself at the Tenth Street branch. It's hard to imagine that in 24 hours this place will be empty for most of the next ten weeks. Matt knows this downtown library's routines like his own house. In fact, he's probably spent more time here in the last two years than he has in his own living room. He tries to imagine the painting that hangs above his mom's answering machine but can't recall if the frame is wooden or metal; is it brown or tan?

Yet he has memorized every fine feature of the portrait of Peter Hardeman Burnett, the state's first governor. A character from a Stephen King novel, his leering gaze stares down visitors as they enter the main doors. The 6-foot square oil sepia-toned photograph taken in the mid 1800s rests atop the information desk on the first floor. You can't miss it. Matt never does. Something about Burnett's icy stare that reveals the hardship of those times, that hints at the first governor's latent racist nature.

When Matt first discovered Burnett's hesitant attitude

toward admitting blacks to the state, he petitioned his town's library to remove the portrait. "He doesn't stand for what we stand for. He stands for hatred. That's not what I want my town to support." Matt had written the library board a letter about three or so years ago when his eighth grade history class was studying the Civil War. Everyone needed to create a brochure on one state and present their views on slavery and secession. When Matt drew California from the hat, he grumbled, hoping for something more glamorous like New York or Oklahoma. Yet when he began researching the state's political history and read more about Burnett and his statements to keep out blacks, he decided to use the project to promote the removal of the library portrait.

The library replied to the 13-year-old's "well-written letter", but avowed that Burnett also represented the state's beginnings as a free-thinking land and because of that (and because his descendants donated the valuable print) his image would remain, 'but thank you for contacting us, and we do appreciate your patronage at the Tenth Street Branch'.

So whenever Matt now enters the building, he returns the governor's glare with his own dissension, averting his prejudicial thoughts and choosing instead to meet the slightly cross-eyed gaze of Susie Mallicksen, his history teacher's sophomore daughter, who greets visitors and directs the elderly to the day's senior activity on the third floor.

After adjusting his backpack on his right shoulder, Matt continues searching the biography stacks for an empty study station. He passes the J-M row and spots a letterman's jacket and pink satchel resting on the floor. The desk sitting adjacent looks empty and unoccupied. Matt figures *finders keepers* and tosses his bag on top of the graffiti-scratched desk top. He pulls the equally marred chair from out of the insert and rests himself on the murky green vinyl cushion. Happy to have found one of the comfortable chairs; the T-W row only has metal seats.

Giggles and whispers swirl their way up and around the dusty bookshelves. Chattering girls scurry past his row, most likely on their way to a rendezvous or two in the Sociology stacks on the third floor. *If these books could talk*, Matt smiles at the irony. With so many phrases, rhymes and facts, you'd think these books had scripts aplenty for centuries without the need to share the superficial faux-sexual encounters of tell-all teenage girls and boys.

Matt pulls his heavy Calculus text from inside his canvas bag. He retrieves his black spiral notebook and a pencil. Unzipping the outer-pocket, Matt withdraws the expensive graphing calculator and neatly sets out the items before him like a surgeon preparing for a procedure.

"Okay, better get crackin'," he shares with no one.

Numbers and symbols have treated Matt well, never giving him grief like they do his two pals. So when he sits alone to study or finish a homework assignment, he feels a gratifying comfort, a satisfaction in the completion of a computation problem. There's no critical thinking or looking at the gray areas. There is a beginning, an algorithm, a solution. You are either right or wrong; and if you are wrong, you'll know it when you check it. Something there is to numbers and symbols. Matt settles further comfortably into the indented vinyl cushion and the hard, unforgiving wooden back. He stretches his thin Nordic legs out beneath the table as he works equations, searching for the ever-changing value of that elusive variable.

"So, if the function of x," he begins then stops. His right foot has found something round. Bending down, Matt spies the orange sphere beneath the desk. "Huh? How'd that get down there?"

He pushes back his chair so he can crawl beneath his study space and retrieve the ball. Rolling it around in his soft hands, his thumb slides past some lettering.

RT

"Hmm, RT," Matt smiles. He places the basketball on the desk top, steadying it so it won't roll to the floor. Finally balancing it between his calculator and textbook, Matt returns to his equations.

More giggles travel down the rows. Momentary distractions. Matt works extra hard to maintain his concentration on the numbers and symbols that jump and dance off the two-dimensional black and white pages. His pencil taps in staccato on the wooden desktop as he wills himself back inside the world of Calculus. It works, and he soon begins dropping equations along the lines, flipping into the back of the text to check odd-numbered answers. In the flow, Matt smiles. *Correct. Move the decimal one more space. That should be a negative there. That x cancels that one. Correct.* One-sided limits done.

After what seems hours but is really only about thirty minutes since his arrival, Matt feels the need to stretch his legs, get some air. Shoving his calculator in his back pocket (doesn't trust that it'll be there when he returns), he covers his book with his bag then moseys down the row and out into the center of the stacks.

He walks down to the first row and takes a left. Biographies A-D. Passing a finger along the dusty spines of the books, he spots a small red clothbound item with the lettering *JMB* imprinted in gold. Admiring the soft fabric stretched around the tiny hardback, he slips it from the shelf and opens to a page of text:

> *...he soon began writing plays. Perhaps JM Barrie's most famous play during his early career was "The Admirable Crichton". This combination of fantasy and social commentary may have set the stage for his best known work (and only piece intended truly for children), 'Peter Pan'. ... it was the play's roots, Barrie's earlier novel, "Little White Bird," which entertained his friends' young boys, George, Jack and Peter, that inspired his classic children's tale.*

Matt closes the book and carries it with him as he returns to the J-M row. Lost in thought with Barrie and the Lost Boys, Matt pays no attention to the long legs travelling in his direction.

Bump!

"Hey! Watch where you're goin' dream boy." Blind to the on-coming traffic, Matt falls back onto the thinly carpeted library floor, losing hold of the little red book and nearly cracking his calculator, which slides out of his back pocket and lodges itself under the shelving.

"Ow! Sorry, I wasn't watching –" Matt pauses his apology as he looks up to see who he's collided with. The out-stretched hand underneath a Black and Red Letterman's jacket extends down to Matt.

"No prob, you had your nose in a book. Hah! Guess that makes sense in a library." Ricky Traeger's gentle smile hides no signs of anger. "Shit happens. Help up?" His hand remains. Matt takes the firm grasp and allows the all-star forward to pull him vertical. An electric current travels up his arm and settles in the small socket of his right shoulder.

"Yeah, I guess. I was just," Matt looks around.

"Here you go." Ricky picks up the little red book, turns it around to see the cover. "JM Barrie, huh. Didn't he write 'Peter Pan'?"

Matt smiles. Why is he surprised an athlete, this athlete, would have any idea who is the author of a classic children's tale? "Yeah. That's him. It's a biography. I was just stretching my legs and found it over there." Matt points behind himself.

"Yeah. My mom teaches English Lit at State. We got stacks of these kinda crazy books at home. She's always trying to get me to read about the authors, says it's not just their stories we should study, we should learn about their lives and see why they wrote what they wrote," Ricky hands the book back to Matt. "I heard he was a little twisted. Him and that Lewis Carroll guy. You know, 'Alice in Wonderland'. I dunno though, I mean, just cuz these guys wrote kids' books and liked kids, it doesn't mean they were pedophiles or anything, you know, I mean, they were probably nice guys and all, and, yeah. Just, they were probably normal. Like us."

Feeling anything but normal right now, Matt finds no words. *Why can't I speak?* he thinks to himself. He stares at the dimples on Ricky's cheek. Well, he actually only has a right dimple. A solitary dimple and some stubble. Probably shaves way more than Matt, than Matt would need to, considering that he isn't doing any shaving now on account of the plan not to shave until…

"Hey, you OK? You seem a little out of it? Did ya hit your head?" Ricky reaches over to feel Matt's head.

Still lost in thought, Matt flinches when he feels the basketball player's warm hand brush across his right ear.

"Sorry, just checking for a bump."

Matt places his hand on Ricky's. Another surge of electricity races through his body. He is frozen, stuck in a moment indefinable, sure there is no turning back now, convinced that what he thought might be true is true. The electricity turns to a warmth radiating within and around his muscles, wrapping itself gently but firmly around the venous layers of his heart, travelling headstrong, determinedly up to his ears, burning, spilling over like paint, no, like molten steel, over his body like an armor. He quakes." Uh, yeah, I'm OK. No bump. I'm just a little spaced out from studying."

Ricky releases his hand from Matt's slight grip. "Uh, OK, yeah. Well, uh, I don't want a lawsuit or something, you know." Another awkward smile as he shoves both his hands in his jacket pockets. "So, uh, I was, uh, actually, I was lookin' for my ball. Lexie said she thought it mighta rolled under a desk, but I couldn't find it. That your Calculus stuff over there in the J row?"

Matt feels a heat rise inside his belly and spread across his face. Maybe he did hit his head. Unsure, he rubs his hand around the crown and back of his skull. "Yeah," is about all he can get out.

"So did you happen to see my ball?"

Matt remembers pulling it out from beneath the desk. Suddenly, he realizes what he did. He walked around the library stacks with it. *Why'd he do that?* But he knew why. So now where is it? He must've put it down when he pulled out the JM Barrie book.

"I think I saw it over in the A row," Matt lies. Well, sort of lies. "I'll go check."

Ricky looks around. "Okay. I'll come with you. I gotta get home. Lexie took off with some of the cheer squad."

Matt smiles, turns and heads back to the A row, hoping the ball is there. Ricky follows. Arriving at the aisle, Matt turns, looks down, and sure enough there's the ball. Sitting exactly where he'd imagined it'd be, had he actually been conscious of carrying it down here. He bends down and picks it up, turns and hands it to Ricky.

"Thanks," Ricky takes the ball. "Kinda creepy in here late in the day, huh? Like a ghost town in the stacks, man. Not a lotta people around."

Matt's heart races, the thumping pounds inside his chest so loudly that he can barely hear his own thoughts, let alone anyone else's words. He smiles nervously at Ricky. *Oh, God, I can't. I want to. I can't.*

"You know my mom is quotin' shit to me, all the time, man, from these authors," Ricky rolls the ball around his large hands, skillfully spins it onto his right index finger. "There's one from Barrie that I remember. It's in his book, 'The Little White Bird'. Ya know that one?"

Matt's heart calms to a steady beat, the thumping has lessened. He can breathe. He tries to remember the words on the pages of the little red cloth book that he holds in his hands. "I know he wrote that book. I don't think I know the quote you're thinking of, though."

Ricky stops the spinning, brings the ball toward his chest, holding it with both hands; he bounces it against his body then places it on the floor, nudging it with his toe to steady it and keep from rolling away. "Can I see that?" Ricky motions toward the small red book.

"Sure," Matt extends his arm handing over the book and shivers when Ricky's warm fingers brush against his as he takes hold of the small tome.

Ricky's eyes meet Matt's. Both boys hold each other's gaze for a moment that feels like a lifetime. Sometimes, when a lion is about to strike its prey, it meets the other animal's stare, holding it steady, letting it know who is in control. This is not that kind of stare. This stare is gentler. This stare is slightly uncertain. This stare asks a question, asks permission, asks for confirmation.

Matt does not look away. Unconsciously, however, he releases his grasp on the book.

Ricky takes it and inhales. Exhales. He moves his gaze to the cover then opens it as his finger travels along the pages, searching. He smiles. "Here it is. See." He steps forward, moving closer so Matt can see the words on the page, smell his lunchtime pick-up game, the remaining aroma of his generic shampoo that whiffs of such familiarity.

He traces his finger beneath the lines and reads:

"The reason birds can fly and we can't is simply because they have perfect faith, for to have faith is to have wings."

He closes the book, hands it to Matt. "It's a good one, huh? It's even in his biography. Whadya think it means?"

Matt unleashes his cataleptic fog, runs his own finger along the spines of other dusty untouched volumes that sit neglected on this library's shelves. He considers the question, regains his composure, and ponders the words of the 19th century writer. "I guess it means that we, that people, are afraid to do things. It's not that we can't do something because we don't have the tools or the skills. We just don't trust ourselves. We don't trust others. Well, that's what I think. I mean, I trust myself. I have faith that I'll pass that Calculus final tomorrow, but I'm not sure I have faith in my mom that she won't be disappointed if I don't. Faith is funny. You just need to have it, just take that step and say, I can do this. It'll be OK." Unknowingly, Matt has shifted his gaze onto the books, speaking more to them than to Ricky. Aware of this now that he's stopped talking, he looks over at the athlete, tries to puzzle out his intentions.

Ricky takes his hands from within his jacket pockets, bends and lifts the ball. Matt twirls the book around as he observes the tall boy, the thick dirty blond curls tucked behind his ears, the one loose strand that flops just above his right eyebrow.

Ricky meets Matt's stare for the third time in the last fifteen minutes. "Faith *is* a funny thing," he agrees. "Sometimes it seems too simple, though, to just trust and it'll all work out, but I guess it needs to start somewhere. Maybe at first with yourself then with one other person then together it can be stronger. You think?"

Unsure if they are still talking about birds and their ability to fly because of faith, Matt takes a chance. "Yeah, I think so. Faith is a choice. You can choose to have it, let go, believe, or you can disown it, let go, believe in nothing. I mean, faith is invisible; you can't see it, and it's hard to believe in something you can't see."

Ricky holds Matt's gaze. Gentle, yielding, soft. "I suppose that's why he says, 'to have faith is to have wings'. Faith gives flight to what you really want." He smiles without breaking eye contact. The smile, too, is gentle, yielding, soft.

Matt smiles back, and with some renewed confidence, replies, "Yeah. I guess everyone has wings. We just gotta find 'em."

6

INCUBATION

Growing up cannot be stopped. Once egg meets sperm, zygote embeds itself in the uterine lining, menses halts, and the female host does nothing more to stop development, the roller coaster reaches its final point of assent and the apex of turning downward gathers momentum. Blood vessels form, organs grow, muscles, tissues, bones assemble within their assigned atomic collections, and before the eyes of the sonogram, a single egg becomes a fetus becomes a baby becomes a life. One and the same. In synchronicity with the mother host, destined to exit into a world awaiting but not always prepared for its arrival. A violent series of squeezes, pushes and assertive thrusts, down and through a narrow, bloody, warm pathway forces this being - willfully or not - out. Its first sound often a cry, whimper, gasp, scream, or worse – silence. Blue. Panic. Shuffling of feet, hooking up of monitors, tubes pushed in, pulled out, injections, a slap, a compression, a gasp, a wail. Tears. Relief.

In the summer of 1974, when Matt West's tiny, wet and wrinkled infant body is finally pushed out by his petite teenage mother into the bright, sterile hospital room at St. Benedict's Hospital in Santa Niña, he greets the world with characteristic silence (or what would soon become the characteristic silence of this young man). His aunt returns the tight grip of her younger sister's hand, tears streaming down her own frightened face. Lee, drained, sore, scared, gathers back a more steady rhythm of her own breath and asks, "Why isn't he crying?"

The OB nurses scramble from machine to sink to drawer, seeming to ignore the bearer of this silent gift.

"Why is he so quiet," Lee tries again, this time directing her unanswered questions to her sister.

"It's OK, baby," Lee responds. "He's just getting his lungs ready. He'll cry. He will." She strokes her younger sibling's wet brow, pushing back her straggly strands of blonde hair.

"Owww, oww! Oh, God, it hurts, ow, help me," Lee screams uncontrollably, gripping again her sister's hand, pulling her down toward the bed.

"What's happening?!" Janie barks at the nurses who seem to have completely forgotten the two women are still in the room. "Why is she in pain? Help her!"

One elderly nurse turns, staring at the two girls as if they themselves are babies. "It's just the placenta. Tell her to breathe and push again. You'll need to coach her. We need to attend to this newborn."

This newborn. The three flat syllables hang in the stale hospital room's air like one of the many white flannel receiving blankets stacked in the corner. *This newborn.*

"Mmatt. Matthew. Tell, *oh God!*, tell the bitch his, *ohhh!*, name is, *whew-whew-whew*, name is Matthew," Lee manages to spit out at her sister between labored breaths as she desperately tries again to push, force, exert what remains of *this newborn* from within her tired body out onto the already blood- and mucous-soaked bed sheets.

Janie laughs at her little sister's cursing. She has maybe

heard Lee utter two other swear words in her short 16 years of life. Not ever at her parents who might have stumbled home one evening knocking a glass of water onto her three-page English essay for Ms. Wells' fourth grade California Mission History assignment, resulting in unplanned weekend rewrites from memory (as this was the 1970s, prior to the common word processors or computers that today store hours of work inside metal boxes, which later can easily be opened and repasted and reprinted in a matter of minutes); not at her own elder sibling who perhaps more than once shunned her baby sister from her bedroom as she gossiped with Allyson Mayes about Carrie Weiss; but one time at a crow that ate away the marshmallow moon of her third grade solar system, and another time at Mr. Mayes' golden retriever who peed on the Fern in her shoe-box diorama of "Where the Red Fern Grows".

Shit! and *Damn it!* Those were the two expletives. And now a third swear word to add to Lee West's small collection of verbal shouts. *Bitch*.

The gray-haired thick-waist nurse turns again and saunters over to Lee and Janie. She must be the relief. Neither girl remembers meeting her when they arrived just 17 hours earlier, Lee gripping her abdomen with both hands as her sister attempted to navigate the hospital protocol and find a room to prepare for their new family member. "Legs up, Honey, you can do this. Come on, sister, push! Push!"

"Ahh! Ergh!" then a sigh as the slimy red folds of mucous and tissue slide out from between Lee's legs and onto the soaking sheet.

"Good girl," commends the nurse as she lifts the gelatinous sack with her white-rubber gloved nurse's hands and places it in a round metal pan. "You know some folks cook this up and eat it. Others, the Navajo, they bury it. Say it's the link of child to Mother Earth. How about you girls, what do you want to do with it?"

Struck by the nurse's newfound interest in them and engaging conversation, Janie finds no words to respond. She turns to Lee who looks from the nurse to her sister then leans forward, the blood having drained clear from her face, hurls her jaw out, opens her mouth and pukes onto the bed between her knees.

"Guess that answers that question." The nurse smiles, forces a small chuckle, turns and tosses the remaining bloody connection of mother and child into a red plastic bin with what looks to Janie to bear some sticker for Nuclear Waste on its side.

She returns with a towel, which she tosses to the elder sibling. Janie wipes the trailing liquid from Lee's face, dabs the sweat from her brow, and finally hands it to her sister to wipe off her legs.

"Okay, momma, up you get. Let's get you moving just a bit with sister here so we can start your contractions and stop the bleeding. Ready, sister?" The nurse, who Janie sees wears the ironic nametag *Mary Payne, obstetrics, RN*, moves to the right side of the bed and motions to Janie to join her as the two support Lee's arms gently lifting her and guiding her to stand on the cold tile floor.

Small dribbles of blood and mucous travel down Lee's thin legs. She wavers a bit, but the two women steady her. Mary smiles, "Good job, momma, here we go, just a little walk."

Another woman moves behind the trio over to the bed, gathering the soiled linens onto the floor, pulling away the plastic mattress liner and returning the bed back in order as if their hotel stay has ended and new guests will soon check in.

Sunlight scatters across the green tiles and Lee sighs at the warmth they deliver to her pale feet. Her attention does not rest long at the chipped red nail polish she observes peeling from her big left toe. All three women pause and look up to the corner of the room where the doctor and a third nurse have stopped their fussing and are now walking toward the women with a small bundle – no bigger it seems than a football - wrapped tightly within a flannel white and yellow hospital receiving blanket.

The nurse hands the bundle to Lee whose eyes water and leak rapidly down her thin Nordic-pale cheeks. Her lips part, her face lifts, a smile involuntarily stretches itself across her freckled face. She gasps. "Oh, he's, he's OK. M-M-Matthew. Janie. My Matthew. He's ... look at him." Lee takes the bundle from the nurse as the two women continue to steady her stance. All five pairs of eyes stare down at the small baby boy. All five pairs of eyes tear up. How can they not.

"Now wasn't that worth all the trouble little momma?"

Lee and Janie laugh. The boy arrived at 21 inches long and 7 pounds 3 ounces. His first numbers. Well, second, if you count the 17 hours of labor, the 2 sisters, 4 nurses, 1 doctor, and this day 26 of the 7th month of the year. Numbers. Matt West's numbers.

Lee turns to her sister. "Oh, God, Janie, he's really here. He's here. Mom and Dad ... I wish ... Mom would have ... she would have wanted ... oh, Janie ... he looks just like Dad. Doesn't he? Look at him, Janie. He's so small. His fingers, they're so, so little and wrinkled." The baby opens its small mouth, puckers, seems to want to say something.

Mary wipes her cheek, "Let's get you settled momma. This little fella looks hungry. Ready for your first lesson?" She looks over to Janie.

"Lee, honey, your boy is hungry. Oh, God, can you believe you are about to breastfeed this little man, and just last week you were studying for a math test? Come on, little sister. Come on. Life. Wow."

And so Matt's world had begun. Set in motion by a death. Greeted with screams. Responding with silence. The roller coaster had reached the top and the descent down had commenced with a turn, a stomach hurl, shouts of fear, cries of glee, and tears of joy. It seems the roller coaster's approach to the top varies, it's the journeys down that move with predictable twists and turns, always reaching some end. Arriving with a mixture of relief and that uncontrollable, instinctive tug to climb aboard again. A morbid masochistic pull for some, a hopeful optimistic jerk for others. However, Lee hadn't quite apprehended that she'd arrived back at the platform. More turns, ascents and spirals down awaited her and Matt. Her baby boy had just begun his own roller coaster ride of life, and as he suckled at his teenage mother's breast, oblivious to all before him, the two enjoyed this moment of quiet, this moment where the future is so far away that it doesn't even matter what it brings.

Santa Niña's Tenth Street public library sits fifteen-feet back from the curb. The winding pathway to its concrete steps bends between the colorful border of various perennials – the lavender spikes of the Lily of the Nile, the fried egg persona of the Matilija Poppy, and the fuzzy red curls of the Kangaroo Paw - inviting thirsty readers inside its double-glass doors like a chilled glass of strawberry Kool-Aid on a hot summer's day. For Matt, the library is somewhat of a refuge, a sanctuary. For ten years, this three-story one block square structure has lovingly held Matthew West within its cement arms without judging, keeping all the secrets necessary, welcoming him back daily, missing him the moment he exits those double-glass doors.

The librarians know Matt like their own child. At the second-floor reference desk, Beverly greets him on Mondays through Thursdays, and Veronica offers suggestions for history projects on Fridays and Saturdays. Sunday remains a day of rest for bibliophiles.

Thus it would make sense that the place Matt feels most comfortable to explore who he really is would be within the familiar walls and stacks of this downtown library.

As Matt returns to his desk to continue his homework, he considers his chance encounter with Ricky. More importantly, he ponders the Barrie quote. "To have faith," he says in a low whisper to himself.

He moves to pull the rigid calculator from his back pocket. It's not there. Matt flashes to the fall, to Ricky, the little red book. About to stand and retrieve the necessary math tool, those long legs appear in front of him once again.

"Hey, you lost somethin'," Ricky extends a long arm before him and offers the object.

"Yeah, uh, I was just about to go, uh, look for it," Matt takes it, grazing his fingers slightly past Ricky's. *Electric volts.* "Thanks." He sets it down gently upon the wooden desk.

"So, how's the job app comin'? Need any help?" He rolls the basketball around his torso.

At first utterly confused, Matt slowly recalls the Shack, Ricky, and the folded piece of white paper he shoved in his back pocket yesterday. "Oh, I haven't started actually." He looks over at his calc book.

"Right. Studying. So maybe tomorrow, after finals, I could help you fill it out." He flashes that trademark smile. "It'd be good to have some intelligent conversation this summer."

Matt grasps the back of the wooden chair, swallows. "Yeah, totally," swallows again. *Why am I so nervous?* "So, you're around this summer? You'll be working?"

"Totally." Both boys laugh, and Matt suddenly feels at ease. Ricky smiles warmly. "Meet you here about 2? Gives us some time to sign yearbooks and all, right?"

Matt considers this, then fishes, "So, Lexie's probably got some cheerleading party or something after school, huh?"

The smile disappears. Ricky casts his gaze toward the dingy floor, brings the ball to his belly then looks up at Matt. Smiles. "Yeah, she's busy."

It's at this point, Matt enters a black hole. After this moment, he can't recall anything, what Ricky said next, who said goodbye first, nothing. The next thing Matt West remembers is that he's back at his study station, adjusting his chair and stretching his long legs out underneath the cold library desk, and turning unknowns into knowns.

Something there is about the world of numbers. Matt has always found a comfort in their ability to provide a known solution. You are either right or wrong. There's no debate, no subjectivity. X is or it is not. Period. When Matt, Miguel and Jesse sat at the back table of Mr. Carney's third grade classroom in Pine Crest Elementary School, only one of them had his times tables memorized. Only one of them could complete two-digit multiplication in his head. And only one of them knew how fast a plane needed to travel to complete a 873-mile journey in ninety minutes.

"What difference does it make how fast it's going if it gets us to where we need to go, huh?" Miguel would ask his number savvy friend. "You get on the plane, you get off the plane. That's all you need to know."

"Yeah. Maybe. But what if you want to be a pilot? You need to know that stuff." Jesse would suggest.

"I don't wanna be a pilot. I'm gonna be – ..."

"Yeah, we know, a soccer star," Jesse and Matt would respond in unison.

"Ugh! Mr. Carney's crazy. Matt, just solve it so we can get to recess on time," Miguel would bark as he'd roll the soccer ball between his feet underneath the small desk.

And Matt would find the solution, scratching out numbers, erasing errors, and circling his answer. Satisfied, the three would share their findings with Mr. Carney who would tap his ominous red marker on the paper before scratching out a big red star at the top. "Well done, boys. You're the first to complete the work. You can be the first in line to recess."

They'd smile, high five each other and slap Matt on the back. On the yard, it would be Miguel's turn to shine as he'd school his pals in the precise techniques of soccer on a dusty patch of dirt near the fifth grade boys' baseball game.

Matt, seated again at his study corral, repositions himself in the not-so comfortable green-cushioned chair. He considers his encounter, birds that lack faith, and the shiver still running along his spine and tickling the hairs at the nape of his neck. He rubs his hand along their track, hoping to reignite the spark. Bringing his hands to his face, he rests his eyes behind their warmth, taking in the memory. *It was real*, he tells himself. *There was a spark*. Yes. Absolutely.

He retrains his attention to the scattering of numbers and words inside the voluminous text. The images not foreign to this boy stand out upon the page like soldiers on the battlefield. Familiar with each, sure of their positions, clear on their paths and next direction. There is no discomfort in the world of numbers for Matt West. Unlike his classmates who might scribble algorithms or sample limits on the soft inside of their forearms, at the ready on test day, Matt has never felt the need to cheat, to have a back-up plan, just in case.

He's not the kind to really write on his own skin anyway. Tattoos and imprints are not yet the *soup du jour* of this generation. Permanent ink imprints exist solely within the soul of this confidence-lacking boy. These imprints tell stories of missed opportunities, moments where fear took charge over chance. That time back in Little League when he would stand in the sunny outfield at right, kicking at the dandelions, marveling at the strong throwing arm of his teammate in centerfield. That time when the two would run in after the third out, high-fiving and smiling and whooping it up as boys do. That time when the sunny smile of his teammate remained one moment longer than usual, when eye contact felt suddenly uncomfortable, when his hand lingered a little longer than usual as he retrieved the ball from Matt's own hand. That time when Matt and Ricky Traeger were teammates for one summer. That one most glorious summer when everything and anything seemed so totally possible until the oh-so-cheery smile of one Lexie Cortes interrupted the glory and replaced it with the black thread that says the world is not that way and so neither can you be. And that thread wound its way inside Matt's heart, stitching a message that said *No, you can't.* And so he didn't.

This day could not be one of those, but this day felt as if it might be. Would he stitch another scar upon his heart, telling himself that today is not the day for love? Today is not the day to take that chance? As he works to complete the last of his review problems, he overhears a scuffle (and is that a giggle?) in the next row. Peering through the shelves of books, he spies another letterman jacket. His heart races until he sees the large hand attached to the jacket reach out to steady himself against the structure.

"Come on, baby, we gotta be sly here, you know. Walls got ears. Books got eyes," he chuckles as the girl runs her hand along his felt red sleeve.

Matt can't make out the faces, but he recognizes the All-State voice of Nate Gibbons. He squints between the shelves trying to make out the girl.

"I know, but Jesse ain't here. He's waiting for me at home. Ain't no one gonna see nuthin'."

Matt swallows hard. Vacuous air rushes through his ears. He takes in quick, shallow breaths. Trying not to hyperventilate, he steadies his inhalations. *Shit!* he thinks to himself.

Boom! Matt jumps at the crash of his text book.

Voices stop in the next aisle, a head peers through the shelf, but Matt is invisible having bent to collect the book.

"Let's go, Rube," Nate whispers. "This place gives me the creeps anyway."

"Okay, I just gotta get my bag."

It's then that Matt glances to the floor. The letterman jacket is gone, but the pink backpack remains. Ruby's pink backpack. But it's too late. Before Matt can gather his own gear and clear out of row J-M, he sees Ruby's slender black leg and short cheerleader skirt step around the corner and into view.

"Oh!" Ruby gasps. "Matt, well, wow, I, uh. Hey. How's it goin'?"

Matt knows she knows he knows. He pauses. "Hey, Ruby, just gettin' in a few more minutes of studying, you know. Calc final tomorrow. Gotta get my notes in order and all." He decides upon the path of ignorance. *I didn't see nuthin'.*

"Yeah, me, too. Well, Econ final. And Spanish." She lifts her backpack and secures the zipper, patting down her hair as she sways. Her skirt swishes, and she and Matt observe its rhythm.

"Yeah. Not too worried about Spanish," his breathing normalizes, he manages a smile. *I didn't hear nuthin'.*

"Okay, well, uh, yeah. So, uh, I gotta go. Gotta check in with my man before I head home."

Matt cocks his head slightly and squints. The smile gone. *Is she playin' me for a fool?*

"You know how Jesse can be. 'You said you'd come by before dinner,'" Ruby mimics a deep voice and laughs.

"Hah! Yeah. He's a stickler for stuff like that," realizing which *man* she is referring to, Matt decides playing the fool is safer. *I ain't gonna say nuthin'.*

"Okay, well, see ya later, Ruby."

"Yeah. Uh, see ya." She turns with a swish. And she's gone.

Damn, what the hell am I gonna do with this? he wonders. Not realizing Jesse's own accidental witnessing of a hallway rendezvous just hours earlier, or Miguel's suspicion of one young lady's hands upon one lughead of a jock's shoulders, he frets over what to do. Should he just flat out tell Jesse what he saw? What he heard? Maybe he should check in with Miggy first. Yeah, Miguel would know how to handle this.

He packs up his backpack and pushes in the green vinyl chair then thoughtfully heads out into the hallway. Thinking he has time to consider his options, Matt casually descends the library staircase, unaware of Ruby's lurking presence at its base.

"Hey," she interrupts his daydream. "So what so interests you about one tall lanky basketball star?"

Matt balks. "Uh, what? Whaddya mean?"

"I mean, what intense conversation were two guys having in the dark corner of the second floor biography stacks?" She flashes a stealthy grin, cocky secure of her collateral.

"What intense conversation was someone's girlfriend having with another guy in a dark row of books inches from my ears?" he bravely retorts.

The two stare each other down. Matt, less confident, feeling he has more to lose. Ruby, not sure what she's feeling since she recently told herself (and Karen) that the spark had dimmed between her and Jesse.

Matt makes the first move. "Look, Ruby, I don't know what you're playin' at, but whatever fantasy is lurkin' in your silly head is nuthin'."

"Oh, so, uh, this bird ain't got no faith then?"

Matt swallows hard.

"This bird ain't gonna take a chance and spread his fairy wings?"

If she were a guy, Matt thinks, I'd punch her in the nose right about now, but she's not, and she could still go to Jesse or Miguel or even Nate and share her *fantasy*.

Truth is, Matt's not sure who they'll believe.

The setting sun strikes a penetrating ray through the wide open library windows on the ground floor. Matt looks past the glare and out into the late afternoon sky. A murder of crows flap wildly across the airy landscape. One trails behind, an eye out for prey, for predators. He observes their muffled caws through the library's thick glass windows. Matt smiles as he considers something that might work in his favor.

"So, you're not at all bothered that I might just share what I heard, what I saw, with Jesse tonight, and that he might just tell the cheer squad what a two-timer you are, and that those girls wouldn't just jump at the chance to knock you off your Junior Girl Head Cheerleader throne, and that you don't think Karen Gibbons isn't the least bit jealous that *you* are head while she's on the sidelines with a gimpy knee? You don't think that jealous little sister wouldn't just run with the others and join in on the scathing, back-stabbing high school girl bathroom talk? Behind your back? And with summer comin', how would you stop it? You'll be stuck at cheer camp with that same group of foul-mouthed jealous girls while Karen Gibbons'll be back here in Santa Niña with her big brother and Jesse and an entire ten weeks of nothing else to do but talk smack about her best friend. If you don't think that'll happen then go ahead and share your silly fantasy with *my* best friends or your lughead home wrecker of a jock.

"See, Ruby, guys just deal with shit. We hear it, and we believe it or we don't. We hash it out. Yell. Hit. Whatever. Then it's done." (At least, this is what Matt is counting on.) "But you girls. You girls are catty and jealous. Your pain is drawn out. Guys don't pretend. He's your friend or he's not. And when he's not, you just don't say anything." Matt has found his steam and he's on a train ride down a track so straight and wide that nothing worries him at all. *Nothing except the truth in his hollow words.*

"So go ahead and share what you *think you heard*, what you *think you saw* with my best friends, with your idiot new boyfriend. Go ahead. And I'll just share what I saw, what I know I heard, and chances are anyone will believe it because it's just what they expect of you. And that's where you are out of luck. Cuz no one expects much of me."

That's not true, really. Matt knows people do expect things of him. Just not this. Feeling no more words ready to spew forth, he idles past her and makes his way under the portrait of Peter Hardeman Burnett and his icy stare, out the double glass doors of the Tenth Street Library, and heads around the corner to Eighth, footing his way back home. His heart races inside his chest, but a smile slowly spreads its way across his face, pushing up a freckle here, forming creases beneath his eyes. A smile so wide, Matt just can't stop it.

It's the first time he can remember when he's really stood up for himself. Stood up for himself without the help of Jesse or Miguel. A strange feeling settles in the pit of his stomach. He doesn't recognize it at first, and he can't stop smiling. What is it, what is that odd sensation?

Is it possible that Matt West is winding down the backside of the roller coaster and arriving at the platform, arriving with a feeling of accomplishment, a feeling of *that wasn't so bad*, a feeling of *I can do that again*?

It's possible that Matt West feels confident, but has that

confidence simply been sitting on the surface, a piece of poisonous plastic waiting to be gobbled up by a confidence-deprived teenage boy whose head is clouded with uncontrollable thoughts about unordinary things that he might do, want to do, that might get him into more trouble than some snooty little remark from a pretentious head cheerleader?

He feels the ground beneath his feet as he reaches the gravel driveway. Pausing for a moment at the border of gravel and cement, the line where crumbly turns to solid, he recalls a saying his mom used to share whenever things were going smoothly. *If it seems too easy, it is.*

Matt starts to unlock the back door then thinks of Jesse and Miguel. He remembers the plan to study together for Calculus. He reaches back in his pocket, checks for his key, backs out, pulls the door shut and heads out across the gravel driveway distracted by the crunching beneath his shoes. A red-tailed hawk circles overhead, surveying the dense backyard bushes for a mouse or small house pet. It won't matter which to the hawk. A meal's a meal.

7

DISCOVERY

When Miguel was small, three or four, he'd crawl up onto his mother's soft lap and sit within the folds of her warm arms as she read to him from a colorful chunky cardboard picture book. His mother would hold onto him while he held onto the book. The small boy would turn the thick chewed upon pages and point to each brightly colored cartoon animal. She would point to the funny lines and squiggles, saying each animal's name. Then she would add, "What does the bunny feel, Mijo?"

"Shy," her small boy would respond, drawing out the vowel so it sounded more like *shiyeeee*. Then he'd hide his face behind his chubby toddler fingers to show her the shy bunny.

"Good, yes, good," his mother would coo. "*Bueno*. And what does the kitty cat feel?"

Miguel would look into his mother's dark eyes and raise his eyebrows, gently cock his head to the left. "Cooreeooos," he would attempt.

His mother would smile, holding in her laughter. "My boy is so smart. *Si*, Mijo, *el gato poquito es* very curious, *muy curioso*." She'd turn the page to Miguel's favorite. "Ooh, and *el leon*, Mijo; how does the lion feel?"

For this, Miguel needed to climb down from his mother's

lap and pull himself up tall, stretching his chest forward and his arms skyward, then he would bend down his arms and place his hands on his slender denim-covered hips and roar a gentle, "Puh-roud!"

Miguel and his mother would laugh and roar and hug. Then Francesca would gather her son up into her arms and gaze deeply into his round brown eyes. She would tell him how important it was to feel proud, to feel proud of oneself for what you have done, proud for what you can do.

This immigrant mother had no idea at the time about the double-edged bite her words held, how the sage advice of a doting mother could transform itself into the twisted and toxic anthem of an angry young man.

So over the years, that feeling of pride has turned on Miguel. Has turned within him like a poisonous venom that courses through the salivary glands of a viper. The cartoon lion has morphed into a deadly beast. Pride has evolved for Miguel from something free flowing and transformative into something stagnant like cement, a barrier that blocks out what it should invoke – a feeling, a desire to do what is right. A sense of pride in one's work to support a family. Pride in one's ability to love and care for those who depend on you. This is not so for Miguel.

This boy's pride has inflated his ego like a Thanksgiving Day balloon. Miguel's false pride has grown over and around him instead of within and throughout him. It is not a structure of strength that supports and upholds all that is good and right in the only son of Manuel Alma de Ramón. On the contrary, this pride has grown around the outside of Miguel like a sticky fungus that keeps out what is pure, what is the light and the air. Miguel's pride has blinded him to what is or can be. Miguel is the lion, a proud and furious lion on the hunt to protect his lair at all costs.

Feeling the soft folded edge of the narrow sheet, Miguel pulls out the crumpled twenty dollar bill one more time. "You never know," he repeats, flattens it out against his pant leg, folds it in half and slides it deep down in his front right pocket. He places the red-handled broom back in its corner, survey's the station and presses the button to lower the garage door.

Crash! Clang!

Miguel jumps and turns. "It's only me, heh, heh, just got such greasy fingers. Can't quite keepa hold of a silly old hubbacap." Al lifts the aluminum disk and places it gently down on the workbench. "Time a to go home, little man. The wife don't like a me late." He smiles and walks toward Miguel and the office door.

"Yeah. The old ball and chain," Miguel jokes.

"Mi Bella *es* no ball and chain, little man. She's the light of my life. I worka hard all day. She worka hard all day. I come a home exhausted. She come a home exhausted. I slumpa in my easy chair. She cook us a tasty a pasta meal with a sweeta Bolognese. Mi Bella es no ball and chain." Al stares deeply into Miguel's eyes, Miguel's guilty eyes.

"I was jokin', hombre. You know, pullin' your leg, your *lega*." Miguel shifts his stance and moves toward the open door. "Alright then, old man. You go home to your Bolognese. I'll go home to my math final."

The two laugh. "But you also go home with extra twenty in your pocket, no?"

"Yeah, that, too. Thanks, Al," Miguel gently rests his hand upon the kindly boss' shoulder. "I'll bring you one of Mama's tamales Friday. You bring me some Bolognese. Sabe?"

"Ok, ok, *ti ho da mangiare, mi mangiare*," Al replies. "I feed you, you feed me. See a you tomorrow." He flips the light switch, pulls the office door shut, then the outside door, double bolts both, and slaps Miguel on the back. "*Tornare a casa in sicurezza."*

Miguel laughs at his ability to translate Al's broken Italian. "You get home safely, too, old man." The 17-year-old hoists his backpack over his shoulder and steps onto his wheels, beginning his journey from work to home.

The agile teen moves swiftly across the station driveway, swerving through the broadening early evening shadows that paint poignant pathways across the pavement, and heads onto Pine Street, down Eighth. He isn't worried about getting home in time for dinner; he's in no hurry. The June evening air is cooling.

Besides, he wants to replay the day. Lughead Gibbons is out twenty, and Miguel Alma de Ramón is up. That's one for the downtrodden. Miguel takes a deep breath in and exhales, pounding his palms to his narrow still a boy's chest. "I am the hawk!" he shouts to the air. A pair of blackbirds flutter out of a nearby palm tree and fly out over the rooftops. Miguel observes their partnering pattern as they circle above and soon return to the tree from where they left. He smiles, pushes himself forward with his left foot and kicks a stone, watching it travel, skipping over cracks and landing on a patch of wet grass.

Miguel considers the stone, its inability to move without the will, the force of another. He recalls a science class lecture about physics, his coach's comments on the field about an object in motion. He adjusts his backpack over his right shoulder, feeling the weight of his Calculus text, laughing at why he even brought it home. After all, he is simply going to read over Matt's notes; there isn't anything more this text can offer at this point. He knows it now, or he doesn't.

One thing continues to nag at the back of his brown neck. He rubs his hand along the prickly ridges of his hairline. *Why did she have her hands on his shoulders?*

Miguel pivots his board to a stop at the corner of Oak. With a pop, he stands his board upright and steadies it with the tips of his fingers. He can see his home from here, but he doesn't feel ready to get there. He leans against the bus stop, sets his backpack and board on the bench, and hooks his thumbs through the loops in his jeans. Not one to wear a belt, but not one to droop his drawers neither, Miguel enjoys the loose fit of his denims, resting on the bony curve of his hip bones. He kicks at the shiny green bus bench, considering the replay in his mind of that squeaky red Camaro and its passengers.

Lughead Nate was driving, resting his right wrist on the steering wheel and hanging his left arm outside the car window, dangling it along the door, trying to play the cool casual driver that he's not, thinks Miguel. *Ruby sat directly behind him tapping her fingers along the seat (his shoulders?) to the thumping bass of Ice Cube or some other rapper.* Not Miguel's music.

He stops here, lost now inside his own song, he taps his foot. Sways his hips. Opting to move his body rather than rack his memory over Ruby's mistakes.

He doesn't advertise it, but he prefers the cooler stylings of Mariah Carrey or Boyz II Men. The in-your-face deep vibrations of 90s rappers stir an anger deep within Miguel. The demand to be a man - that to be a man means strength, power, dominance – irritates Miguel. Or so he says.

"You feel threatened, hombre, that's what I think," Jesse would say. "*You* wanna be the man, not Tupac or Ice Cube. You want the girls to thump to the beat of smooth movin' Miguel Alma de Ramón and his wild left foot. I got it right, amigo, you know I do."

He did. Miguel would deny it, but in his heart, he knew his friend had pegged him. Miguel competed with every alpha male that stepped foot on the pot-holed streets of this little town and even with those whose deep harmony busted through some lame speaker system in a squeaky old Chevy. The two go hand-in-hand, according to Miguel. Play the violent rap, you are the violent rap.

When he can, Miguel pumps some C + C or Boyz II Men on his boombox. He enjoys the gentle rhythms pulsating up through the arch in his right foot, tapping in time, extending along the path of his calf muscle and resting in the narrow boy sockets of his bony hips. Caught up in the moment of himself, Miguel unconsciously begins bopping his head and gyrating his hips to the imaginary beat of Zelma and Co.

Completely lost, forgetting the station, Nate, Ruby, Miguel takes up partner with the bus stop, blurts a lyric or two, "let the music take control," he spins, writhes his hips, "let the rhythm move you". He turns to face the street, just in time to see the giggling faces of three SNiHi freshmen in the back seat of their mom's sedan.

"For the ladies!" Miguel shouts. "It's all for you, ladies!" He blows kisses as they speed on; the blonde driver steals a glance in her review mirror at the discoing teen.

The car's taillights remind Miguel why he stopped here in the first place. He sits down on the green-coated bench and places the board beneath his feet. He rolls it back and forth as he considers the possibility of Ruby cheating on Jesse. Today's events fog his mind, but he clearly remembers yesterday afternoon at the Shack. Ruby's bright smile as she exited the Camaro. Her play to keep the peace between Jesse and Nate. *Why would she defend that big lug?*

It's true, Miguel's never been Ruby's number one fan, but she is his best friend's girl, and there's something to that. Actually, there's more than that. There was that one time. There's always that *one time.*

Miguel tries to forget it, but he can't. He tells himself that Jesse and Ruby weren't an item then. Well, that *is* pretty much the truth.

It was eighth grade, Ruby and Jesse were just flirting with each other at that point. In fact, they'd been flirting for nearly all of middle school and even back in the fifth grade.

Ruby had lost most of her toddler body-fat and was just about the best looking eighth grade girl in town. That, according to the three boys. Jesse hadn't made any moves on Ruby since the Orange Growers' Picnic back in 1978. Grade school was a lot of *girls got cooties* time. It wasn't until the middle of fifth grade that he really noticed Ruby Newton again. It was about then that Miguel noticed her, too.

He held back, on account of Jesse. He put his attention on Lucy Peña and Leslie Taylor (Carlos Sanchez had moved back to Texas after fourth grade). He held back until that one weekend in May at the end of their eighth grade year. That one day under the bleachers of SNiHi when Miguel had scored a hat trick for the Santa Niña Strikers and Jesse and Matt were both home sick with some stomach bug. Ruby and Lucy decided to use their cheer skills (ordinarily reserved for the Pop Warner football teams) to root on the town's number one 14-and-under Strikers and the wild left foot of Miguel Alma de Ramón.

After the game, Lucy's dad picked her up. Miguel told Ruby he'd walk her home. He had meant to put in some good words for Jesse because earlier that week, Jesse had confided in his pals that he was thinking of asking Ruby out, to go steady. He figured it would give him something to do over the summer while Matt played Little League and Miguel traveled with the Soccer Club.

Miguel had told his pal he might as well get some girl time

if he wasn't gonna flex his muscles. "You gotta practice the ole' lip-locks while we dominate the grassy fields and them sideline girls cheer us on. You get your action, little man, we'll get ours." Besides, Miguel wanted to say but never did out loud, Ruby was lookin' good. He'd noticed her, and he knew she had noticed him. But Miguel always put his friends first. Almost always.

Not exactly sure where things went awry, Miguel remembers it started to rain, one of those freak warm late spring rains the town often got before the scorching days of summer set in. The two took temporary cover under the bleachers before the lightning and Ruby's shrieks. Miguel instinctively wrapped his arms around her for protection, but he soon felt the warmth of her body and the curve of her hips and those firm newly budding breasts sitting against his chest. Ruby felt something, too. Embarrassed, she moved her body away from Miguel's.

"Oh, shit, I'm sorry, man, it just happens, you know," Miguel squirmed a bit and crossed his legs.

Ruby laughed. "Yeah, I know, it's just, I, uh," she paused.

"Let's just forget about it. Let's just wait for the rain to stop." Miguel rested his arms against a metal cross bar and peaked through the seats up at the cloud-covered sky. Then he felt her hand reach around his chest. He turned.

"Ruby, there's somethin' I've been meanin' to tell you," Miguel started.

"Shh," she placed her finger to his lips then took her other hand and pulled him toward her. She felt it grow again.

Miguel lost all power, all will; he couldn't remember his name. And he surely couldn't remember Jesse.

The next thing he knew, hands roamed everywhere, Miguel's, Ruby's. Their lips explored, passionately pulling in each other's tongues. Miguel's hands started to explore Ruby's body, cupping her breasts, reaching around to her buttocks, travelling back around to the front of her body, down. His hands ventured into places they should not have, and there was no resistance from Ruby. After their rain-soaked encounter, Ruby remained a virgin. A virgin until the day she joined Jesse at Matt's house when Lee was at work.

Miguel decides that if it's true that Ruby's cheating on Jesse with Nate, well, then, he'll tell Jesse everything. He has to. The guilt is eating away at him. Not sure if tonight is the night or not, Miguel considers cutting down Oak to Jesse's. Then he remembers the plan to study at Matt's. He lifts his backpack over his shoulder and secures the board under his arm as he walks the remaining block down Eighth past Cypress.

Digging his hands inside his front pockets, Miguel stops in front of his parents' home. He observes his mother's vibrant flowerbed that outlines the front, adding contrasting purples and whites to the home's own brazen display of color.

Back in the 60s, Mexican immigrants arriving in California attempted to carve out neighborhoods that reminded them of home. Seeking also to stand out, wanting their homes to add a bright contrast to their difficult lives, families created their own mix of pigment. Popular at the time was Mexican costume designer Ramón Valdiosera. He adored bright colors; his most beloved and copied, *Mexican Pink*, a kind of hot pink similar to fuchsia, found itself slathered on the stucco walls of numerous homes in Southern California.

Including the Peña-Alma de Ramón home.

It's not necessarily the feminine color itself that bothers Miguel but the brightness, the demand to be seen, the squeal the hue emits as passersby pass by. Many stop. To admire, some, yes. To ogle, many. True.

It is the ogling Miguel cannot tolerate. Their pale-faced

stares mock his family's pride. They do not understand the heritage, the honor the screaming tint holds for this family. They cannot comprehend its depth.

Martin Waters understood, and that is why he took the job to paint the modest single-story home in the Numbers back in 1969.

Miguel bends down and grabs the evening paper from the driveway before he opens the unlocked back door and enters the Mexican Pink homage to one Ramón Valdiosera.

"Mama, you home? Mama?" Miguel drops the paper on the kitchen table and follows his nose over to the stove where a pot of tamales steam. He lifts the lid.

"*Oye, mijo. Deja eso!*" Miguel ducks in time to miss the slap on the head. He lowers the lid with a clang, spins and runs out of the kitchen.

"Mama, I gotta go to Matt's and study for math. One hour. Okay?" Already in his room, pulling his shirt over his head, Miguel cannot hear his mother's response. Tossing the soiled white Tee on the floor, he sniffs his underarms then pulls a clean shirt from his dresser drawer.

His mother leans against the door frame. "You gonna pass that test, *mijo, si?*"

"Yes, Mama, that's why I'm going to study." Miguel takes a peak in his warped bedroom mirror that hangs over the back of his closet. He rubs his hand across his hair. "Time for another shave soon, Mama, no? Gettin' a little straggly."

Mrs. Alma de Ramón bends down to lift the dirty shirt and tosses it in Miguel's closet where a pile of clothes forms an amorphous blob inching its way out. She shuts the door. "Tomorrow you are finished. Then my boy is a senior. You will be our first graduate, mijo. I'm so proud of you."

Miguel turns. "Aw, Mama, stop. I'm not there yet." He

reaches inside his pocket, pulls out the neatly folded bill. He opens his mother's clenched fist and places the twenty onto her soft warm palm then folds his hand over hers. "For you, Mama. I got a tip today." He kisses her cheek.

Francesca Alma de Ramón pulls her closed fist to her chest and takes her other hand, raises it to Miguel's head and gently caresses the soft fuzz. "You make me proud all ready, *mijo*. You make me proud everyday." She embraces his cheek in her hand and squeezes gently. The two generations hold each other's stare. Miguel pulls his mother toward him and hugs her for a moment. Holds her.

Miguel steps back and places his hands on his mother's shoulders. "I'll be back by 7:30, Mama. Save me some tamales. Maybe Papa can eat with us. Maybe tonight, we wait for him."

"Aye, good idea, Miguel. Let's wait." She grabs his hand and swings it softly. "Adios, Miguel. Say hello to the boys."

Miguel moves past his mother and out of the bedroom. Passing through the kitchen, he shouts, "Adios, Mama!", slams the back door and bounces across the driveway, grabs his board, and pumps his way down to First street, a few quick blocks over to Jesse's.

Francesca, still holding the twenty in her closed fist, looks around her son's room. "*Aye, dios, mios.* Such a messy boy." She places the twenty in her cleavage and pulls the navy comforter over his bed. She fluffs his pillow and pulls the blinds down for the evening. As she turns to leave the room, she looks over at his desk observing its near cleanliness. *Why even have a desk,* she wonders. *The boy don't ever use it, always studying at Matt or Jesse's.*

Unable to contain her desire to clean, put things in order, Francesca straightens a stack of papers, opens the wide center drawer and lays two pencils in the narrow tray. She pushes the drawer shut, but something blocks its path. Jiggling it, the entire apparatus is now stuck. She tries again, shakes the drawer up and down, pulls, tugs, pushes, tugs. *Crnnkslpsh!* The entire wooden tray dislodges from the desk and both it and Francesca crash to the floor.

"Aye!" she shouts to no one. Seating herself upright, she brushes some pencil shavings from her lap and begins to gather the spilled items one by one, returning them to the drawer, which itself must be turned upright. "What a mess, Miguel. Why so much stuff that you don't even use." More of a statement than a question.

Carefully, she sets the items inside the drawer, surmising their proper location in the partitioned tray: A black permanent marker, pad of yellow sticky notes, two retractable pens (one black, one blue), roll of clear tape, rectangular green lidded pencil sharpener with yellow daisies adorning its plastic holder (empty now, its contents scattered across the thin blue carpet), a tiny pink eraser (that looks partially gnawed), half a dozen small metal paperclips, a wooden ruler, a small key (perhaps to a bike lock?), and thirteen cents in change (a nickel and eight pennies).

As Francesca steadies the drawer and carefully guides it back along the tracks, into its proper location, she wonders which of the items could have caused the jam. She closes the drawer and pushes forward the small wooden chair. She exits, only to return within moments with the house vacuum. Impossible for a housecleaner to leave her own home so untidy, Francesca finds an outlet and starts up the beast.

She attaches the hose so she can reach around and beneath the furniture. As she maneuvers the machine, allowing it to suck up the array of shavings and other debris, the vacuum crackles and grinds as if gnashing its teeth on some bones. Francesca pauses her task, depresses the on/off switch and sets the vacuum upright next to the door. Curious about the gritty objects upsetting her machine, the round housecleaner stoops down and peers under Miguel's bed. Lowering herself, she stretches her short chubby arm as far as she can reach, trying to grasp the item she has spied resting at the foot of the bed near the wall.

Pressing her left cheek to the bedframe, she extends her arm as far as she can. Her fingers come upon an item. Its jagged edge pierces her skin as she tries to grab hold of it. Her reach comes up short. She locates a pencil from the desk drawer and uses it to extract the unknown debris from within its temporary cave.

As she sits back on the floor, knees bent like a kindergartner at story-time, Francesca moves the pieces about on the carpet with the yellow wooden pencil. Initially annoyed at these stubborn non-vacuum suckable things, she soon understands what's before her.

"Aye!" she screams and quickly shimmies back from the voodoo-like items. She breathes, rights herself and moves to the doorway, resting her hand on the vacuum as if this modern machine will protect her from such evil.

She studies the items, small bony fragments that appear to be exactly that. Bones. Moving an inch or two back, bending slightly, she turns on the ceiling light as the setting sun withdraws its illuminating support.

What is this, she wonders. More importantly, what is this doing underneath the bed in which her son sleeps?

Assuming a new sense of courage, Francesca takes another small step toward the bony and feathery objects which silently mock her timidity. After a moment more, telling herself this thing - these things that sit together as one - is not alive, assuring herself that it won't attack her, she walks over to the desk, pulls out the chair, sits down and reaches to place the objects on the hard surface.

Observing the smooth texture of the tiny items, she pushes them together with the pencil, believing they form some sort of puzzle. Gathering courage, she takes a finger, running it along the smooth feathery texture. Convinced now nothing is about to jump up at her, Francesca lifts the feathered item. It's about the size of her palm. She returns her finger over the delicate surface and beneath it.

Confirming her initial instincts, she says aloud, "*Un ala. El ala del un ave.*" She is certain it is the wing of some kind of bird. Its brown variations and firm texture suggest perhaps it is a strong bird, a hunting bird, maybe an eagle or a hawk. No longer afraid, Francesca finds the wing and small bone fragments fascinating. More so, she finds the reason her son has such an object curious.

Did he kill the bird? she wonders. *Where did he get such a thing? Did he steal it?* Suddenly concerned the items might be dirty, carrying some sort of disease, she places them back beneath the bed, as far back as the stoutly woman can reach.

She stands, wipes her palms on her pants, walks out of Miguel's room, down the hall and into the bathroom where she scrubs clean her hands for about two minutes. She returns to his room, retrieves the vacuum, turns off the light and returns it to the utility closet.

Francesca decides that tomorrow she will venture to the library and check out books on bird skeletons. She wants to know what kind of dead carnage her son keeps hidden beneath the bed that he lays his head upon in the evening.

8
A CRACK

Balancing upon the slippery steel ribbon of the useless and obsolete rail track, Jesse deliberates over the afternoon's events. *They were kissing.* He's sure of it. Yet only moments prior, Ruby had nibbled on Jesse's own ear, whispering promises to *him*, promises she couldn't keep, sending that uncontrollable and exhilarating shiver throughout his body. He runs his hands down his denim-covered thighs as if he might simply rub away her memory.

Damn her! How could she? The pity that has been wallowing in Jesse Waters' knee caps turns, burns, gurgles upward into his belly, forming a fine pool of lava waiting to evacuate, to launch out of his body and onto the cracked pavement at his feet. He swallows, clenches his fists, and stares down upon the worn track bed. Spits. He is John Henry, hoisting hammer upon nail, pounding and grinding, sweating and toiling, doing all it takes to get the job done. Not stopping for pretty girls. Not considering the noon-day sun that burns its rays into the deep pores of his black skin, his mocha tan, seething milky brown skin.

He kicks at the raised steal track that rests slightly above the aggregated tar road. The town, too lazy or too proud, decided to build around the historic rail line rather than follow through with the costly task of removing it.

Exhausted, hot, Jesse sits down on the curb, hidden between two parked cars, and opens his backpack. If there were ever a time he needs something to relax him, it's now. Uncle Winston says it's harmless, he does it all the time. Jesse's never actually tried it. In fact, Winston said he'd kill Jesse if he ever caught him smoking. He told his nephew that it was OK for adults because they aren't developing anymore. Well that was Winston's lame reasoning when Jesse caught him smoking a joint behind Grandma Celia's rosebushes last month.

Jesse flicks the lighter he keeps with the two joints he found in Winston's bedroom Saturday night when he babysat the twins. He places the small hand-wrapped paper tube to his dry lips and inhales.

Cough! Cough! Jesse gasps, spitting out much of what he inhaled. He tries again, this time slowly. Just a small cough. He sits for a few minutes, drawing three more times. He tries to keep in as much as possible. That's how's he's seen it done in movies. Soon he's feeling it.

The air around him closes in. His hand shrinks and grows before his eyes. He leans back, feels the warm soft air embrace his cheeks, caress his heart. He lies back against the cool grass, closes his eyes, opens them, stares up into the vastness of the blue sky. He inhales then sits up and snubs out the joint, placing the remaining piece along with the lighter back inside the baggie and into his backpack.

He stands. Teeters a bit, steadies himself on the hood of a white Camry. "Dang. Whoo!" Jesse totters some more. Gathering his bearings, he stretches his neck back and peers up skyward. A lazy hawk circles above. Jesse follows it for what feels like hours. The bird keeps circling and circling. Jesse recalls Miguel's ruminations over embodying a bird. What had Jesse said he'd be?

Oh yeah, an owl. A great horned owl. Jesse laughs. He laughs some more. For some reason, the idea of flying over town as an owl is the funniest thing ever.

Beeeepppp! A car whizzes past the day-dreaming youth who desperately tries to shut out the world around him. Barely flinching, he turns toward the departing blue Audi, hurls his backpack from his shoulder in its direction and raises both middle fingers in classic adolescent posture. No words escape his lips, just the simple universal gesture.

The car continues down First Street, ignorant or indifferent to the boy's complaint, remark, plea.

Jesse's thoughts are sporadic. No timeline contains them. He is no longer an owl in flight over town. He is a child at an orange grower's picnic. It is the moment when Ruby Newton entered Jesse's life. The moment. Yet at *this* moment, he can't quite latch onto that *one* moment. As if it's covered in grease, lubricated by distance, slowly vanishing through the vapors of time, Jesse reaches back into the cavernous regions of his short-lived memory trying to grasp one slippery moment before it escapes his jealous mind forever.

He wants to take love hostage, hold it captive inside his angry body. His head spins. Love. It is here now. It is gone. Ever. Never. Forever. Jesse spins himself, extending his arms, taking flight. He crashes into the side of a parked car and bounces off, nearly falling to the ground.

Falling. Falling in love. Falling out. In.

Love does not enter lightly, tapping one on the shoulder and whispering gently, *I'm here. See me.* Love booms into a room, into a heart, tumbling over anatomical furniture, tripping over the slippery arterial pathways into the moist and beating center of being. This is how Jesse remembers remembering Ruby. She boomed into his life, raising the thumping of his organ to deafening decibels. And when she did that, he kissed her. He's sure of it. Even though he was only 3. He remembers it like yesterday. Or was he 4? Like forever. Like never.

He cannot see the whole moment. What Jesse does remember, however, is that day at Matt's. The first day at Matt's, and the last day at Matt's. The day he emptied the trash, washed the sheets. The day he didn't tell Ruby about a mess in the bed, about a hole in some latex, about the possibility, the probability that some of his, that some of that, that some leaked out of him and into her.

This possibility of a probability travels within the thought tunnels of Jesse's burning, aching, lovelost mind. He resides inside. In the burning. Imagining his hand travelling along the naked curve of Ruby's smooth hip. In the aching. Feeling the firmness of her tender thighs and buttocks as they tensed and stretched beneath him. In the love lost within the deep brown pools of her dark round eyes. His fists curl. He pounds his thighs. He screams at the top of his lungs for all the world to hear.

"Ruby!" he shouts. "Ruby!" he screams. "Rubeeeeee...." He is spinning. He is standing. He is still. He is moving. He is lost.

Jesse doesn't know it yet, but he is running - and at a ridiculous speed - along the slippery track of the defunct and forgotten Santa Niña Rail, down First Street, past Pine, through the intersection of Oak where the Stop sign bends at a 75-degree angle because Leslie Taylor arrogantly decided she really hadn't had that much to drink behind the bleachers at that football game last winter against Grove High, and down toward Grove Street, toward home, toward Momma. He shouts and screams and runs. And the tears trail down his black cheeks, his mocha cheeks, his coffee brown cheeks and fly off into the wind as if they don't really belong to him. But they do.

And maybe if he didn't blink, wipe away that one tear and close his eyes for that one second, Jesse might see, maybe hear the honking, the beeping, and the screeching of tires in time. But he doesn't. And the small black Honda driven by Leslie Taylor's dad, the car that just weeks ago sat on the floor of Al's for a squeaky brake problem, might not need to swerve and test out those new brakes. But it does.

Tires screech. A man screams. A horn honks. Mr. Taylor slams into the tilted Stop sign, nearly righting it back to its 90 degrees. His airbag deploys and his glasses fly off at the violent burst of plastic. Jesse does a near 180 and spins with and against the black Honda and over the hood of a parked white Toyota Camry. He tumbles to the ground, falling in between the two Japanese imports made in America. Crunching glass grinds into the soft palms of his hands and knees. He rolls over and onto the curb.

The confused driver pours himself from the dented vehicle, sans eyeglasses and steadies himself on the bent trunk of his car. He squints down the street in search of the person, he's sure someone was in the road, but can't bring into view anything but fuzzy cars and trees. He moves around the front of the car, surveying the damage. It's then he spies the legs jutting out from behind his vehicle. His heart sinks. He flashes to a business meeting at lunch today at The Peel. *It was just one Martini, and that was at least three hours ago.* The irony of his situation and his daughter's does not escape him.

"Are you OK?" he moves around and sees the boy. "Son, are you OK?" He bends down and touches the boy's left leg. *Moans.*

Jesse opens his eyes as a crow glides overhead and alights on the electric pole. It caws. "Am I dead?" he asks. *Wishes.*

Mr. Taylor breathes deep and lets out a relieved sigh. "No, son, just a bit tumbled about. What were you doing in the street?" It's a concern more than an accusation.

Jesse looks to the black bird as if he has all the answers. "I dunno." He sits up, shakes his head a bit and looks over at the guilty man. He takes in the scene, remembering the hallway, the kiss, her hands. "Shit!" He's not dead. Today happened.

"You're Jesse, Harold Waters' boy, right? Look, let me help you up. I can walk you home. You can walk, right? I mean, did I, I don't think I, did I hit you?" Taylor steadies himself, leans against his bruised car. *Jesse Waters*, he muses, *what are the odds of that?*

The two eyes meet. Jesse runs his hand along his aching thigh, his aching right thigh. "Ow! I, uh, shit!" As he turns over his stinging hands, dazzling shiny shards of glass poke up from his tender brown palms, like thousands of sea stars scattered across the sand. He looks back at Mr. Taylor. "No, you didn't hit me, Mister. Maybe. I dunno. I think I rolled over that white car. Maybe you missed me," *unfortunately*, he wanted to add. "I'm OK, Mister. Just gotta get this glass out. And, uh, my leg hurts. I'll be OK."

"Let me help you." Mr. Taylor moves to hoist Jesse up by the elbow. Jesse holds his arms up as if he's just sanitized for surgery. His palms sting. His leg pulsates. He's dizzy. "I got you, there, lean over a bit on me. There you go." They reach the curb, and Jesse notices the Honda. He feels a sense of déjà vu.

"Ah, shit, you're Leslie's dad. Man, I, uh, I guess I shouldn't've been walkin' in the road. I was a bit, you know, out of it. I mean, I ain't high or anything like that, just, it's, well, it's …. It's been a rough day."

"Yeah, I hear that," Mr. Taylor looks back over at his crumpled Honda. He laughs a bit then rubs his eyes, runs his shaky fingers through his gelled back thinning brown hair. Rex Taylor sits on the City Council. Jesse can't remember if he's the president or just a councilman. He forgets that in small towns like Santa Niña, the president of the council – the one who gets the most votes – becomes the mayor. Rex Taylor did not get the most votes. "Well, I gotta find my glasses, son, and then I guess I better call a tow."

"Man, I'm sorry, Mr. Taylor," Jesse lamely offers. "Can I help?"

Mr. Taylor looks over at Jesse's hands, which he notices are trickling blood. "You better get home and have someone help you with that, I think."

Jesse looks down. "Yeah, I guess." He tries to pick out one long piece of glass. "Shit! Dang, they're in there, huh?"

"Get some aspirin, soak them in ice water, and you won't feel a thing," he pats Jesse on the shoulder. Jesse wonders how Leslie's dad knows so much about taking out glass. "I suppose you have some studying to do tonight as well? Last day of school, finals and all. I sure am sorry you were on the road when I was."

Jesse considers this. Looks over at the Stop sign and down at his legs. All in one piece. "I think I was probably lucky it was you, Mr. Taylor. Anyone else, and, well, I mighta not been so lucky to have just glass in my hands."

Taylor isn't so sure of this logic, considering what happened last time. However, he wasn't the driver. True. He was drinking, though, so that couldn't have helped the situation. Still, this time is different, he tells himself. He finished that lunch hours ago. In fact, if the cops were to breathalyse him right now, he's sure they'd simply find a case of bad breath. But really, what are the odds it's Harold's boy?

Rex Taylor smiles. He cannot suggest the boy should be sorry, that he shouldn't have been wandering in the middle of the road. It's fate. Or is it destiny? He's not sure of the difference right now. His face stings. He reaches up to his right cheek and feels a dull bruise forming.

"Yeah, those air bags might save your life, but I think they can give you one helluva bruise." Jesse himself has never been in a car accident, but he remembers his dad telling him about Uncle Wayne and the irony that airbags started being used in cars a year or two after his accident.

"Yes. Well, I suppose we can count ourselves lucky today, Young Mister Waters," he begins tapping along his face, searching out other bruises like landmines. "Just cuts and bruises today." He looks over at his car and frowns.

"You should take it over to Al's on Pine. He's awesome. He'll fix you up." Actually, Jesse isn't so sure Al does body work, but he can't think of anything else to say.

"Sure, I know that place. Good idea." For the first time, Taylor notices the small crowd gathering on the sidewalk. He looks over at them. "We're fine. Looks worse than it is." He looks to Jesse.

"Yeah, all's good here. Lucky day."

"Are you sure you don't need an ambulance," inquires Mrs. Weiss. She is truly concerned and not just being nosey. Actually, the crash was loud enough to be heard throughout the entire block. Those who aren't on the street looking are probably not yet home. "You don't look so good Rex."

"Oh, no, I just need to find my glasses," he replies recognizing Carrie Weiss' mother's voice more than her blurry face. "You're just not used to seeing me without them. They must be in the car somewhere." He nods over at the stationary vehicle that sits up against the Stop sign like a drunken sailor.

At this, Jesse peers in through the passenger window. He raises his hand to shield his eyes from the glare; the movement itself pulls at his skin where he wishes it didn't. "I bet they flew onto the floor, Mr. Taylor."

Mrs. Weiss moves closer. "Why don't I call your wife, Rex. You're going to need help getting home." She looks over at the Stop sign. "And probably a tow."

The two parents meet eyes. Taylor lets out a small chuckle, remembering their girls' own event with the same sign. "I suppose I won't need to fill out so much paperwork this time being that they'll have me in the system."

"I'll give Suzie a call then," Mrs. Weiss takes his comments as confirmation that he could use his wife's help with this mess.

"Thanks." Mr. Taylor turns to Jesse who by now has regained his balance and a throbbing feeling in his hands. "How about you then, son. Can we help you home?"

Jesse looks down the street. First right, trying to spot his backpack then left toward home. "Naw, I'm good. Just a few houses down that's me. I can make it just fine. Thanks, though, Mr. Taylor, and, uh, you know, sorry and all. You don't really need to talk to my parents, do you?" Jesse'd rather not deal with his mother's 'I told you to stay out of the road' lecture or his dad's 'tell me you got more sense than that, Jesse, tell me you do' speech. Then he remembers sitting on the curb. Spinning. He looks again for his backpack.

"I'd say we're even Mr. Waters. Just glad no one was hurt this time."

Not sure if that's a threat or if Mr. Taylor is just a bit confused, Jesse just smiles. Maybe he's talking about Leslie. Although Leslie only had a few scrapes and bruises herself. Maybe he means Jesse might not be so lucky next time. Well, one thing's true, Jesse thinks, those airbags are life saviors, and he's glad Mr. Taylor didn't get more badly hurt because Ruby is such a cheater. "Me, too," he manages.

Mrs. Weiss leaves the scene, presumably to call Mrs. Taylor. Most of the other lookee-loos also return to their previous tasks having observed no need for ambulances or police cars, just a tow truck for now.

"Jesse, I'll need to let the police know what happened to the post maybe. So that might mean getting you involved, but

I don't think there'll be any problems for you. They'll just need a statement, you know." The world is starting to make sense again for Mr. Taylor, although his head is beginning to throb.

"I suppose," Jesse responds, looking down at his hands then over at the sign post. "But, really, do you think they'll even notice, or care? I mean, look at the sign. It's practically upright now. It's like you almost fixed it." Jesse pauses at this thought, *an accident that can be reversed, returned to its previous nearly upright state.* He wonders if he and Ruby could be uprighted. He doubts it, with more than a 15-degree knock to their relationship. How is it even possible to straighten this mess out? He kicks the bits of glass and watches them scatter. His thoughts move on, unable, unwilling to sit with the pain, the heart-ache. "It's not my fault, though. It's hers."

"Hers? I'm not following," Mr. Taylor scratches his head. "Who's *her*?"

"Huh?" Jesse returns. He looks up. "Oh, uh, sorry, wrong number." He tries a laugh.

"Ha ha, I see. You OK, Jesse? I mean, Mrs. Taylor is on her way and we can see that you get home safely." He looks down First Street, hoping to see his wife, not sure if she'll walk or drive. Heck, he's not even sure she'll come.

"I'm good, Mr. Taylor. Really. Just thinkin' of other stuff. You know how it is," Jesse smiles and steps from the grass to the sidewalk. "I'm gonna head home. Need to get these glass things from outta my hands. They sting. I'm gonna try your trick with the ice water. That sounds like a good idea."

"Yeah. It should help. It'll still hurt some, though." Rex Taylor walks around his car and bends inside the driver's window. "Aha!" He opens the door and reaches down beneath the now deflated airbag. He pulls himself out and stands raising his hand in the air in triumph.

Jesse laughs. "Right on, Mr. Taylor, your glasses!"

"Yes, better," he says as he sets them gently upon his slightly bruised nose. "Well, I'm going to just grab my briefcase here and start walking home. Suzie should be on her way. I'll save her a few steps." He grabs the case from the passenger seat and closes the door, starts to lock it then laughs and simply shuts it.

"Good one, Mr. Taylor. Well, sorry again. I guess I'll just see you 'round." Jesse pauses, unable to shake hands, and not entirely sure what is the proper good bye to the man you caused to crash into a Stop sign.

"Alright, Jesse. We'll check on you later. Glad you are OK."

Jesse turns and continues down First. *OK? No, Mr. Taylor, I ain't at all OK.*

Jesse reaches for the knob on the back door, inserting the key and turning the handle with the tips of his fingers, trying desperately not to use his entire palm, he somehow manages to open the door then pull it shut with only a slight grimace.

He checks the clock. Just past 5. He knows his mom is still at school correcting papers, and his dad won't be home until after 6. That gives him a good chunk of time to clean up his hands and figure out a reasonable story about his ripped jeans and cut up palms. However, with the guys coming over soon, that's another distraction. Jesse's undecided whether distractions serve a useful purpose now or not.

Searching the medicine cabinet for some aspirin, he finds Tylenol and decides that'll work. He laughs, thinking that now is not the time to become a purist. He pops the cap and tosses two in his mouth, cupping his hand under the bathroom faucet to slurp up some water. He tilts his head back; as he leans forward, he catches his reflection in the mirror. It's the first time all day. His eyes are bloodshot, probably from all the screaming and yelling earlier. *Had he cried, too?* He can't remember. He walks to the kitchen for some ice. Every move is painful. His leg throbs, his head aches, his hands sting. If he hadn't already cried, he could do it right now.

He manages to fill a small metal bowl with several ice cubes, adds water from the kitchen tap. He dunks his hands inside. *Yikes!* He quickly withdraws them. *Don't be a baby, Jesse.* He places them in again, slowly, searching for a sense of comfort in the cold. He lifts the tweezers he'd found in the bathroom cabinet.

His hands bloody and numb, Jesse awkwardly maneuvers the eyebrow tweezers, pulling one shard at a time from his left hand. He drops each on a napkin. He goes for more, repeating this tedious task about eleven times, every so often stopping to dab the bright red blood with a tissue. One hand complete, he places both hands back in the freezing water observing how much ice has melted and how the water isn't actually so much freezing as it is just plain cold and uncomfortable.

Next, he starts in on the right hand, which is much more difficult considering he's not very skilled with his left. Digging deeply into the flesh of his tender palm, Jesse works tirelessly to remove the sharp slivers of glass. His skin tugs angrily at each piece, reluctant to release the intruders. Using a thin sewing needle that he found in his mother's craft box on the counter, he bores the fine end under his skin, gently encouraging each sliver, one at a time, to release itself from his body. He thinks he could spend the entire day digging out the shards, but in the same moment, he wants to stop, give up and press his hand further into the counter to embed each sliver there permanently – a reminder of the pain. Each sliver, a memory, a stab into his heart, tearing away any thought of forgiveness.

Instead, Jesse forges on, eventually completing the daunting task. He soaks his hands in the bowl of water, adding warm tap water, hoping to quell the throbbing. Leaning over the sink, he lowers his head against the stainless steel faucet. He closes his eyes and lets the tears fall as images of Ruby wander aimlessly across the dull landscape of his thoughts. That bright smile in history class that would say *only a few more minutes of boredom then we can hang.* The shapely silhouette of her girlish figure wandering down the gray hallways of SNiHi. The swish of her cheer skirt. The lilt in her laugh. The tilt of her head. The deep round eyes that soaked him in. The touch of her soft lips against his.

Over.

He could feel it.

Over.

The realness of the end surges through his body, winding its way around his arms and legs, crashing inside the pit of his belly, seeping out the corners of his eyes, dropping reluctantly into the dirty, tepid bowl of water that does not sooth his aching hands.

Ruby.

Over.

Real.

A pounding thunders inside his head. A loud knocking. He lifts his hands up and beats his bruised fists against the hard counter top. "Agghhhh!" he screams. "Aghhhh!"

"Jesse!"

He gulps in the air, exhales.

"Yo, Jess!"

He turns his head, catching the clock. *Shit. Miguel.*

Jesse picks up the soft terry dish towel with the yellow and orange stripes and black bees along the fringe. He wraps his hands tightly. The firmness feels good.

"Yo, Jess, what's goin' on, man. Why you screamin'?" Miguel enters through the unlocked back door. He leaves his board outside, leaning it against the stucco wall, making sure to avoid the small potted flower pots that sit in neat rows along the driveway.

The curious friend eyes the towel wrapped around his hand like a bandage.

"I, uh, I just, uh, scraped up my hands, that's all," Jesse walks back to the sink and unravels the towel.

"Damn, bro, that's nasty."

Jesse smiles. "Yeah, it's nasty, bro." He motions toward the tiny pieces of glass still sitting along the counter top like fallen soldiers on a battle field.

"Shit, man, whadja do, crash through the window?" Miguel turns and scans the kitchen, believing he'll find evidence to confirm his crazy idea but sees nothing.

"Nah, I, uh, just kinda had a little accident on the street."

"Accident? With what? Your feet?" he laughs.

Another smile. "Kinda."

"Damn, you's crazy, bro." Miguel turns Jesse's wrists to examine more closely the puffy red palms and tiny dots of dried blood that scatter across the landscape of his brown skin.

"Yeah, well, I was just a little, kinda, I dunno, distracted." Jesse tosses the towel across the counter into the corner by the toaster. "I don't wanna talk about it right now, man."

For a moment, Miguel thinks maybe Jesse knows. Thinks maybe that lame rusty red Camaro took a detour down First Street just for show. He tries a bite. "You with Ruby? She hurt?"

Blowing cool air on his throbbing palms, Jesse pauses, looks over at his friend, remembering his screaming. "Shit, man, she's with fuckin' Gibbons. I saw them. Shit! I saw them in the hall. Fuck her!" Jesse's fists bawl up again, and he's pounding them against each other. He draws them into his own chest and grimaces. "Aghhh!"

"Yo, bro, chill, man. Are you sure? I mean, like, she's

tutoring him and stuff, and she's always with Karen and all, and are you sure? I mean, what'd you see?" Miguel, afraid to ask the question, turns instinctively away and walks over to the fridge. Opening the white door, he peers inside and grabs an orange.

"I saw what I saw." Jesse is sitting now, his head slumped down, his hands hanging between his legs.

Miguel moves to the sink and starts peeling the orange. He glances out the lace-curtained window thinking back to Al's and the bird's nest and that back window and those hands on his shoulders.

Jesse looks up. "She was kissin' him, Mig. They were *kissin'*. Right there in the hall. In school. Like no one else was around. I saw them." His last statement spoken almost as a plea – or at least that's how Miguel heard it.

"Nah, you musta seen someone else." Miguel does not believe his own words, and he's sure his friend hears the skepticism in his voice.

"It was them, Mig. I saw it. It's over, Mig. Over." Jesse pulls his swollen hands up to his burning eyes. He doesn't want to cry in front of his friend, at least not in front of Miguel. He knows it'd be different with Matt. It's always different with Matt. Matt gets stuff like feelings and all. Miguel. Miguel's probably thinking how he's gonna jump Nate or something.

The ripe orange sections burst as Miguel pops them one by one into his mouth. "Fuck him!" Juice sprays. "Fuck him and his pretentious whip of a sister!" He shakes his hands of the juice then turns on the tap.

"Yeah." The meek syllable is all Jesse can add to his friend's predictable outburst. "I guess."

"Shit, he's an ass, and she's an idiot for falling for him. You're lucky to find out now about her rather than later, man. You know?" Miguel turns toward his friend. "She ain't worth it,

Jess. It's not worth it."

"I guess," Jesse looks up then glances back around the kitchen. "Let's just study for math and forget about all this. Where's Matt?"

Miguel grabs the orange and yellow striped towel and dries his hands. "He's comin' from the library. He'll be here in a bit. When's your mom home?"

"Soon," Jesse looks up at the clock. Just past 6. "Hey, Mig, you got your board?"

"Yeah, why?"

"Gonna ride down toward the bus stop and see if you can find my backpack? I kinda dropped it, or threw it. Somewhere."

"Haha, you loco, man," Miguel dusts the top of Jesse's head. For once Jesse doesn't stop him. The last thing he cares about right now is his hair. "Yeah, I'll go. Be back in a flash."

Miguel heads out the back door and jumps on his board.

With Miguel out of the house, Jesse lifts his bruised self and heads down the dark inner hallway to his bedroom. Opening his door, he falls onto his crumpled galaxy blanket thrown off this morning in his hurry to get to school. His hurry to see Ruby. Not that she's the reason he gets up every morning, but knowing her warm smile will greet him in first period sure makes the thought of going to school a lot more inviting. He rolls himself up inside the fleece throw, closes his eyes and takes in the whole ugly day's events. Curling himself up in a fetal position, he squeezes into his chest then pops himself upright, nearly losing his balance as he's caught inside the tight wrap of the blanket and almost falls off the bed.

He unravels himself, reaches for the closest thing he can find and hurls his pillow like a torpedo hard against the closet door then turns and punches his mattress. A vibration hastily echoes its way through the coiled springs while a fist imprint like a tiny crater sits in the center of the solar system. The dark blue bedcover's space age background taunts his chaotic universe. He closes his eyes. An astronaut floating in space. Three more violent punches hit his bed.

Jesse lies there for a moment. Still. He breathes. This is all he can do. Wants to do. For now.

Miguel ignores the Weiss' kids' plywood ramp that sits at the driveway edge. Any other day, and he'd shoot right up the quarter pipe to practice a grind or stall. Today, however, is not one of those days. Miguel has a mission. He pumps the ground with his left foot, gliding along the smooth sidewalk, and keeping his hawk's eye on the street, searching in between cars. Having no idea of the exact details of his friend's afternoon adventure, he imagines Jesse running and tripping, maybe shoving his hands through someone's side window. The backpack could have slipped underneath a car.

Miguel jumps off his board and lets it slide into the grass. He walks into the street and bends his body low so he can spy underneath cars. Nothing. He stands and walks toward the bus stop.

"What the -," Miguel stops. "Damn, someone needs drivin' lessons." Miguel walks up to the black Honda observing the crumpled hood and askew Stop sign. A closer look reveals small shards of glass on the pavement. He takes in the scene.

Moving to the center of the intersection, Miguel bends down again. There it is. Lying in the gutter on Oak just behind a black Ford pick-up. Miguel realizes that he rolled right past it on his way over to Jesse's. He walks over and picks up the canvas bag. Noticing the open zipper, he turns to see if anything has fallen out. He knows Jesse usually carries his sketchpad and pencil case with him, but he's not sure if they're inside the bag. Miguel sits on the curb and carefully dumps out the contents into the dry grass.

A hawk circles over head and lets out its evening call, but Miguel doesn't hear it. His gaze fixes on something far more interesting. An envelope addressed to Mr. and Mrs. Harold Waters. It's open. At first, Miguel wants to toss it aside. It's not what he's looking for. He's looking for the sketchpad (which Miguel doesn't realize is what drew Jesse back inside the building earlier today where he happened upon Nate and Ruby and their lips; the sketchpad is still back in Locker 2053 on the second floor of SNiHi). On a closer look at the envelope, Miguel observes the return address: *Santa Niña Unified School District, Student Truancy Department.*

"Damn, bro, what mess you got yourself into?" Miguel knows these letters. He's received about a half-dozen of them, several each year of high school. They are usually about his excessively late tardies to fifth period after lunch, or, in the case of freshman year, cutting sixth period PE so he could perform his own soccer conditioning over by the Grove then meet up with Cindy Tompkins after the junior high let out. Cindy had flunked third grade, so by eighth grade she flaunted the round curvy body of a high school freshman and enjoyed the affectionate attentions of the SNiHi athletes. Her favorite, though, was Miguel Alma de Ramón. Cindy was also a star on the soccer field. In fact, last year, her family moved to LA so Cindy could prepare for a professional soccer career – despite the fact that there were no professional women's soccer leagues around yet in the U.S.

Miguel considers opening the letter.

"Hey, Mig, what's up?"

Startled, he drops the envelope and places his hand before his eyes shielding the setting sun's glare. "Yo, Matt, *¿qué pasa?*

"*No mucho, amigo,*" Matt returns, making some proper use

of his two years of high school Spanish. "Whatcha doin on the curb with Jesse's backpack?" Matt looks around, expecting perhaps to see his friend.

"Ah, nuthin'," Miguel replies, returning the contents, including the envelope to the bag's interior. He misses the small Ziploc sitting in the bottom. "Just on a retrieval mission for our boy. Seems he had some sort o' accident and dropped his bag. He's home." Miguel nods down First Street.

"Oh," Matt sticks his hands in his pockets. "He get into some mix-up with Karen? Nate?" Matt fishes.

"Nah. Well, not really. Actually, I'm not sure what happened here, but, well, that fool got himself into somethin'. His hands are all messed up from pieces o' glass." Miguel stands, slings the bag over his shoulder and gestures toward the Stop sign. "So he says."

"Dang!" Matt removes his hands and begins walking toward the crash site. "Who's car is that?"

"Not sure. Jesse says he was walkin' home and there was some kinda accident."

"Hmm," Matt runs his hand along the crumpled front end of the vehicle. "You say Jesse's OK, though?"

"Yeah, he's got some scrapes and all, but, uh, yeah, he's, uh – shit, man, he ain't cool at all!"

Matt turns. A red flush races up his cheeks. Sure that Jesse knows, that Ruby beat him to it, told, and has planned her denial of anything going on with Nate, he turns to his friend, "Whaddya mean?" Matt prays. Hopes.

"Just that, well, Ruby, she, uh," Miguel pauses. "Let's go back to Jesse's. It's better if he tells it. I might mix it all up."

"Uh, OK, yeah, sure." Not sensing any awkwardness from Miguel, Matt settles on the assumption that his friends don't know anything more than they knew this morning. He picks up his pace to keep time with his sure-footed friend.

Miguel turns, places his hand on Matt's shoulder. "Somethin' tells me we're gonna need to mommy this boy. He's got a story to tell. His heart is busted bad, amigo."

Matt swallows. Maybe she didn't tell him. As they head down First Street to the Waters' home, Matt wonders if he has the wings necessary to share his own story.

9

A DIVIDE

Miguel pumps his left foot gently against the smooth sidewalk, gliding easily over cracks, keeping an even pace with Matt. The afternoon sun begins to fade, hiding behind homes and trees, bringing with it a much-welcomed drop in temperature. A host of sparrows dive and dart overhead, clearing the air of insects for their evening meal. The boys share no conversation. Their friendship is easy; more importantly, both boys carry weighty thoughts on their minds. One struggling with how to console his other best friend about a girl and how he even might have, probably did, see that she had her hands on that other guy's shoulders. That maybe he'd suspected something all along and just never shared this suspicion with his friend. What kind of friend did that make him anyway?

The other besieged with similar thoughts regarding the boyfriend/girlfriend issue; more so, playing over the scenes in the library with one tall basketball forward. For this friend, feelings bounce inside him like a pinball game, hitting off levers, sending unescorted fear and worry ricocheting about his body.

Lost in thought, Matt trips on a crack.

"Easy, dude," chides Miguel who flips up his board and carries it along the drive as the two arrive back at the Waters' home. Harold Waters pulls into the driveway behind them. Vanessa, who sits in the front seat, waves wildly at her brother's pals.

Despite her youth (Vanessa will turn 13 in about a week), the younger sister of Jesse Waters has always been somewhat of a keepsake to Matt and Miguel. Perhaps it's her devout adoration of her older brother or maybe her constant cheerfulness at the arrival of his friends, or it could be that neither Matt nor Miguel have any siblings of their own, let alone a little sister. To them, she's the *group's* little sister, and any of them would do anything for her. That includes beating up - or aggressively intimidating - a certain snotty-nosed seventh grade boy like Richard Talbot who might have spread a nasty rumor about Vanessa and Ethan Jones.

Last October, when Vanessa ran into Jesse's room crying, holding a crumpled note, and fell into her brother's arms like a puddle of water, Miguel took up the call. "Ain't no one gonna mess with you, little lady. Don't you worry, we gonna handle little Richard Talbot," Miguel had assured the tearful girl. Vanessa didn't try to stop him. She didn't think Miguel's machismo could erase the horridness of what had been written with black ink on that crumpled sheet of binder paper. She felt hopeless.

Miguel sensed that, and that was not acceptable. Three days later, Halloween, Miguel made plans to greet the Pine Crest Junior High exiting crowd, especially one skinny little Mexican boy who didn't even have the sense to hold onto his own heritage and his father's good name. Miguel had left sixth period 15 minutes before the bell, telling Miss Thomas he had a stomach ache and wanted to catch the nurse before dismissal. She handed the junior the plastic glow-in-the-dark Jason mask he had earlier tried entering class with, told him she hoped he felt better and not to eat too much candy. Miguel faked a sick smile, thanked her, winked at his pals, and made his way to his locker for his board.

Pumping hard and fast down Blackbird Lane, Miguel arrived at the corner of Seventh Street in about five minutes, just seconds before the 2:50 bell clanged inside the junior high and hundreds of adolescents poured out the doors, down the steps, and onto the sidewalk. Miguel shoved his board inside a leafy bush and walked purposefully toward the school's outer courtyard. The day before, Miguel had gone into Vanessa's bedroom and pulled out last year's Pine Crest Pine Needles yearbook. He figured Richard Talbot couldn't have changed that much in the last year. He took in the round pimply face of the boy, eyeballing his distinct Hispanic features – the small round nose, brown skin, and floppy black hair. *We could be cousins, little boy*, Miguel laughed to himself. Santa Niña claims a majority Hispanic population, recently surpassing the White residents by about two percent. The two races comprise about 67 percent of the 1990 Census. The other half ranges from Black and Vietnamese to Hawaiian and American Indian.

Richard Talbot's family migrated from Mexico about the same time as Miguel's. His father died of cancer less than six years ago. Rumor says it was due to the pesticides used in the Grove. Richard's mother remarried last year (Victor Talbot, proprietor of Talbot Electronics on Tenth Street, seven doors down from the library). Mr. Talbot adopted Richard (formerly *Ricardo*) and his brothers, dropping the boys' father's name, Mendoza.

Miguel spotted the gangly 12-year-old as he strolled across the courtyard with about three other scrawny boys. With complete confidence teetering on sheer cockiness, the high school soccer star marched straight toward the boy, "Talbot? Richard Talbot?"

The boy froze. His friends scattered like ants at a drop of rain. Richard looked at the nearly 6-foot muscular frame of this high school boy.

Miguel studied the weak structure of Vanessa's insulter. He considered his original course of action, his violent intentions, the boy's trembling, the gathering crowd. "You," Miguel jabbed a pointed finger into the small boy's flat chest. "You, Talbot, keep your lame-ass business to yourself and stay the fuck out of Vanessa Waters' life." Miguel paused, moved in closer and whispered in the timorous boy's ear: "Say one more word to her. About her. Near her. And I will find you again. And that next time, I will pull you from this nosey little crowd of junior high busy bodies and into a quiet, dark, secluded corner of this gossipy little town and beat the livin' crap outta you. *Sabe*?" Miguel took in a breath, calming himself, and placed both of his large hands on top of the now severely shuddering shoulders of Richard Talbot. "You got it, amigo?"

To the credit of this shaken little seventh grader, he managed to utter two very important, well-chosen words that probably saved him anymore lectures and certainly a trip to the emergency room, or, at the very least, Pine Crest's nurse's office, from this towering teen. "Yes, Sir."

At this, Miguel laughed, patted the boy's shoulders - this time, more gently – stepped back near the circling crowd, laughed again, jogged over to the leafy bush, grabbed his board, and road off. Just before the arrival of two teachers and the vice principal.

"What's going on here, kids? Talbot, what're you up to this time?"

"N-n-nuthin'. Just, just gettin' goin' to trick-or-treat, that's all."

"Okay, then, get going. Everyone. Get going."

The crowd dispersed, including Richard who wasn't sure

what had just happened but knew it most likely had a lot to do with his stupid threat to Vanessa Waters for saying *No* to the Fall Fling and *Yes* to Ethan Jones. *Stupid girls,* thought Richard. Still, he planned to stay well away from Vanessa. Even if she was the prettiest thing he'd ever seen. He had no intentions of spending any more quality time with her body guard from SNiHi. *No, Sir.*

As Miguel pumped his board home to Eighth Street, he considered his own violent threats, his own *idle* threats. Miguel had no intention of *beatin' the livin' crap* out of anyone, let alone a meek 12-year-old. Still, this vengeful fire sizzled in his gut, racing out of control, licking at the pride within his being. Miguel knew he needed to get a handle on his anger. Soon.

"Hey, guys, whatcha doin?" Vanessa chirps as she hops from her dad's non-descript four-door and bounces over to Miguel. The usually macho teen pushes Jesse's backpack tightly against his right shoulder and wraps his arms around the giggling girl.

"Hey, Beauty Queen, *¿qué está pasando?* Lookin' prettier than a rose in bloom, little girl." Miguel lets go as Vanessa giggles harder.

"It's all good in the hood, amigo," she laughs then turns to Matt, whom she offers a more formal greeting. "Hey, Matt."

The awkward, less confident teen, moves toward Vanessa and shares a gentle hug.

"What's that?" she teases and hugs him tighter, wrapping both arms around his slender waist and pressing her head into his chest. Matt returns the squeeze. Vanessa chimes, "Better!"

"Okay, Nessa, leave the boys be. Let's get inside and take out Momma's chicken." Mr. Waters walks over to shake the boys' hands. "You two big appetites staying for dinner? You're always welcome."

"Nah, Mr. Waters, we gotta study. Math final tomorrow, ya know. Last day and all. Seniors in the house," Miguel laughs at his own corny line.

"That's right. Seniors. Well, seniors gotta eat, too, though." Harold Waters walks toward the back door carrying a shiny brown leather briefcase and looking a bit less perky than his adolescent daughter.

"We're just gonna go over some notes, Mr. Waters. My mom's gonna be home soon ya know. I'll eat with her. But thanks for offering. Appreciate it." Matt falls in behind the man and steps gingerly inside the kitchen.

"Yeah, Mama's got tamales on the stove. Can't miss those." Miguel closes the door behind himself and the two boys turn down the hall toward Jesse's room.

Miguel pushes open the already ajar door and finds Jesse still sprawled across his bed, face hanging over the side, feet dangling to the floor.

"Dang, bro, ain't you up outta that frump yet? Come on, man, she ain't worth it." Miguel swats Jesse's feet, pushes his legs, tosses the backpack to a corner of the room, and sits down beside his forlorn pal.

"Let him have his moment, Mig," Matt tries. "They've been together a long time. Let him have this moment." Matt moves aside some papers and plops his backpack on Jesse's metal desk top. "You talk to Ruby, Jess? After school? She come by?"

A tightening spreads across Matt's abdomen. He swallows. His dry throat grips a small trickle of saliva. His heart beats loudly in his ears. Biting the inside of his lower lip, he looks toward Miguel who's found a greater interest in removing the dirt splotches that mar the white rubber along his sneakers.

Jesse rolls over, tosses his arm over his eyes and grunts, or moans, or something. An inkblot watermark stains the starry background of the soft duvet. He pulls himself up and immediately throws his face into his hands. His elbows rest upon his thighs. The heartbroken boy rocks slowly back and forth as the two buddies watch helplessly, unsure of when or how to intervene. Jesse looks up, drops his hands between his legs and utters, "Never gonna talk to her again."

"That's the spirit," chirps Miguel.

"Aw, come on, Jess. You just feel that way now," Matt attempts some realism. "What exactly happened between you two anyway?" Still fishing.

Jesse looks up at Matt, who imagines the terrified face of this lifelong pal at 7 witnessing the oblivious Mrs. Weiss driving right over his cherry new bike. "Three words. Lips. Nate. Ruby." He stands, stretches, punches at an imaginary something near the ceiling. "Oh, one more word – idiot. Me."

"That's two."

Matt swats at Miguel. Miguel shrugs his shoulders.

"So, you saw Ruby kissing Nate? Where? At the library? Did you follow them?" Casting another line, wondering how much Jesse might know about Matt's own adventure at the library, his conversation with Ruby on the stairs, Ricky. Matt shifts, leans against the metal desk, clears his throat and bites his lower lip.

"Slow down, amigo, he's still takin' it in." Miguel rests a reassuring hand on Jesse's tense shoulder. "Spill it, dude. She broke your heart. Spill the poison now so it don't fester."

Jesse and Matt laugh. "That's a *Manuelism* if I ever heard." Matt and the boys had grown accustomed to the elder Alma de Ramón's words of wisdom. A few years back, Matt dubbed them Manuelisms. More respect than mockery; though the boys laugh, the lines stick with them always.

Jesse sits back down on the edge of the bed, his body less tense, the friends' therapy taking effect. He sighs and takes the cue for a story. Miguel sits down upon the metal chair while Matt rests his lean frame against the desk.

"It's real simple, actually. I went inside the building after you all left and saw two dark figures at the end of the senior's hallway in a liplock. I mean, what more is there?" Jesse lets out a short laugh.

Matt fishes again. "So, you never went to the library? This happened at school?"

"Yeah, school. Why did ya think it was the library?" Jesse pauses. "Wait, what the, what happened at the library? Damn! Don't those two know nuthin' about discretion?"

"Huh?"

"Discretion, Mig. It means like being hidden, not so out there for everyone and their mother to see," Matt explains.

"Oh, yeah. Nah, they don't seem to know nuthin' about discretion."

Jesse just rolls his eyes, turns to Matt, "So, uh, what happened at the library?"

Matt shifts, pivots his right foot into the brown carpet. He looks over at Miguel for a sign. The boy seems to know about as much as Jesse. Matt relaxes. "Nuthin', really, except, well, I kinda heard them, you know. Well, this was way after school, after you woulda seen them. So, I guess they met up at the library. I mean, it's ..." A ping at the window interrupts the conversation.

The three heads turn in unison, and Jesse reaches across the bed to push apart the plastic blinds. Through the cream-colored slats he can see Ruby standing in the driveway in her cheer sweats. Seeing Jesse, or at least the open blinds, she motions with her finger for him to come outside. Unbeknownst to the boys, she's been calling the Waters' house phone for the past 20 minutes, but Vanessa has the line tied up with her own intense conversation with Mary Pence about Ethan Jones.

"Shit!" Jesse lets go the blinds and flops back on his bed. Without looking, Matt and Miguel know exactly who's standing on the sidewalk.

"Leave her there, man. She don't deserve your time."

Drawing from his own motives, Matt agrees. "Yeah. Let her stew. She broke your heart and that severs any obligation to console her own guilt."

Miguel looks over at his pale friend, raises that eyebrow, and adds, "Yeah, what he says."

"Shit, shit, shit! I hate this. I want to see her. I want her to say I was seeing things. I mean. Maybe I was. Maybe it wasn't her. Or maybe it wasn't Nate."

At this, Miguel decides to share what he knows, what he thinks he saw, what he is now 99% sure he did see. "I saw her, too, man."

"What?" Jesse and Matt return in unison.

"I saw them at Al's." Matt relaxes, exhales a breath he didn't even know he had been holding. Miguel continues, "She had her hands on his shoulders. At first, I thought I was imagining. They drove into the station after school. Dumbhead had a bird caught in his axle. She had her hands on his shoulders. I'm sure of it, man, sure of it. Lughead. She was kinda funny with me, but I kept thinkin' I was crazy. Now I know who's crazy. Her. Ruby. She's the idiot, bro, not you. Her and that lughead Gibbons."

Miguel pounds his fist. Jesse shakes his head. Another ping at the window. He doesn't turn this time. He looks up at Matt. "You, too, huh. The library, right. That's what you were tryin' to say earlier. You saw her at the library."

Matt shrugs, lowers his gaze at the thick brown shag carpet that separates his feet from the hard floor, a foundation that right now feels more like the surface of a pool, any moment his feet might fall through, and he'll tumble inside an abyss so dark and fluid that he will have lost hold of any reality he's known. Freefalling. No handles. No railings. Unknown. Travelling at speeds so fast they'll feel static like when you are racing along a rollercoaster track strapped inside a metal car. You are moving, but you aren't. The air is racing through your hair, but you are locked into the same spot you sat down in when the ride began. Moving but going nowhere. Returning to where you began. Exhilarating and frightening. Lost but in the same place.

He exhales. Unmindful of the breath he's been holding. Standing at a precipice, a defining moment, moving from a place of pure security and dishonesty to an unknown landscape of truth and fear. The truth he utters could change his life forever. Will change his life forever. Is that a bad thing? Why is living a lie so much easier? It's not. It's safer, maybe. Not easier. You must constantly hold back, be sure not to reveal too much, too much of you. That's not so easy. Matt wants to let go, to fly. *Does this bird have wings?* The line brings more comfort than worry. To have faith, it's true. *Does he have faith? In himself, his friends? His mom?* He inhales, glances at his pals, two boys who have always been there for him, who have stood up for him when he couldn't, who have made him laugh when he'd wanted to cry, made him feel safe when he was so afraid. He wants to tell. He wants to hide. He exhales. Should he reveal this truth, or should he confine it to the narrow stacks of the downtown library?

"Matt, I know you did," Jesse's voice breaks through the fog, but Matt hears *I know what you did*.

He loses his grip on the desk, slips then catches himself, looks up at Jesse, Miguel.

"Tell him," Miguel prods. "We all saw. We all know."

Matt, still trapped in his own mind, believes he has been found out. "I, uh, I," he swallows, wants to cry, wants to shout, takes in another breath, lets it out. "I wanted to tell you, both of you, you know, I just..."

"Damn, bro, spit it out. You saw them. So, you saw them, I saw them, Jess saw them. Damn, we don't need details. Just say it. You saw the two-timin' bi—"

"Don't say it, I know it, OK, I get it!" Jesse shouts. Another ping, two of them.

Convinced Ruby's gonna bust the window, Miguel vaults over the bed, pushes the blinds aside, slides open the frame, and shouts, "Go away! He don't wanna talk to you! Scram! Go curl up with big lughead and leave Jesse the fuck alone! Git!"

Ruby flips him the bird and walks down the driveway toward the sidewalk. No intention of leaving, she stops, turns, arms folded.

Miguel slams shut the window, and now Jesse thinks Miguel is gonna break it. "Cool your jets, man. She ain't gonna leave till I go out there. She's stubborn." He stands up, pulls open his door and storms out of the room.

Matt and Miguel follow.

Vanessa sets down the receiver on the hall phone. She turns as her brother and his friends storm past her like soldiers to battle. "Where're ya'all goin' in such a hurry?" she intercedes. No one stops to answer. Figuring that maybe they're going to play some hoops or pull a prank on the Weiss kid, she turns into the kitchen where she finds her dad reading the newspaper.

"Where's Jesse and them headed?"

"Huh?" Harold Waters looks over the paper's business section at his youngest. "Who?"

"Jesse and the guys," she responds impatiently. "Didn't you see them go out the front door?"

"Uh, no," he turns the page, looks back at Vanessa whose

crinkled face suggests he should know what his son is up to. "Where'd they go?"

"That's what I'm sayin'! Where are they headed? I mean, it's almost dinner, right? Where's Mom? I'm hungry." She moves toward the refrigerator but stops as something catches her attention through the laced curtain hanging over the sink.

Turning toward her father who has resumed his interest in the paper, she moves closer and pushes the curtain aside enough to reveal the four figures on the sidewalk. All but Ruby have their back to her. Ruby's waving her hands about while Miguel's pointing his finger at her like a woodpecker, almost touching her sweater, and Jesse's just got his hands wrapped around the back of his neck staring down at the ground and twisting his body this way and that. Then Vanessa sees Matt. He's moving himself back from the group. His hands lodged deep down inside his jean pockets; he's staring purposefully, intensely, directly at Ruby. Vanessa can't hear any words, mostly just sees Miguel's mouth moving rapidly while Ruby seems to break through with a word or two now and then. Jesse's still twisting, and Matt's still inching backward. Then Ruby points her finger at Matt, her arm straight out like a rifle about to shoot. She yells something. Matt drops his head, pulls his hands up to his face, shouts something, and then he just runs, bolts, torpedoes across the street and down First. Vanessa loses sight of him.

As she returns her vision to the group, she sees her brother's face, his mouth slightly agape, his right hand upon his chest as if he's just been shot or maybe about to pledge allegiance to the flag, and the left hand coming to rest on top of it now as if his heart is hurting. His eyes look toward the empty spot where Matt had been standing. Jesse remains, staring, holding his chest, open-mouthed.

Vanessa knows this look. Disbelief. Confusion. Fear. She

looks back at Ruby whose hands now cover her face, her eyes, her mouth. Her head bobs. Is she crying?

Back to Miguel. His hands rest on his hips, and he stares down at the ground shaking his head. He looks up at Ruby. Vanessa is sure he's swearing at her. His lower lip keeps pulling in under his upper teeth, and he seems to be spitting. Vanessa is scared now. She lets go the lace curtain and turns toward her father. He remains seated at the small wooden kitchen table reading the daily paper, sipping a beer from a silver can, oblivious to any turmoil brewing outside. Feeling his daughter's eyes on him, he looks up.

"What's goin' on baby girl?" he folds the paper and sets it down upon the table, stands, and walks toward her. She's shaking, arms wrapped around her body. She looks up at the window and back toward her father. The few remaining rays of afternoon sun spill in across the kitchen floor, scattering amorphous white spots like blemishes across the green linoleum.

"Somethin's wrong, Daddy. Somethin's wrong with Matt or Jesse, or … somethin's not right." She looks back up at the window. The curtains shake. The front door slams. Suddenly, Jesse bolts through the kitchen, down the hall and slams his bedroom door. An invisible hand sweeps across the lace fabric.

"Seems the boys got some trouble goin' on." Harold Waters releases his daughter, pats her shoulder. "Suppose it's my turn now."

The reluctant father moves down the hallway. He knocks gently on his son's door. "Jesse." Nothing. "Jess, son." Nothing. "I'm comin' in." He pauses and enters.

The room is dark. Harold reaches blindly along the wall for the light switch. Finding it, the room fills with a dusky glow. Jesse lies folded on the bed. His arms wrapped tightly beneath his face, his knees bent upon the floor as if in prayer. He is still.

Harold Waters' large frame nearly fills the space. Pulling up the desk chair, he surveys the room, observing his son's tidiness, the canvas backpack resting quietly in a corner of the room, the neat pile of clean laundry sitting upon the four-drawer wooden dresser. The only askew item seems to be his son himself.

"Listen, son, whatever it is, it'll pass." He waits for a response. Jesse doesn't stir. "Is it Ruby? Trouble with the heart, son? Tell me. Let's talk, Jesse." Harold again looks around the room, hoping for inspiration, evidence, something to guide this already awkward conversation. He breathes in deeply. Exhales. "Son?"

After what feels to Harold like hours, but is surely only moments, Jesse lifts himself up on his hands, digging his elbows into the soft mattress. He turns toward his father. "It was Ruby. At first." Tears fall down his brown cheeks. "Now, it's, it's more." Jesse averts his father's gaze. He can't find the words, the strength. "It's too much, Dad." More tears trickle in silence down his unblemished skin and gather into a stream along his curved fists that sit solidly beneath his chin.

"Can't be so bad, Jess. Broken hearts do mend, son. I know this." Harold crosses his legs, leans in closer to his boy. "What seems like the end of the world, what feels like such darkness, that passes, and you are stronger for it. I know this."

Jesse looks back toward his father. Still in a state of genuflection, he lowers his face upon his balled fists, rolling his forehead over the bumpy knuckles. He had nearly forgotten about the narrow shards of glass that only an hour earlier shot piercing pains throughout his body. He remembers. Jesse opens his fists and stares down at the crisscross of Band-Aids plastered over his palms like a kindergartner's art project.

"What's that? You get in a fight, Jesse? Is that what's going on? A fight with Miguel? Matt? What happened?"

Jesse lifts his body and moves to the bed's edge. He lays his hands out before his father and looks up into Harold Waters' now frightened eyes. "Not a fight, Dad. I just kinda, I fell on some glass is all. I wasn't payin' attention. It's OK now. I don't even feel it anymore. But it's all just too much. This," he waves his hands, "this is nothing. This is just a distraction."

Harold stares at the plastic bands of adhesive that traverse his son's small hands, hands that reached for his just a few short years ago, hands that he grasped as he swung his son high in the air like a helicopter as he squealed with delight, hands that look so much like his own, like his father's, his brother's, like Wayne's. Harold swallows, takes Jesse's hands in his, folds his own warm fingers around his son's, looks down into his eyes. "These are your future son, you gotta take care of them. Like your grandpa, your uncles, me. These hands hold the tools that paint your future. You're talented Jesse. Don't let it all go to waste over a girl." Jesse pulls his hands away.

"It ain't just Ruby! Shit, Ruby's just another distraction. It's more than that, Dad. Way more." He inhales deeply and stands. "I mean, it was Ruby. At first. Now it's Matt. I mean, I dunno. It's just everything. Everything at once. God, today is the longest fuckin' day of my life, and it's not even over." He turns, "Dad, I did somethin' stupid. I almost got hit." He paces the room. "I almost, I just, I dunno. I was just distracted, and I wasn't thinking, and Mr. Taylor, he honked, I know he did, he must've, he said he did, and I just wasn't thinking, I was so angry and then there was all this glass and we couldn't find his glasses, but we did, and he said something about this time I was lucky or that this time he was lucky or, I dunno, I was jus-" Jesse stops. Stops pacing. Stops talking. He looks at his father who's staring out the window into the darkness that has become the night.

"Mr. Taylor is right. You were lucky this time and so was he."

"What do you mean *this time*?"

Harold unfolds his legs, stands. "Son, sit back. It's time I told you a story about your Uncle Wayne. If there ever were a time, this must be it. It's gotta be. Sit down, Jess."

The unsettled teen rests back on the edge of the bed and watches as his father now takes up pacing the room. His hands sting again. He blows on them, rests his elbows on his knees and lets his arms dangle as he stares up at the towering structure that is his father, a man who's always been there. A well-made fence, protecting, guarding, keeping the unwanted out, the beloved inside.

Jesse can't imagine Harold Waters not being there, being who he is. He wants to be seven again, wants to be that small boy who sat on the lap of this man, folded within the warmth of his arms, shielded, loved. What has been ten years feels like a hundred. Today feels like ten years all at once. This morning he was kickin' it with his pals, two guys who've just been *the guys*; and wasn't it just lunch time when he was holding the curvy body of one Ruby Newton in his own lap, feeling the softness of her skin just beneath her tee shirt, resting his hand on hers? Wasn't that just today?

Harold clears his throat and sits down beside his son. He places his palm on Jesse's knee then moves it to his back, caressing the hunched form, stalling for the right words then returns his hand to himself, placing both upon his knees. He doesn't know where to begin.

"I don't think Wayne was really thinking. At the end of this, the lesson we learn is that. He wasn't thinking. Not thinking gets you in trouble. In your Uncle Wayne's case, it got him killed. And someone else, too. Two others. Three all together.

Just not thinking.

"God, it feels like yesterday that all of us, me, Winston, Daddy, and Wayne, we were up them ladders painting houses. Winston'd be trying to tell me and Wayne the best way to lay on that paint. Me and Wayne laughin'. Wayne sayin' somethin' like 'don't matter how you lay on the gray, bro, gray is gray'. That'd get Daddy laughin', too. Those were good times." Harold pauses, wipes a tear that spills down his cheek, over his memory's smile, looks at Jesse.

"Your Uncle Wayne was a good man, well, boy, really. 24. That's not a man yet. That's still a boy. In my mind, he's always that little boy. Impulsive he was. You're not so much like him there, son, but you remind me an awful lot of Wayne. Momma was right when you came out. Same big round eyes as him. Same smile. All smiles. All happiness you were as a little one. Just like Wayne. We hadn't actually meant to give you his name at all. Your momma thought'd be kinda, I dunno, creepy, or ominous. She just didn't want her first born having the name of someone who died so recently. Then when we all took a good look at you, and when your momma heard my momma say how much you reminded her of Wayne and how you were her little angel, well, Amelia couldn't resist. You were, no doubt about it, Jesse Wayne Waters. And that was OK with her. Still is."

It's now Jesse's turn to stroke the strong form of his father's back. He does so despite the sting and throbbing of his palms.

Harold continues. "That night when we got the visit from the officers, they'd gone to Daddy's house first. He asked them to tell us. He couldn't, couldn't make the call. Never got to see him cry, but I know he did. We all did.

"Anyway, the officers told us that it wasn't just Wayne, that it wasn't just that he'd been drinking, there'd been another car. The people in that car'd been killed, killed by my brother because he hadn't been thinkin'. Rex Taylor was in the passenger seat next to him. Officers told us that *he* was so drunk, he didn't barely have a scratch. Funny how that happens. And, later, Rex told us that he didn't even remember snappin' on his seat belt. He's sure Wayne did it. They'd been at Sal's on Tenth celebratin' someone havin' a baby or getting' married or somethin'. They'd decided Wayne was the most sober, so he should drive home. After all, they figured, it was only a few blocks. Well, you see how that worked out."

Unaware, Jesse's left hand still lay upon his dad's right shoulder. He moves it down to his leg. "Yeah, I know. Still hurts, huh, Dad?"

"Hurts? Yeah, I suppose. But it's not the same hurt that you're feelin' now. It's more an ache, a kinda dull throb that makes this hole in your heart that you can't ever seem to fill up. Some days it's a quiet kinda ache, and other days, well kind of like today, when somethin' jars your memory and makes it feel like today is not today, but it's *that* day, seventeen years ago; it's a sharp, piercing, penetrating ache. A stab."

Harold stops, looks at his son's hands and remembers the real reason he wanted to tell the story of Wayne. "When the officers came to our door and told us about my brother, they didn't say the names of the people in the other car. I didn't think to ask because, well, I wasn't in a thinkin' state at all after such news. Later, there was an article in the paper. That was hard for Daddy, seein' his son's name and the people he'd killed. They had two daughters. When I read their names, I knew I'd never forget them." He pauses again and looks at Jesse. "Their names were Janie and Lee."

At first, Jesse's just listening. Not hearing. Then it hits him. "Wait, no, wait, what? Dad, no. It's a coincidence, right? Come on, man, that's weird. Lee? Lee West? Matt? Dad?" Now Jesse's feet feel like they are about to crash through that same floor. Slowly the world begins swirling and spiraling around him and within him. His heart pounds violently in his ears, the air rushes toward him like a vacuum. He gulps, catching his breath, stands, throws his hands to his head and turns around inside the tornado, the vacuum, the melting world that is his room yet is slowly disappearing. "My Uncle killed my best friend's grandparents? What the? Dad, why didn't you ever tell me? Does, does Matt know? Lee? Shit, she's gotta know by now, huh? She must. Wait, Dad, do you still have that paper? Do you?"

At some point during Jesse's rant, Harold has stood and placed his arms around his son, trying to steady his body within this spiral. "Jesse, calm down. I couldn't have told you. How? I, I just couldn't. I knew one day I would. I didn't know when. Now I do. This is when I needed to tell you, when you needed to know. Whatever is going on with you and the boys, with Matt, well, this is the time you needed to hear this. You and Matt have this strange sort of connection. Call it spiritual, or call it fate, I don't know what it is, but you boys are linked. Right from the start. Ya see, Jesse, if Lee's parents hadn't've been killed, well, she probably wouldn't've gotten pregnant, and well, you know, she -"

"She wouldn't have had Matt. Yeah, I see. But still, that's not gonna be any comfort to Matt." Jesse, who had still been spinning, flailing his arms about, suddenly stops. "Does Matt know, Dad? Does he?"

"I don't know, son. I've never really spoken to Lee about it. We've actually never talked about it. There was just this one time when you two were in first grade, and you wanted Matt to have a sleepover. Lee dropped him off and came inside to meet us. We'd never really talked as parents before. We'd seen each other at school events and such, but we'd never really spoken. She was so young. I think she kind of avoided the other parents. Then that night, she came in the house, and she saw the pictures. The family pictures. She saw Wayne's high school portrait. It was the one the papers ran with the article. She just stood there staring at it. Amelia didn't know why. We'd not forgotten their names, but we just never connected Matt's mom to the Lee in the paper. She didn't say anything, but we all saw how she'd looked at the picture, how she'd stopped and stared.

"After she left, after she'd left Matt, Amelia and I looked at Wayne's picture then at Matt. It'd been just about seven years at the time, and we knew what Lee knew at that moment, and that's all that any of us ever said, or didn't say."

Despite his original intention to console his son about whatever was disturbing him, Harold realizes he's complicated matters. Jesse sits back on his bed, this time he lies all the way down upon his pillow.

Harold turns toward the door and places his hand on the knob. He cups the cold metal lump in his large warm palm, resting momentarily before turning it. He looks back at his son. "You never know why things happen, Jesse. You don't. You just need to follow your heart. You need to trust. There's a plan. God has a plan, son. Uncle Wayne and Grandpa Martin are up there right now playing cards with the Wests. I just know they are. And all o' them are lookin' down here sayin', 'ain't it nice how those boys became friends, became best friends, how they look out for each other in a way we couldn't do for ourselves'. Whatever it is between you and Matt now, son, whatever happened today, remember that your heart knows more than your head. That's why you need to think. You need to pay attention to your next move. I know you will because you always do." Harold opens the door. "I believe in you, son. You've got a big heart. Big hearts forgive, big hearts comfort. It's gonna be OK." He shuts the door.

A parent's natural instinct, no matter what the species, is to protect its young. Jesse can't see any sense in holding onto bits of anger toward his dad, toward his mom. For all they knew, not telling Jesse was the right thing to do. So now it's his turn.

His grandfather pops into his mind, seeping through the rubble dust that is today's avalanche of secrets, of pain. He understands, it's a matter of simply closing his eyes and making that choice. His friends are not cans of paint, but they are the foundation of his world. He must choose. He must spin and ask, *what are ya feelin' today? Are ya feelin' a bit blue or a bit o' cowardly yella?*

Jesse laughs at his grandfather's legacy, that Zen style of paint selection. He understands that the choices rest inside him. The answer is there.

It's time now to spin and choose.

As Jesse lay back on his bed, he realizes they never actually studied for tomorrow's math final. He hears Vanessa shout that dinner's ready, but Jesse isn't hungry. He closes his eyes. All he wants is for the day to be over.

Tomorrow's math final is the least of his worries.

THURSDAY

A bird's lifespan varies. How long it lives, as with humans, depends upon how it lives. Birds in captivity reportedly live up to twice as long as their counterparts in the wild. It's no wonder the National Audubon Society devotes resources to restoring and preserving the natural habitats of birds throughout the world. It proudly displays its inspirational namesake's portrait on its website. So sits John James Audubon, replete with canine by his side and rifle in his arms.

10

A WING

The tardy bell rings at 7:55, and Matt finds himself seated inside his Spanish class, his journey here a blur. He has been up since 5 tossing and turning, reviewing math notes that were not reviewed last night, taking another chunk of time *to look at* his Spanish notes, maybe eat something, take a shower and quietly exit the back door. Outside, when he realizes it's only 6:45, he decides to walk to his last day of junior year. He does not deny to himself that this is an excellent way to avoid Miguel's conversation on the bus.

This is not how he imagined the last day of school, the day before summer vacation, the day students count down to from the very first day school begins. *This* is not the day Matt has been waiting for.

Inside Señora Castañeda's room, the air rests like a stack of bricks upon his shoulders. Matt cannot shake the intensity. He finds his seat in the fifth row center, sets his backpack on the floor beneath his desk, wipes his palms along the soft blue denim covering his thighs then brings them together in a kind of prayer position beneath his chin resting the weight of his head upon the slender peak of his index fingers. He inhales, closes his eyes and calls in the images of his Spanish text, wishing now he'd had Miguel's photographic memory. But he knows he doesn't really need that. He's sailed through most of the year with a 93%, and he doesn't imagine that bombing the final will really affect his grade. Still, Matt West does not like to fail. He prefers all goes as planned.

The second bell rings as Ruby Newton enters the room. She seats herself two rows up from Matt, turns, and makes brief eye contact as she places her backpack behind her. She swallows a smile that hovers inside a sea of guilt, fear, anger and even sadness. The disparate feelings tumble inside her like bubbles in a tipped over soda bottle darting around the artificial space with no visible escape.

"*Buenos días, clase. Bienvenido a su último día de año. ...*" Señora Castañeda speaks on about this final day of class, what she expects, what she hopes and more. Matt tunes her out. Had he tuned her in?

As he clears his desk, a balled up paper shoots across the room and lands at the heal of his right black Converse. A perfect shot. No one else moves, their minds preoccupied with foreign words and phrases so dense that their thoughts hold room for little else. Matt stares down at the crumpled mass. His eyes shift to the right then left, his head steady. Only one person in the school possesses such a flawless aim. Matt glances toward Señora, slowly turns his head to peer at other suspicious faces. He swallows, turns to the back.

Ricky flashes a wide smile, his single right dimple folds in and Matt falls inside. He mouths *good luck, you'll do great*. Matt eyes the paper ball still sitting at his feet, smiles, looks up and sends back an awkward thumbs up. He bends down to collect the attention-seeking wad; unfolding it, his blood races wildly inside his body. Señora moves absentmindedly about the room distributing tests. Matt nervously taps his pencil on his desk, unaware of the smile spreading across his own face, stretching from one freckled ear to the other.

He peels back the crumpled layers of paper and flattens out the sheet upon his smooth wooden desktop, using the Spanish test as a shield, pressing the multi-page final firmly atop the creased note. He scans the room for Señora and spies her talking to Julia Finn up front.

Matt isn't sure about Julia's story. She's been in many of his classes at SNiHi, and she always sits up front. She doesn't wear glasses, so he's unclear as to what the preferential seating is all about. Now and again another teacher comes in to chat with Julia or the classroom teacher. Sometimes she leaves the room.

As if on cue, the door opens, a round black woman stands in the door frame. Julia gathers her belongings. Señora hands the woman the test, exchanges quiet conversation and the two exit.

Señora moves over to her corner desk by the window, sips her coffee, takes another glance about the room, and sits down with a stack of papers and red pen. This is her honors group; she doesn't worry about cheating. She steals a quick peek out the sunny window then begins her task of scoring yesterday's tests. The clock rests at just past 8:15. The bell won't ring again until nearly 10.

Matt slides the blue-paper final from atop the note. A single penciled line is written across the center of the paper:

A poet is a nightingale who sits in darkness and sings to cheer its own solitude with sweet sounds

Matt recognizes the line from English class. It's Shelley. Miss Carson had all English 3 students choose one line from a Shelley poem or piece of work, memorize it, write a speech about it, and present it to English 2 students. This was Matt's line, yet he wonders how Ricky would know since he wasn't in his class and that event took place months ago, before Matt admitted to himself any feelings for the popular ball player, before he remembers even speaking to Ricky in Spanish class.

Matt neatly folds the paper and tucks it inside his pocket then returns to the test at hand. At least he tries to; his mind wanders, his attention rests upon Shelley's words, Ricky's intentions. Does he consider Matt a faithless bird who sits alone in the darkness? Does he pity Matt? Or is Ricky the solitary winged creature hiding inside a cave of lies, his song a chance to be free?

Unsure, confused, lost himself, Matt desperately struggles to steady his mind and concentrate on the Spanish final. Señora stands, strolls about the room, up and down the aisles, pauses to survey a student's paper, moves on. Her summer heals click clack upon the hard school floor tiles. An early morning heat wave ignites oven-like conditions inside the soundless classroom. Señora ambles back toward her desk, leans over and cracks open the window. She sits down, peruses the room once more, satisfies herself that her *estudiantes* are working diligently and earnestly, and resumes her paper-grading task.

At the end-of-period bell, Señora stands, applauds, announces, "*Felicidades, mis estudiantes. Que tengan un verano encantador, y te veré en septiembre*". She moves to the doorway to collect their tests and wish each a personal goodbye.

Hundreds of test-dreary students fill the SNiHi halls. Most

seek out friends for secrets on the last upcoming final. Many head to the bathrooms for personal needs or a stealthy smoke. Several head straight to the next class.

Matt is eager for none of this. In the hall, he might run into Ruby or Ricky. He's unsure what either might say to him and has stumbled repeatedly in his own mind as to what he might say to them. His last class of the year is Miss Thomas, and it is there that he must face the two people he fears most. The two he cares the most about. He hasn't spoken a word to either Jesse or Miguel since last night, since Ruby's confession, since Ruby's vomit of secrets spilled out onto that First Street sidewalk, since Matt froze then ran down the street home like a child late for dinner, like a zebra from a pack of wolves, like a little boy lost.

"Matt!" It's too late, someone's spotted him. "Matt! Wait up!" He refuses to slow down. He heads toward the staircase, extends one lanky leg after another climbing up to the second floor. His timing is all wrong as a throng of freshman descend the stairway, giggling and holding yearbooks. They push past Matt who is more than just invisible to them.

"Matt!" the voice is nearer. Then a tug on his sleeve. "Matt, didn't you hear me? Hey, we have at least another ten minutes before the second bell." He recognizes the voice and turns. "Geez, *loo-weez!*, those long legs of yours sure do travel fast!"

"Sorry, I guess I was just thinkin' of my Spanish test and stuff. I didn't hear you. It's noisy, too, ya know."

Lexie smiles. "Not more than usual. You must just be thinkin' so hard in Spanish that you can't hear my English." Her broad toothy smile nearly blinds Matt; it's perfectly straight white structures play off nicely against the detailed red and black pinstripes of her cheer skirt. Cradling her books against her flat bosom, Lexie twists and turns upon the balls of her Keds, teeters up on her tip toes in an attempt to reach the eye level of this gangly Nordic junior.

"Yeah, something like that." Matt leans back against the cool white-tiled wall while the two wait out their time on the landing as hoards of students continue their climbs and descents on the south corridor stairwell. "So, uh, last day, huh? Seniors in about 80 minutes." He lamely attempts a smile, still avoiding eye contact.

Lexie reaches out for his hand. Her long fingers wrap around his thumb and forefinger. He meets her gaze. Her smile is warm, friendly. Her brown eyes are bright and clear. "It's OK, Matt," she whispers as she leans in. "I know. Ricky and I, we just, we're just, just friends. It's like a screen. He's the handsome basketball forward. I'm the cute little cheerleader who wants to get into Stanford and doesn't need some silly high school romance interfering with her dreams. He's my safe boyfriend and I'm his muse. We're friends. Best friends. No one knows. You're the first. We trust you. Ricky trusts you." She releases his hand, brushes back a fly black strand of hair and flashes more of that movie star smile.

Speechless, Matt swallows, looks around at the moving bodies unaware of this reveal, this moment, this about to be a huge life-changing moment. Then he thinks of his mom, of Jesse and Miguel. "I don't think I have the wings."

"The what?" Lexie moves closer as if he she didn't hear him right. "What wings?"

"I can't. I can't be me. My mom, she has plans. She-"

"Your mom," Lexie interrupts a little loudly then quiets. "Your mom. I bet your mom loves you, Matt. I bet your mom would want you to be you. You know that, I think. She's just your excuse. Ricky told his parents last summer, but he also told them he didn't think he was ready for everyone at school to know. And you know what?"

"What?" Matt rolls his eyes, sensing this cheerleader's pep

talk has just begun.

"They're not, but if you guys wait for them to be ready, you'll miss out on you. You said it. In just over an hour, we're gonna be seniors. We'll be the top of the school. The leaders. Don't you want to be a leader, Matt? Don't you want to clear a path and blaze a trail? Or do you just want to sit on the sidelines, waiting for someone else to come along and blaze that trail for you? And will you even be ready then, or will you just make another excuse? Will you just sit by like a bird on a telephone wire waiting for someone else to go first?" She pauses, smiles at a sophomore who just made the varsity squad. She threads her hand through the crook of Matt's right arm and guides him up the remaining flight of stairs and down the hall to Room 210.

Matt considers her words. His heart beats louder than ever. He can't remember a single thing he studied for this math final. He's sure he'll fail it. His mind is a fog. He is lost. Is this the roller coaster's climb or descent? Is there a turn ahead? His feet move across the floor. Jolts of electricity race through his body. And just when he thinks he can't feel any more misplaced, he spots Jesse and Miguel entering the classroom. Lexie stops, pulls him aside.

"Look, Matt. I know you're scared. I get it. I would be, too. Some kids may be a bit naïve, immature, narrow-minded and all, but I don't think you give the rest of them enough credit. Besides, you're pretty likeable. You're a nice guy, you're real. That's probably what Ricky likes most about you. You two are a good match."

The tardy bell rings. The two don't scatter in a hurry. A minute or two late won't much matter on this last day of school. Matt looks toward Room 210 then back at Lexie. "Maybe. I don't know. I gotta go." He pauses, licks his lips, swallows then runs his thin hand through his dry hair. He looks down at her.

"I'm supposed to meet Ricky at the library. You gonna be there?"

"You don't need me, Matt." Lexie stretches up on her tiptoes to plant a delicately soft kiss on his left cheek. "I believe my work here's done." Matt doesn't think Lexie's smile can get any wider. She turns away, pivots back, leans up to his right ear, "Why do ya think there's a *man* in *romance*, honey? You can do this."

He smiles back and watches this cheery cheerleader, this screen, this muse skip down the hall to Miss Carson's. He mumbles to himself, "I guess I better bring my wings."

Lexie disappears inside the classroom.

Matt draws in a deep breath, exhales as he enters the room. Miss Thomas, finishing roll, sees him, smiles, says nothing. She takes her pencil eraser to the blue attendance log, rubs out a name, signs it, and slips it under the bright red over-sized paper clip tacked to her door frame. As Matt makes his way to his seat, he keeps his head down, desperately avoiding eye contact with his pals, which isn't easy. They sit right behind him.

Lost within himself, Matt doesn't feel the warm breeze that creeps in through several open windows, stealing across the classroom like so many escaping secrets.

Miguel feels it. He squirms in his chair, adjusts his freshly pressed white Tee, pulling up at the shoulders to allow some of that air inside, hot or not.

The Santa Ana winds generally roll through Santa Niña at the start of the school year, carrying warm, stale inland air across the dry desert floor and settling into the softball mitt crevice that is this inland valley. They threaten fires in the dry grasses of the hills and fail to offer any relief from the 90-degree heat that bakes the area in late September. Today's winds aren't the traditional Santa Ana's, but they are stale, hot, and surely invite a fire.

Vientos del Diablo. Miguel can't take it. He pounds the desk with his open palms, "Damn, *ese*, it's hot. We can't take a final in this heat, man. Come on, Miss Thomas, give us a pass. Let's just go out for some ice cream."

The class laughs, used to the volatile junior's outbursts, more often humorous than threatening.

Miss Thomas scoops up the group's test packet from her desk that sits next to an open window and takes a characteristically slow walk over to Miguel's seat, depositing small stacks at each row. The breeze pushes at her back, and she feels the heat envelop her own body, empathetic to her students' desires to exit this oven but intent on administering her exam.

"Miguel," she whispers, "it's hot, yes. It's always hot." She looks over at Matt whose head hangs, his hands clasped and pushed through the space in his thighs. "You'll have to do your best when it gets hot. There's nothing I can do. I know you're ready for this test. OK?" She smiles (a smile that melts every boy in the room, and Miss Thomas knows it; it's a Mona Lisa smile). She leans closer. He takes in her sweet perfume and can almost see down her green gauze blouse dotted with tiny yellow flowers, but he stares straight ahead. "Focus on the math. It'll be over in an hour. Then you can take care of the important stuff. That'll be with you for a lifetime."

Miguel looks up, glancing for a moment at the freckles that pepper his teacher's neck and the space between her breasts, looks into her eyes then peeks over at Matt, Jesse and looks back. *How does she know? Does she know?* He tilts back his head, cracks his neck and straightens up. "Yeah, OK, whatever."

Miss Thomas rests a soft hand on his right shoulder, gives a gentle squeeze and a pat and moves back up to the front of the room.

She turns toward the class and says simply, "You may begin. Good luck." She steals one more glance over at Matt's downcast body, sighs, and returns to her desk where she sits and stares out through the open window.

The students settle, a few squirm, readjusting to a level of comfort in the hard plastic chairs, stretching out legs that are too long, tapping pencils eraser-side down, scratching out computations in the blank workspace and filling in open bubbles neatly and darkly being sure to stay inside the lines.

Matt lifts his pencil like a crowbar and wields its weight against the clean spaces that surround the numbers and words. He moves effortlessly through the exam, so sure of his skill that comes second nature to this bright boy. He works without thought without attention but with precision. He does not make a single error. He will score 100%.

Miguel will fail the exam but manage to pass the course having accumulated a B average throughout the year thanks to Matt's help.

Jesse will pass with a 73%.

Unable to sleep last night, Jesse arrived at school at 6:30, finding Miss Thomas inside boxing up supplies for summer break. She gave him a few sample math problems to work out on the board while he shared his own tribulations.

Nothing she heard surprised or shocked her. Miss Thomas knew all their stories. She couldn't help it. These boys didn't merely walk through her life, they walked inside it. She held each in her heart like a piece of herself. She believed in them, in their courage, in their strength to do the right thing. This she told Jesse.

Something she didn't share with Jesse was a piece of paper she had found in the back of a reference book turned in last week. Tucked between pages 97 and 98. As she was stacking the books on Mr. Wallace's cart, a text fell to the floor and Miss Thomas spotted the white sheet of paper sticking out between the math pages.

At first, she thought it was nothing but notes from an old English assignment; Shelley's musings on poetry. Then she spotted Matt's name in the top corner. She'd give it to him this week, she thought. Then she read the scribbled phrases he'd written in the margins of the paper.

```
Poet = love
Darkness = choices that offend others
Sweet sounds = people who don't care what you are
but love you anyway
Auditors = ?? potential lovers???

I can't share my song because it scares people away,
so I have to sit alone with myself. My song is my
courage?? That I get from my friends???
```

Miss Thomas can't read anymore because he has erased the words and scribbled over the invisible markings. She picked up the book, opened to the front inside cover, saw Ricky's name. She put the book back on the cart.

This morning, she does not share any of this with Jesse. Even after he spills all of the tell-all prior evening. The sidewalk. Ruby. Ricky. His Uncle Wayne. It is too much to contain within his adolescent heart, too much to withhold. He knows Miss Thomas understands this, so he shares all of it. All of it.

Matt glances toward the round school clock that sits casually above the door. Its blasé hands rest between the black numbers, oblivious to the impact of their movement, they simply tick, tock, move, slide from one number to the next, judging nothing nor no one This is the comfort Matt West finds in numbers. He sets down his pencil, the nubby end dulled by his etchings, the eraser gnawed by his errors.

Unaware of the eyes studying the back of his head, the stress creases along the rubber piping of his shoes, he sits. He waits.

They are his auditors, keeping him in check, assessing his moves, wary of the consequences that may fall into his path. They care, but they are also 16, 17 years old, full of youthful uncertainty, adolescent narcissism, masculine stereotypes, and narrow ideas of love.

As if reading his mind, Matt turns to Jesse, looks him straight in the eyes, stares for what feels like hours, searches for those sweet sounds. The bell rings, and the lilt of Miss Thomas' voice interrupts the exchange.

"I believe I have everyone's test," she scans the room as students begin to chatter, attempting to restrain the excitement that is at this point summer vacation. "Well then, I guess we're finished. Your year has ended. Summer has begun. I look forward to seeing you all walk the senior hallway next year. Have a safe summer."

Students cheer and applaud, for themselves, for their beloved teacher. Several stand and swap high-fives, hugs, cliché farewells. Miss Thomas catches Matt's eye and offers a sweet smile as she tucks a fly-away strand of hair behind her right ear. "Be well," she offers to the room, her gaze still holding Matt.

A figure breaks his line of sight with his teacher forcing Matt to readjust his vision. "Hey." It's Miguel.

"Hey," Matt returns.

Jesse steps in. "Hey."

The three stand, separated from the outside movement as if

held snug inside a jar of cotton balls. Or, from another perspective, a jar of tacks.

Miguel attempts to elevate the conversation, "Good thing that wasn't no English test. Seems we three are lackin' some smart vocab." He smiles at Jesse unable to lock eyes with Matt.

Jesse smirks. "Yeah. Words aren't comin' to me so good right now. We should go to the Shack or somethin', Matt? Ya think? Thirsty?"

Matt's hands dig into his front pockets, he stares at the cracked tile underneath a student desk. Over the year, much dirt has collected in the crooked crevice. He's observed its dark line grow darker from September to January to now. He looks up at Jesse. "I gotta go to the library first. I got some stuff I need to take care of. Uh, you guys go ahead."

"Well, when can you meet us?" Jesse's voice reveals a sense of urgency, one he's been feeling since his dad shared that uncomfortable conversation with him last night. He wants to tell Matt, ask Matt if he knows. He can't take anymore secrets.

"I dunno, depends." Matt catches Miguel's stare out of the corner of his eye. He turns. "You goin' to the Shack?"

Miguel dexterously twirls his test pencil between his fingers before he rests it like a cigarette and taps it against his forehead. He looks directly into his friend's eyes. "Yeah. I'm gonna be there. You gonna be there?" He tucks the tool behind his ear. "I ain't got nowhere else to be."

Matt wishes he'd added *and no place else I'd rather be*, but he doesn't. That would be expecting too much from his macho friend. Trying not to read more into Miguel's words, he quietly replies, "Okay. I'll see you guys later then."

"Yeah, later," Jesse nods.

Then Matt hears it, not realizing the breath he's holding.

"*Hasta luego, amigo.*"

The words, the sounds, the hard Mexican accent against the familiar almost English words. Three words. Three Spanish words. It didn't matter what they were. Just mattered who said them. That was the sign.

Once, back in the sixth grade, Matt had refused to let Miguel copy his math homework. He'd ranted that Miguel needed to start doing his own work. For three days, Miguel didn't say a word to Matt. On the following Saturday, Matt and Jesse showed up to Miguel's soccer game. The two friends rarely ever missed a match. They came to support their friend, watch in awe of his wild left foot. When Miguel spotted the boys in the stands, he waved, ran out on the field, his white and black jersey, number 5, billowing in the wind around his thin pre-teen body, and scored a goal in the game's first two minutes. From the field, Miguel shouted to his pals, "*Aye! ¿qué hay de ese pie, muchachos?*"

"*Salvaje, salvaje!* You the wild one, Mig!" Matt shouted. The foreign exchange from that day on marked the signal for the end to any rift in the friendship. The Spanish words meant peace, and for that they hold a special meaning just to him. And maybe to Miguel.

Matt breathes, turns, nods at Miss Thomas and exits Room 210.

For now, there is peace, unlike the explosion of secrets last night that ripped through years of bonding. He teeters. His friendship sits on a cliff, ready to collapse just because one boy doesn't know how to handle the revelation of another boy. But now, something's changed. It's as though a bridge has formed out of nowhere, in time to delay the ruin of this bond, this union, these years of racing broken bikes up and down the Numbers of a small Southern California town, years of watermelon seed spitting contests, fart contests, *I dare you to do that* contests. There is peace, a pause, a moment when three friends can say maybe we are better than this, maybe we are not the stereotype of male bravado, maybe we are soft, maybe we can accept what is to many so not acceptable. We are friends, and friends hold on. Friends let friends be, be who they are. Because that is the right thing to do.

Maybe.

Boys are like this. Trouble comes. Trouble goes. Words wait. After all, words don't come easy, and what doesn't come easy is often best left tucked away inside a cupboard of confusion, locked with the key of temperance. Words full of fire and emotion, like the bucking hind legs of a rodeo stallion, deserve space, deserve time to be tamed.

11

AN ENCOUNTER

Francesca hums as she gathers soiled items from her son's bedroom floor, dropping them casually into her basket as though plucking grapes from the vine. She examines each, smells the underarms, shakes them out deciding which could get away with one more wear, which are overdue for a spin in the Maytag. Her boys have each left for the day. Manuel picked up an extra shift at the store, and Miguel snuck out of the house before either could wish him good luck, or anything.

Last night, he'd come home around 8, said pretty much nothing to his mother, kissed her cheek, placed his hand on his belly and shook his head, kissed her cheek again as she removed heavy china plates from the pantry (heavy china plates that her clients no longer needed, wanted, and thought perhaps their sweet housekeeper might be able to find some use for in her more modest kitchen; it was true, they were right, Francesca was not an overly proud woman, and she appreciated the opportunity, out here in the Numbers, to set her bungalow's kitchen table with fine china that once found itself on the granite counters of those grander homes on the other side of town where all the houses, all the stately houses, stood tall inside their suits of gray armor. Francesca was pleased, and each time she pulled one of the heavy china plates down to set upon her wooden dining table that sat in her kitchen that needed someone to fix one of its wobbly legs, she felt part of a club which she knew she would never be a true member), and Miguel walked down the hall to his room, closed his door and didn't come back out until he left the house like a cat burglar this morning.

Manuel told his wife not to worry. "Boys need their own space, too, Mama. Your boy will be fine. He's probably just nervous for his test. We want him to pass, right, Mama; we need him to do well. Let him be." So the two parents sat down together for a quiet meal of tamales and rice. It was Miguel's favorite, but this night he would go to bed not hungry for much of anything.

Before Manuel turned in for the night, he gently opened his son's bedroom door and peaked inside. A cascade of moonlight lit a surreal path from his window and across the dark bed cover. Manuel waited for his eyes to adjust then he carefully walked over to his son's window, drew the curtain and stood over the bed. He watched his son's breathing and the up and down movement of his shoulders. This was not a boy at peace, Manuel thought. This boy is troubled. Manuel knelt beside his son, placed his warm palm on the boy's soft round head. He tried not to stroke the soft fuzz of hair but rather hold his hand over the skull like a priest blessing an infant. He stared at his son, just yesterday a boy, tomorrow a man, still so young, still so full of anger.

Manuel sang. "*A la roro niño, a lo roro ya; duérmete mi niño, duérmete mi amor.*" The words fell from his lips in soft waves. He knew the song by heart; it was part of his heart. He lifted his palm from his gown son's head and pressed down upon the bed's side frame as he hoisted his square body up. "Sleep well, my boy," he whispered before he turned to exit the room, closing the door gently and making his way down the hall to his wife. Miguel made no movement.

This morning, as Francesca starts to leave her son's room, she pauses. She stares at the wooden desk sitting idyll by the bedside of an empty bed. She remembers the wing, *el ala del ave*. Setting down the half-filled laundry basket, the round mother makes her way toward the furniture, stepping delicately across the shag carpet as if moving through a minefield on her way to retrieve bodies of fallen comrades. She cannot shake this sense of fear, this apprehension. Moving her fingers across her chest, to her sternum and lips, Francesca sends a brief message to her god, bends down, finds the feathery brown appendage and tiny bone fragments in the corner, gathers them up, and quickly drops the strange items into her laundry basket.

Standing, she lifts the basket and carries it into the laundry closet. The heavy square white beasts sit inside the makeshift utility room, and Francesca hums while she sorts the light from the dark, the heavy from the delicate, leaving small piles across the narrow shelf that protrudes along the wall, just above the machines, low enough for the small woman to reach, high enough to avoid the vibratory shaking of the decade-old appliances that spin and whir, quiver, quake and shudder as they toil to make clean what the Alma de Ramóns have made dirty.

The city bus lurches down Oak and snorts exhaust into the hot day. Francesca elects to walk the two long blocks to the library instead of risking a jog for the bus which stops 100 yards ahead of her at the corner of Oak and Eighth. Though it is mostly empty, having deposited its morning fill of schoolchildren at least three hours ago, she does not want to huff and puff up to its accordion doors, too out of breath to say good morning to the driver, sweat trickling from her clean brow. She does not like others to see her struggle. She chooses to continue the walk and maintain her steady breathing, her dry clean brow. She adjusts the canvas satchel upon her shoulder and across her bosom, feeling the bony wing in the corner beneath her sweater (many summer residents seek out the library's air-conditioned interior during the 100+ degree days, yet for some hot-blooded immigrants from south of the border, the air inside feels more like an arctic blast than gentle relief, so Francesca always brings her knitted orange sweater). The walk will take no more than 25 minutes. She knows she could use the exercise.

Reaching Ninth Street, Francesca takes in the smoother lawns and duller exteriors of homes too close to the downtown to stand out like the abodes deeper inside the Numbers. She eyes a baby blue bungalow with its cement porch and white picket fence, its single red rose bush surrounded by yellow and white daisies and a trim green square patch of lawn. An American flag flies from its porch post, flapping in the quiet breeze, rippling for attention on this quiet last day of school June morning.

This particular home is no stranger to the stout housecleaner. Without opening the front wooden door, she can see down its inner hallways to a nursery and master bedroom, a tidy living room with a large boxy television and multiple-speaker stereo, the wrap-around leather couch that dominates the front room and the litter of red, yellow, and blue plastic baby toys scattered about the short ivory shag carpet forcing pedestrians to practice acrobatics and a housekeeper to crawl beneath furniture in search of fist-sized shapes and jingly soft balls.

Francesca has been cleaning the Watson's home for four years. She's known the Mr. and Mrs. pre-baby, pre-domestic turmoil. She cleaned the master bathroom after Mrs. Watson's first miscarriage, after Mr. Watson's 24-hour bug, after the couple returned from a visit over the border and brought back Montezuma's revenge all over the white tile of the nautical-themed chamber.

But these are the tasks she does not mind so much because these are the times a guilty white middle class family hopes their kind and quiet Mexican housekeeper will keep to herself, and so they tip her. Manuel told her to return the money. "They cannot buy your silence. How dare they think you talk. Who. Who are you going to share their puking and diarrhea and bloody mucous with? Who? Are you going down to liquor store and blabbing to Mr. Le about loose bowels of couple on corner of Ninth and Oak? How dare they! How dare they."

At this, Francesca calms Manuel, ignores his broken English, tells him they only gave her the extra 20 or 40 because of all the hard work of bending and scrubbing and scouring and scooping. "They are only being kind, Manny. They only wish to apologize. They do not want to buy my silence. Manny. This is not *The Godfather*, this is Santa Niña, this is just a gesture. Manny, we can keep it. It goes in the Left Foot Jar."

Manuel calms. Francesca places the bills inside the ceramic jar with the black-markered foot sketch, Miguel's college fund. The family deposits all extra bills and coins inside. What they don't need today, they will wait for after Miguel gets into college, after Miguel has signed in LA or Argentina or maybe even Mexico. Today, the jar holds three-thousand seventy-two dollars and eighteen cents. The family has been stuffing it since Miguel took his first step at eighteen months and toddled right over to the black and white cloth ball in the Alma de Ramón living room and kicked it up and over the coffee table into the hands of his father.

The next morning, Francesca returned from the flea market

with the pickle-jar sized ceramic urn, placed it in the corner of the front room, dropped in two dollar bills, and announced, "This is for our Miguel and his wild left foot. This boy, Papa, this boy is going places, and we need to get ready now."

Francesca reaches the intersection at Tenth Street as the signal turns green and the lighted letters flash in the gridded box. She ambles quickly across the four-lane road, reaching the landscaped pathway of the downtown library just after 11:20.

Susie Mallicksen is not yet seated at the information desk beneath the iron glare of Burnett, so Francesca is left to decipher the colorful chalk letterings of the library's various sections and locations. She locates nature books on the second floor, paws the small hard item inside the corner of her Orange Grower's Picnic canvas bag, and makes her way up the curving staircase.

While his mother sets off to discover the meaning of the wing, Miguel marks the last item on his Calculus final and turns over his scantron. Had she simply asked Miguel, he would have told her all about the hawk nest outside the fence of the Shack and how one of the caretakers stood paralyzed as he eyed the dead bird, and how Miguel found a discarded paper bag that he used to scoop up the bird and take to Al's. But she didn't. Anyway, if he had told her, he might also have had to tell her what he does in the Grove at night when no one else is around.

He sits back as his teacher darts about the room, collecting completed exams, whispering "good job" to each. She stops at Miguel's desk and lifts his test. "Whaddya think? Am I going to be pleasantly surprised?"

"Hah. Yeah, pleasantly surprised I failed." He twirls his pencil and stares into the back of his friend's head, the head of a stranger, today, the head of someone he's not sure he knows anymore. "I guess life's full of surprises, though."

"Sometimes, yes, mostly, I suppose," she adjusts the tests, cradling the stack in the nook of her right arm like a newborn. She places her left hand on the distracted boy's shoulder. "You know, though, Miguel, sometimes it's good to be caught by surprise. It keeps us on our toes, keeps us from being, you know, so complacent, so–"

"Com-what?" he interrupts.

She smiles, squats down beside his chair. "Complacent. Happy with the way things are. You know, Miguel, sometimes the way things are isn't so, so right. Sometimes, the way things are is very wrong. Surprises make us stop and think, stop and take hold of what's right, what's wrong, what needs to change." She stops, distracted by noises across the room. "It's like on the soccer field, you have to keep moving, keep dribbling, keep trying to get the ball back. Your goal is always the same. To score. To defend. To support the team. Right?"

Miguel simply stares ahead.

"Even if you're winning, you can't be complacent. You can't just expect the win. You need to be ready. Always. Support the team. Win or lose." She stands as the talking escalates and walks over to investigate the chatter, leaving Miguel to ponder her words.

Ponder he does.

Matt turns over his test and presses his head to the cold desk, forehead prone, eyes closed, hands folded in his lap. Lexie's words battle his own, teasing his heart; he burps, a small puddle of bile forces its way up his throat. He swallows it. The acid pools in his belly, his empty belly, his troubled mind.

Miguel turns toward the window, not looking for something just trying to replace the present scenery. He spies two robins pecking at the moist ground under a shady Oak. Too far away to see exactly what one's pulled up in its bill, Miguel can safely assume it's a worm. He leans in toward the window as the one bird moves into the other and nibbles at the hanging, squirming insect. The holder of the meal stands still, allowing his mate to share, not flapping off to claim the entire prize to himself. Not surprised his mate wants to share. Miguel imagines if he were this bird, he'd probably peck out the other's eyes; first, swallow the meal then peck out his eyes. Miguel doesn't like to share, and he doesn't usually like surprises. He does like soccer, and despite his famed wild left foot, Miguel has won the team's Leadership award twice. Though his fiery temperament has cost him more than one yellow card, his fight has always been for the team, not for himself.

He looks back at his friend's blond head, trying to understand what is different about it today from yesterday. Yesterday when everything was the same, when everything was just like it always is. Damn, who knew 24 hours later his world would be turned upside down. He glances back at Jesse and his broken heart, still scribbling away at the test, still punching in numbers into his calculator. His hands bandaged, he pecks and pokes, lithely cradling his pencil, hoping he's pressed hard enough to complete the bubbles.

Miguel blankly stares. Back to Matt. Then back at Jesse.

Three Musketeers. He laughs. *Guess we can't all three like girls, we'd be fightin' over 'em all the time.* Miguel pauses at this thought. Why hadn't it ever struck him as funny that his pal never had a girlfriend, never tried to lay claim to one of his, never got caught under the bleachers like Miguel. You think you know someone, expect you know someone, expect that because you get along like brothers that you are exactly the same. But you're not.

Surprise.

Miss Thomas stands up front, speaking. Saying something. Miguel does not hear these words, he's listening to his own.

Inside the tall stacks of books, Francesca threads her way through the many shelves like a rat in a maze. Her right hand gripping the mysterious appendage through her canvas sack, her left hand running across the dusty titles in search of the one printed on the yellowing index card she pulled from the narrow drawer of the catalogue bureau.

She spots it. "The Reader's Digest Book of North American Birds". She withdraws the heavy book from its shelf, finds an empty desk and seats herself with her bag still at her side. She stares at the cover and the stern eagle in flight then turns to the index in the back. Her English might not be perfect, but Francesca has always been the best reader in the house. Before arriving in America, her father had taken her and Manuel and conducted English lessons on the back adobe patio in the sweltering Mexican heat. The two, only fifteen at the time, far more interested in each other than they were in mastering another language. Ignorant at the prospects a bilingual world could bring them. Adolescent ignorance knows no international borders.

Francesca hums as she leafs through the pages, admiring the feathery creatures, preferring the small wrens and sparrows to the predator hawks and eagles. She spends more than two hours simply reading about all kinds of birds; the cheery Robin, that harbinger of spring, the tiny Hummingbird whose male sort entertains the female with twirling acrobatics, and the Laysan Albatross that lays just one buff-white egg at a time, raising it in a large seaside colony with others.

Having satisfied such aviary curiosities, she decides to turn to the item in her bag. Wary of the eyes and ears around her, she carefully extracts the wing from its hiding place and sets it on the desktop. She continues to the index and runs her finger along the words until she finds the section on Hawks. Turning the pages, she hears a scuffle in the next aisle. She looks up, peering through the row of books just above her head.

"I wasn't sure you'd make it. Figured you'd be thronged by fans demanding your autograph in their yearbooks." Francesca recognizes the voice, soft, friendly. Definitely Matt West.

"Haha, yeah, well, uh, just a few. Can't sign too many or the signature loses its value, ya know." The boys laugh. Francesca cannot identify this second voice. Worried Miguel might walk around the corner, she shoves the wing back inside her bag and closes the book. Quietly. She sits. Waits for the boys to finish their conversation and move on so she can, too.

"But, yeah, I signed some. You got yours?"

Matt shifts the bulk of his backpack. *The Rind* weighs heavily inside, but he isn't sure he's ready for Ricky to actually put words down in ink. Ink's permanent. You can't erase it. Matt pauses.

"Well, uh, maybe later. So, you got your application?"

This Matt willingly withdraws from his bag. "Yeah. I was gonna fill out some, but I guess I got caught up in studying and stuff." Stuff like Ruby Newton and the sidewalk.

"It's OK. I found mine in the back office at the Shack. We can pretty much copy most of it. Except for the personal stuff." Ricky unfolds the paper he had stuffed in his back pocket. "Old Man Connors never checks his filing cabinet. Once he hires someone, he forgets why. He only cares you show up on time and clean up good. He'll like you. You're clean. He always says, 'keep it clean, boys and girls'. I think he means our mouths, too, you know, no swearin' and stuff. But, yeah, he'll like you. Can't think of any reason why he wouldn't." Ricky flashes that sweet smile, that dimple, and Matt falls back in. "- so, where then?"

"Huh?" Matt returns, shakes his head slightly.

"Where should we sit? Here?" Ricky motions to the single study corral.

"Yeah, OK, but it's only got one chair."

"That's OK," he says as he pulls out the wooden seat. "Here ya go, handsome. I'll just rest here on the desk."

Unused to such gallantry (Matt's usually the one to pull out a chair for his mom, never a girl, certainly not a boy), he balks.

"Have a seat. It won't bite," Ricky smiles as Matt moves toward the chair. "And neither will I," he whispers into Matt's right ear.

Matt shudders, shivers, tingles. Ricky pushes in the chair as Matt scoots forward. He sits on the desktop, flattens out his application next to Matt's, smiles. Perhaps sensing Matt's hesitation, observing how he's leaning slightly away, just a bit toward the left, Ricky attempts to ease his thoughts.

"It's OK, Matt. We're gonna figure this out. I want to. I talked to Lexie after school. We're gonna 'break up'," he says posting quote fingers in the air and smiles. Again. The smile alone is a paralyzing drug injected right into the adolescent heart of Matt West. At first, it scares him, this paralysis, this shudder, this feeling. Then he relaxes. Ricky places his hand on Matt's, caresses his fingers. "Really. It's OK."

Francesca gasps, covers her mouth. She cannot believe what she sees. These boys. Two boys. Matt. Miguel's friend. What is this? They are, they are together? She's not sure what she feels, what she thinks. She at once wants to run, run home to her boy, run home to find him. Will he be alone? Will he be with a girl? A boy? The thought wrestles inside her as it has for so many generations, tradition v. change, past against the future. What would Manny say? She cannot contain the uneasy, queasy feeling churning in her belly. She is surprised.

She can't help but watch the two. Will they kiss, will they

touch each other more? There? She knows she should turn away. She can't. She watches. The tall boy places his hand on Matt's, he moves his fingers along his, they stare at each other. They smile. Then the boy starts writing on the paper. They talk. Matt places his hand on the boy's knee. The tall one covers it, holds it. They stare and smile some more. She cannot turn away. She wants to, doesn't want to. She is afraid, but she no longer knows why.

The boys do nothing more. Francesca sits back, looks at the cover of her bird book, the stern eagle. She considers these two boys, how gentle they touch each other, how quietly they speak. She places her palm to her chest and feels the rapid beating of her heart, grasps the cross at her neck. Tears roll down her cheeks. Her mind inside swirls. She is dizzy. The room around her spins, too, and she feels the whole floor will soon give way and she will tumble down inside the very molten core of this earth.

She raises her hands to her face and sobs in silence. She does not want to be heard, to be seen. Not entirely sure why she is crying, she wipes her tears, stands, adjusts the bag on her shoulder and exits out the back end of the aisle. She leaves behind the book, the boys. She does not turn back.

"There you go then. Done. Looks good. No way the old man won't hire you now. I mean, if he doesn't hire you, why the heck did he hire me?" Ricky bounces off the desk, lifts his own application, refolds it and slips it in his back pocket.

Matt folds his paper in half as well and slides it inside his backpack. He stands and lifts the bag to his shoulder. A quiver runs through his body, a vibration. He hesitates then clears his throat. "Thanks. I, uh, I guess I'll drop it off tomorrow, see how it goes."

"Might as well take it in today. I got a shift starting in," he pauses, looks at his wrists, laughs. Ball players don't usually wear watches. Ricky looks around for a wall clock, spots one. "Dang, it's almost 3. My shift starts at 4. I told my mom I'd stop at home first. Hey, I'm gonna catch the bus home, but why don't I meet you at the Shack. I can take your application and put in a good word to Old Man Connors. Whaddya say?" The smile. The dimple.

What can Matt say but, "Yeah. Okay. Sure. I'll meet you there." Not feeling the same confidence as the star forward, Matt retreats a step. "I'll see you in a bit then. Thanks for the help."

Sensing the boy's uneasiness, Ricky takes his own step back, smiles and quietly offers, "Great. I'm glad we got a chance to do this. It'll be fun hanging out this summer. I'll show you the ropes."

Matt swallows, blushes.

"You know, around the Shack and all. Where kids stash condoms. Where the ants collect. Fun stuff. You'll see." He hesitates, runs a finger along some book spines. "Remember, you can't sprout wings without faith. No wings. No flying. Flying's fun. OK?"

The familiar metaphor comforts Matt. "Yeah. OK. Just give me time. My wings seem to be buried a little deeper than yours." He returns a half smile, just the left side.

"No prob. But you know you can do this, Matt. You can. We can. I won't let you fall if you don't think you can fly." With this, Ricky Traeger turns and heads out of the second floor stacks, down the main stairs and out to catch the 51 bus.

We don't always recognize that flash, that brief shadow of movement from a not knowing to a knowing, a shift from fear to faith, from restraint to courage, unaware as we, in a simultaneous instance, straddle a precipice between the past and future, holding a handful of each within the same palm, unconsciously letting go those finer grains of the past, the ones we've rubbed smooth from so much wear, so much gnawing, so much doubting, allowing them to quietly spill out through the spaces between our fingers while holding steady to the newer, coarser grains of the future. This was that flash, a defining moment for Matt West.

This time, he observed it with a mindfulness so clear and sure, it was as if a whole new day had risen inside the narrow confines of the stacks on the second floor of this oh so familiar library.

Could it be that the genetic conduit bent and torn from so much abuse by those West men had now begun to straighten, to veer back on course, back within the lines? Like a rollercoaster car righted on its track, made steady again on the rails, Matt West's gathering of just an ounce of courage, just a smidge of faith might well have shifted that DNA, returning it to its rightful path, its daring descent toward a platform varnished in faith, polished with hope, a shiny surface from where any bird with the smallest of wings could surely step forward, drop off and take flight.

Matt runs his hands through his thin blond strands, strands that share headspace with a touch of red, Nordic red like his grandfather, and he starts to laugh. He laughs so loud, he has to cover his mouth with both hands. He can't stop laughing.

12
AN EVENT

The Shack spills over with jubilant jabbering teens celebrating the end of another school year, welcoming the wide-open days of summer. The inland valley heat bears down on the electric crowd, weighing upon their heads like a heavy hand as glistening droplets of sweat spontaneously erupt then spill down their youthful complexions, over hummocks of acne forming rivulets inside the narrow cleavage of perky breasts, gathering within the creases of their genitals. A heat that confuses racing libidos with rising mercury. They paw and poke each other, in jest, in courtship, baiting one interest with the jealous moves of another.

Superficially united in one purpose – to celebrate summer - the hormonal adolescents divide themselves into factions about the hangout, slowly initiating that much anticipated transformation from school to vacation, from ignored classmate to potential lover. A bird's eye view suggests pods of colorful amoebas, morphing and vibrating within their own select genetic families. The jocks have discarded their heavy jackets in exchange for muscle-boasting cut-off tees. The cheer squad has swapped mini-skirts for spandex, tight sweaters for sexy midriffs. This toxic female unit winds its way around the Shack like a snake hunting its next prey, sneering at the lesser packs, finally coiling inside the den of narcissistic athletes. A few tables away, a tech-savvy throng curls itself about an umbrella table, sipping Swirls and downing fries, laughing at inside jokes outside on this 100+ degree Santa Niña day. Smatterings of those who don't quite fit into one stereotypical high school clique scatter themselves in twos and threes about the venue, whispering, giggling, glaring and sulking. This marginalized set that often finds itself caught in a web of not wanting to be part of a defined group while hoping not to be left out, unseen, disregarded.

Jesse and Miguel, a unit to themselves, move about the landscape like geckos, able to blend into any crowd, settling most comfortably within a cadre of outsiders, high-fiving, head-nodding, and dirty-joking, exchanging knowing looks at the juicy rumors, disapproving bobs and tongue clicks at the more scandalous tales.

The boys mingle at this libidinous cocktail party like honored dignitary arriving fashionably late. The two opted for a slow walk from school, taking time to recount the past 24 hours, Ruby, Matt and Jesse's tumble in the street; they now sport near empty backpacks, the one artificial reminder that the day began with school. Miguel's shoulder-sling bag crosses his body military style, while his beloved skateboard clings to the strap, secured by a bungee. Jesse's traditional Jansport weighs heavy with *The Rind* yearbook and a plastic sandwich bag still resting at the bottom of the sack unnoticed.

Miguel attracts more attention than his broken-hearted partner who follows the former around like Peter Pan's shadow. Only this shadow has no intention of escaping, taking flight, encouraging mischief. Jesse Waters hangs his head low, taking more interest in his scuffed Chucks than the pretty girls in their scanty summer attire.

"Come on, Jess, you got some change for a Swirl?" Miguel asks, at once trying to jog his friend out of his self-absorbed misery while equally hoping to score a few quarters to complete his handful and quench his thirst with some sweet orange nectar. Young or old, every Santa Niñan loves a Swirl.

Jesse digs in his right front pocket and drops two quarters and a dime onto Miguel's brown palm.

"Nice one. Let's get some magic juice for that jilted heart of yours, man." The two boys walk over to the shaded canopy of the front counter. Miguel drops his change on the sticky surface like a five-year-old who's just smashed open his piggy bank. "One Swirl, Old Man."

Old Man Connors greets the youth with distaste, gathering up the coins and depositing them in the cash drawer. Typically, the owner doesn't show up on the scene until near closing, but today being the last day of school, he hedged bets that his staff would need an extra hand. They do. At least 60 or 70 teens fill the tables or lean under the canopy, seeking shade that drops the outside temps to maybe 90.

This old man isn't quite an old man; however, to anyone under 20, he sure looks the part. Hunched over due to a damaged nerve in his back, Billy Connors has not yet seen his 40th birthday. A promising football career was cut short by a near-death experience about ten years ago. Back then, he had a full head of hair, stood just under six feet, and carried the ball an average of 5.6 yards each run. No Walter Payton, Billy Connors was a SNiHi star, All-State superstar, and promising rookie LA Ram. He had survived the death of Caroll Rosenblum and the move by his widow to Anaheim Stadium, but he saw only three seasons on the field. Now the 35-year-old Connors watches his former team struggle on the field as he does in life, imagining neither has much longer in the spotlight.

Had he not decided to race inside the two-room structure of

Ms. Elisa Jensen to save her 15-year-old blind poodle and find himself in the middle of the city's now-historic Panoramic Fire of 1981, he might not now be wiping up the sticky orange trails of arrogant and apathetic teens. But he did save Macie, he did suffer second-degree burns on his hands, head and back. He did, and those scars, of course, run deeper. His football career ended the minute the doctor told him the fire had damaged his nerves, and he'd be lucky to walk straight let alone run.

So now the slightly hunched, bald and scarred mid-thirties former athlete sips the sweet juice of a Swirl allowing it to wash away the bitter taste of regret. Each day is easier. Each day he forgets more, regrets less. But then some cocky footballer walks up to the counter, reminds him of his feats on the field of SNiHi, his trophies that decorate the boosters' Wall of Fame, and he must feign gratitude and begin again as he swallows a little more disappointment that tastes so much like a Shack Swirl, the bittersweet nectar, magic juice.

"Thanks, ese," Miguel takes the Swirl and shuffles his pal over toward the fence near the back side of the Shack. "Yo, want some medicine, my man?" Miguel squats down, looks about then slides off his backpack and zips open the side pouch.

Jesse looks down. "Whatcha doin, man?" His eyes widen as his pal withdraws a small flat bottle filled with brown liquid.

"Just a little celebration to end our junior year. Come on, ese, don't be a pussy on me now." Miguel unscrews the cap then removes the lid from the sweet drink. He pours out some orange and adds in some brown, twirls the straw, sips, considers the mixture, seeking balance and just a bit of bite, adds a drop more brown, twirls, sips, smiles as he replaces the lid, screws back on the liquor bottle's cap, secures the taboo item in his bag, stands and holds the now darkly orange liquid out to his friend. "Drink up, ese, mama's sweet magic will make *allll* your troubles disappear."

For a moment, Jesse hesitates, his hands remain dug down deep inside his pockets as he turns to survey the scene out front. He spies the lughead. A bitter trail of bile edges up his throat. "Fuck it," he mumbles and takes the drink.

Miguel laughs. "Now you're talkin', man. Who needs to be a part of that fuckin' fake party out there. We got our own goin' on back here. Yow! Aye, yai, yai, yai!" The boys laugh at the clichéd line. "Yeah, that's me, man, all Mexican. Mexican and proud! Arriba!"

The boys lean back against the wire fence, not caring about the dirt catching in the lines of their jeans or the dust gathering on their pristine shoes. They drink. To celebrate. To forget. They drink. To go.

And they laugh and shout. And drink some more.

The mid-afternoon sun continues to penetrate the celebratory crowd and ripening fruit in the Grove. The Valencia oranges peek in the summer months, holding in a sweeter, juicier meat after the wet spring rains unlike their seedless kin, the Navel, which lay dormant at this time of year. Grove workers have taken a midday break, seeking their own solace in a small shed that sits at the far end of the property. Far from the Shack and its celebrants, far from the sounds, smells and games. They are not eager to return into the field of trees and shower them with water, so they enjoy the quiet within the tool shed, their homemade sandwiches and a few sections of orange.

Back around inside the Shack, Billy Connors tosses a wet rag to his employee. "Yo, late bird, you missed the worm, you get to wipe."

Ricky catches the cloth, smiles, turns to peer out at the chatty customers, his classmates, teammates, smiles again. "No problem, Old Man. It's a beautiful day to wipe away slime." He laughs to himself, not sharing his joke with the owner. Nothing is going to stop his day, this day that has begun moving forward, inching gently along the tracks into the Fun House, inside the winding darkly lit pathway of the House of Love. Ricky beams.

"Glad someone's havin' a good day," Connors mumbles to himself, then a little louder, "Must be nice to be in love."

"Huh?" Caught with his hands in the cookie jar, Ricky turns back toward his boss. "Whatcha say? Love? You in love, Boss?"

"Hah. Me? Yeah, I'm in love with all you greedy little buggers who share your allowance with me everyday then scratch your lovebird initials into my nice white tables. Yeah, that's me, Billy Connors loves You!" The old man turns away from Ricky. Whistling an unfamiliar tune, he heads to the back freezer for some more meat patties, so he needs to shout the last part, "Your girlfriend's lookin' for you, lover boy! That oughta put a hole in your parade float!" The rest, if there's more, is lost inside the cold aluminum walls of the freezer.

"Yo, Old Man River, your song is flat and off key." Ricky opens the side door, wrings the cloth out by the wall, grabs a plastic bin and joins the party. He spots the cheer squad and decides it's time to start the fight with Lexie.

"You got any more coins, man?"

"Nah, that was it. Jus got lint now."

The two laugh, having quenched their thirst and completed part one of their celebration. Miguel digs back inside his bag. "Then I guess we ain't gonna sweeten our next dose." He unscrews the cap and takes a swig. "Ahh!" Shakes his head. "Nasty stuff, man!" He hands the bottle toward Jesse. "Go on, doctor's orders."

Jesse's ready. He's been watching Ruby flit from her girls to lughead. He takes the bottle, bends his elbow twice. Longer on the second gulp.

"Whoa, slow down, amigo! Gotta save some, ya know." Miguel takes the bottle as Jesse tilts his head forward then back wondering when the ship's gonna dock and why the sea's so choppy today. Miguel looks out at the crowd. "When'd Matt say he'd be comin? Do ya remember?" He takes one last swig. A long one. Screws on the cap and sets the bottle between his crossed legs.

Jesse doesn't hear Miguel; right now he's digging in the bottom of his own bag looking for something else.

Cradling the waste bin on his left hip, Ricky moves about the tables with his rag, wiping up spills, scooping up trash, and exchanging superficial chatter with some of the girls, all while keeping an eagle on Lexie who's sharing her own very close conversation with Greg Tyler. Greg's the outgoing team captain, a graduating senior, and a total ladies' man. He's chatted up Lexie before, but he doesn't realize today is his lucky day.

"Hey! Lex? What the... Yo, Greg, back it up." Ricky sets down his bin, tossing the rag inside and takes up a steady pace toward the two cozy teens.

"Ricky, hey, it's not what you think."

Really, that's her best line?

"Yeah, Traeger, we're jus talkin'. Nuthin' big. Cool yer jets, man."

On cue, the crowd moves in, circling the trio. "Dude, lay off. Come on, it's the last day. We're jus gettin' the summer party started. Come on, man, take a chill." Anthony Tran places his right hand on Ricky's shoulder. "Yo, let's take this down a notch." He turns to Lexie. "So, you gonna add somethin' to this and keep it all cool? You jus chattin' with my man Tyler, right, Lex? Innocent, right?"

"Yeah, that's it. Just chattin', Ricky," working on her Oscar, she tries to take his hand in hers.

Working on his own, he pushes it away. "Nah, you weren't jus 'chattin', Lex." He eyes Greg. "Neither was you."

Anthony and the rest fall silent. But feeling the fire's reduced to a sizzle, most move back to their previous interests, their fries, Swirls and gossip (to which they'll now add this scene).

"Just chattin', Ricky. Really." She looks up at her all-star boyfriend, knowing the jig's up, knowing she'll need to find a new ruse, knowing it's not going to be Greg Tyler. She turns to find her own pals. Ruby's still over with Nate's crowd who decide this scene isn't going to amount to anything exciting. Had they believed a real fight was starting, they'd be over in an instant, over to watch, to watch one guy beat up another guy. Don't matter who's fighting. A fight's a fight for these boys. Besides, the football crew's already reached its own verdict on the basketball superstar. The boys aren't surprised to see the Ricky-Lexie saga end. Not surprised at all.

It just means less competition with the girls for them. They don't much care who this all-star likes, and for a group of small-town nobody athletes, this fact sets them up a notch in the world of acceptance.

Nate Gibbons does not own this notch, however. He can't help but add his own lines to the story. He moves away from the field to the court. "Hey, Tyler, need any help?"

Greg Tyler turns toward the beefy running back, somewhat surprised at the offer. "Nah, it's cool, man. Like I said, we was jus talkin', that's it."

Just a few feet of dirt separate the two teammates, while Lexie has moved a safe distance behind Nate. Greg and Ricky maintain eye contact. Neither wanting to be the first to back down.

Actually, that's not true. Ricky would like it to end now. He'd like it all to end now. The lies. He starts to say something, searches for the words. Wants so desperately to just lay it all out, but he can't. He's stuck. The words must be perfect, he thinks; after all, he has a lot riding on this.

And the *lot* has just arrived.

"Aha!" Jesse smiles. "Now we're talkin'"

"Huh? What?" The loud voices and moving pods of voyeurs have held Miguel's attention for the past few minutes. He can't quite make out who's yelling at who, but the energy doesn't lie. Something's brewing outside the Shack. "Whatchoo doin now, Water Boy? Somethin's goin' on over there. Les take a look."

"Water Boy. Hah, you hadn'ta called me that in a while. Hah. Water Boy. Well, Water Boy's got somethin' fun for hiz pal. Lookee here arribo amigo."

Miguel turns, tries to correct his focus, which has suddenly turned fuzzy. Like his speech. He grabs at the white object in Jesse's hand. "What the? Whatcha got there, my man?"

Jesse pulls away his hand in time. "Jus a little prezzie from my good Uncka Wins, Winston. Good Uncka Winzzton. Haha!" He pulls out his lighter. "Come on, we gonna amp up this partayyy. Screw lil missnewton! Screw her!"

Jesse's only once tried a party stick before. That was yesterday when he almost ended up roadkill. Miguel's choice of dessert has typically been a stolen can from his dad's stash in the garage or a swig of Al's flask in his office behind the cans of Penzoil.

Miguel's never smoked a joint. Never gotten high. He's always opted for the depressant, the alcoholic downer. Just like his dad.

"So, we gonna smoke that or what?"

Jesse lights the stick while Miguel finishes off the whiskey.

"Pass it over, man." He throws the bottle against the back wall, shattering it into a zillion little pieces, startling a host of sparrows from the lamppost, but drawing no attention from the fertile crowd out front.

Jesse laughs, dropping the lighter to the dirt, and slaps his buddy on the shoulder. "Arriba!" he shouts.

Miguel inhales.

Ruby moves up behind Nate. "Come on, Nate, leave'em be." She threads her arm through Lexie's then takes her hand and tugs at the footballer's belt loop. "Let's go finish our food. Come on, Nate."

Matt stands at a distance, his backpack hanging off his right shoulder, the folded application in his other hand. He observes the collection; though most have dispersed, Greg, Ricky, Nate and the girls remain huddled.

He looks around for his pals, not sure where to move next. Lexie spots him.

"Yeah, it's cool now, Nate." Lexie wraps her hand over Ruby's. "Ricky, I'm sorry. This isn't working." She takes her other hand to her face and starts making sounds.

Ohh, she's good, Ricky thinks. *Yeah, you get the Oscar, girl.* He looks up at Greg. "Well, whatever. I got work to do." He turns, picks up his bin and rag and moves toward the building.

"Hey, when'd you get here?"

"Just now. Well, a minute ago. What's goin' on? Where's Miguel and Jesse? You seen them?"

"Nah. Just finished a little of my acting class." Ricky relaxes. Smiles. "Ready for Act two?"

"Huh?" Matt looks back over toward Ruby. She has her arm around Lexie whose head is buried down in her lap. Ruby strokes her back. She looks up and sees Matt. She tries to smile, tries to send a message, *hey, I'm on your side. I got this. I'm sorry. I'm a jerk. I'm gonna fix it. I'm sorry.*

Ricky grabs the paper. "Come on, let's go have a chat with the old man.

"Whoowee, man, I'm flyin'! Jus like that hawk. That's me, circlin' my prey, lookin' fer my mate. Yeah, lazy circles in the sky." Miguel leans his head back against the fence.

"Good stuff, huh." Jesse finishes the last bit. Not being regulars, the boys have only their fingers to hold the small stub of cigarette. Feeling a bit high in the sky himself, Jesse decides to snub out the remainder.

"Yeah. Good stuff. Damn, I'm feelin, feelin out there, man." Miguel turns toward his friend. He slaps his hand down gently on Jesse's shoulder. "Problee a good time as any to tell ya some stuff."

"What stuff?" Jesse moves his finger around in the dirt, transfixed by his creation of swirls and figures.

Miguel gathers his hands behind his head, looks again up toward the sky, squints, turns back toward Jesse. "Did ya think you an' Ruby were gonna be like forever, man? Did ya?"

"Huh? Yeah, maybe. I dunno. What difference does it make now anyway?"

"Yeah, none, I guess. But, uh, ya know she's not the most faithful, man. She's uh, she likes to flirt and stuff, ya know."

"Yeah, I know, but I don't think she ever gave it all up to anyone else." Jesse turns his head toward the crowd. "I mean, it's not like she was screwin' that fuckin' lughead while she was with me, man."

"Nah, but I bet she is now, man."

"What the fuck? You on my side or what, dude?"

"I'm on yer side, man, relax. I'm jus sayin' I think she's friendly, ya know, with the guys. Always has been."

"What the, whaddya mean *friendly*?"

Miguel stands up now, feeling the world closing in on him. *Whoa, too fast.* He reaches for the fence, lacing his fingers through the links. "Look, man, there's some things you should know about yer girl, thass all."

"Yeah, like what?" Jesse stands now, holding onto the same fence with his right hand, eyes on his pal.

Miguel pulls away, shoves his hands in his pockets, kicks the dirt. "Stuff. Things."

"Don't gimme that, dude. Stufffff. Thingzzz. Come on, man," Jesse moves toward Miguel. "Dish it!"

"Look, Jess, it's nuthin. It was a long time ago. You weren't even together yet."

"When? Who?" Jesse moves closer toward Miguel. "Who, man? Tell me!"

"Back off, man!" Miguel pushes Jesse's shoulders and stumbles back toward the fence.

"Who!" Jesse pushes Miguel back. "Who?! Who?! Who?!" He thrusts his finger into Miguel's chest at each word.

Knowing he has to share the truth, wanting to purge himself of this secret, Miguel moves away from the fence, away from Jesse.

"Me."

As though he didn't hear this, Jesse looks toward Miguel. "What did you say?"

"It was 8th grade, man. You weren't even together. Not yet. And it was rainin', and we din't really even do anything. I mean, we just messed aroun'. And-"

Jesse takes a step. *Crunch.* Another. *Crunch.* The shattered whiskey bottle dots the ground like pebbles. He bends over and lifts the largest piece, a long shard that extends from the lip. Jesse laces his forefinger inside it, holding it up like Captain Hook. Anger is sobering, and he finds more ease in his speech. "What the fuck, man?! You're my friend. You're my friend, man. Aren't you?"

Miguel, not used to being on the other side of anger, steps back. "You weren't together yet!"

Jesse steps forward.

"We din't do it!" He steps back.

Crunch.

"Come on, man, she's the cheater, not me, man. I'm yer friend, Jesse." Miguel stops moving. "I am." He swallows. "I am, man."

"Hey, Old Man, ya need some extra help this summer?" Ricky hands Billy Connors the folded application.

"Who's this? Another superstar athlete?"

Matt extends his hand. "Matt West, sir."

Billy laughs. "Didya coach him, Traeger? Tryin' to butter me up with some manners, are ya?"

Ricky smiles. "That's right. I'm doin' your dirty work, Old Man, finding good clean employees for this greasy joint."

Matt shifts his backpack. "This'd be my first job, sir. You can see that on my appli-"

"Don't tell him that," Ricky whispers.

Billy looks over the application then up at Matt then over at Ricky. "Well, we'll try you out, kid, but no askin' for vacation days or stealin' fries for your girlfriend."

Ricky laughs. Matt swallows hard. "Don't worry, sir. I won't."

"Alright." Connors pauses, turns, picks up a Swirl. "Here kid, better stock up on the magic juice now. And, you, Traeger, grab a rag. He's all yours. Show 'im the ropes."

"You got it, Boss." Ricky dumps the contents of the bin into the waste can and hands it to Matt.

"What? That's it? I got it?"

"Yes," Ricky smiles. "Here, gimme that." He pulls Matt's backpack from his shoulder, slipping the bag down his arm and off his hand where Ricky lingers his own for just a moment, wrapping one finger around Matt's. Just for a moment.

Matt shudders.

There's a banging at the front counter. Shouting. Ricky and Matt look up. It's Ruby.

"Come on! Now! It's Jesse and Miguel! Come on!"

The bin and backpack drop to the floor as the two boys race out the side door and around to the front counter where Ruby was just standing. They see her move around the side of the building. They didn't need a road map, actually. The whole Shack crowd has pushed its way to the back now.

"Come on," Ricky pulls Matt.

"Wait. There're my friends."

Ricky has moved to the other side of the building. "I know. Come on."

"Put it down, Jesse. Come on." Ruby moves in close to her ex. The rest of the crowd stands back. Miguel leans against the wall becoming part of the plaster itself. Jesse totters.

So does Miguel.

The clear glass spike juts from Jesse's dark hand. The clock ticks. Captain Hook is angry.

He turns toward Ruby. "You! You're the reason. I know about you two, you two-timin slu-"

Oomph! Miguel barrels into Jesse's left shoulder, knocking both boys and the glass spike to the ground.

"Get off, you big lug!" Jesse pushes Miguel's chest.

Miguel sits atop his friend, pinning his arms back. "You gotta cool it, bro. Don't be comin' at me if you don't mean it."

Jesse squirms, kicks, spits.

"Ain't gonna make no difference, man, I got you. Chill." Miguel turns toward the onlooking crowd. When he does, Jesse frees his right arm and knocks into Miguel's unguarded left jaw.

The boys tussle, dust flies, legs kick.

Matt stands back, not sure how to intervene, or even if he wants to. He thinks Miguel could kill Jesse if he wanted to. For this, he considers stepping in. He makes a move toward his friends, the tumble of dirt and legs. He is saved.

Bang!

The crowd quakes.

Bang!

Miguel and Jesse turn toward the sound. Billy Connors' arm aims skyward, his pistol extending from his stubby fingers. "That's it. Enough! Go home! Everyone! The Shack's closed."

It's then that Miguel spots Matt behind the old man, and to his left, Ricky, and Ricky's hand hanging there right next to his friend's, so close. Almost touching.

Most of the kids desert the grounds. It's almost 5. Tonight's graduation; most seniors left at least an hour ago. The rest decide now is a good time anyway to head home and get ready to cheer on their friends, brothers, sisters, cousins, neighbors. There are balloons to buy, flowers to choose, cards to sign. Tonight's a celebration. Another group has completed their education, is ready to move on, ready to step out into the world as college students, unskilled workers, wanderers, dreamers, procrastinators. The choice is theirs.

"Dang, that was nuts!" Ruby grabs onto Lexie.

"I know. They looked pretty wasted, too, don't ya think?"

"Yeah. I've never seen Jesse like that. I mean, Miguel, I've seen him sloshed. He's always stealin' beer from his dad and stuff, but I've never seen him like that."

"Yeah, he was totally drunk."

"Nah, I didn't mean that, I mean scared. Miguel was scared. Of Jesse."

"Well, I'd be scared, too, if someone was comin' at me with a sharp dagger," Lexie laughs. "Come on, ya goin home to get ready? We gotta be there by 7, before the parents and stuff start showin' up."

"Yeah, I'll head out in a minute. I kinda wanna check on Jesse." Ruby wipes her cheek.

"Rube, it's not your fault, you know."

"Yeah, well, maybe. I dunno, it's just lately, I'm so moody and all. I'm just stressed, I guess. It's OK. I just wanna talk to Jesse, make sure he's OK, ya know."

"Yeah, it's OK. You can get a ride?"

"Yeah. I'll get one from Nate."

"Sure. Right. Well, don't worry, Rube. It'll be OK. Anyway, I'm on edge, too. I think I'm gettin' my period. Maybe you are, too."

"Hmm, yeah, maybe that's it." Ruby steps in and hugs Lexie. "Thanks." She stops, pulls back. "Dang, look at me. I completely just forgot everything else that's gone on here today. You OK, Lex?"

Lexie smiles that wide toothy smile. "I'm OK, Ruby. I'm OK."

"Good. You're strong. I'm gonna check Jesse. Not so sure about his strength. I'll see ya later."

The girls hug once more. A single crow sits on the wire and caws. Lexie walks around the other side of the building.

"Wow. Crazy stuff." Ricky pushes the broom along the dirt, gingerly sweeping up the broken glass. Matt bends down with the dust pan, sets his Swirl to the side.

"Yeah. Jesse's been kinda whack lately. Him and Ruby split

up, and, well, he's not takin' it so well."

"Ya think?" Ricky laughs.

"Hey, you guys OK? Matt? You OK?" Lexie bounces over to Matt. She takes the dust pan from his hand and sets it down. "C'mere." She wraps her arms around his narrow waist, rests her head on his chest.

Matt looks over at Ricky who smiles, shrugs, "Ya gotta give in. She won't give up."

Matt returns the hug.

"Aw, come on, Matt West, you're gonna have to do better than that. Gimme a real hug. Give one, get one. Come on."

Matt leans forward, moves his hands around her back, criss-crossing them up to her shoulders. He squeezes.

"Better! Much!"

Matt laughs, pulls away. Lexie releases him.

"You know, those two let their emotions run them too much. They gotta get a handle on things."

"Yeah, well, it's been kind of a crazy week."

"Yeah, well, still. That Miguel, he's a live one, but Jesse. Wow, I didn't know he had that fire in him."

"They're guys, ya know. Guys get angry and they just kinda let it out. That's how it goes."

"Really? I dunno. My guy over here, tall, blond and adorable. He doesn't explode a fuse like that. He keeps his cool, talks it out. I don't think he's ever gotten himself into a mess or trouble like those two. Right, Ricky?"

"I guess. Maybe." Ricky continues moving the broom along the dirt, pulling himself further away from this conversation, knowing just how Momma Lexie likes to play these things.

"I'm just sayin', Matt, those boys are trouble for you. Miguel for sure. He's always gettin' into fights and stuff. Why do you hang out with him, anyway. He doesn't really seem your type?"

"My type? You mean I can't have guy friends. Just friends.

Who are guys?" Matt takes a step away.

"No, that's not what I meant. I meant, well, you're just hanging out with boys. A boy can't teach you how to be a man, Matt."

"We're all boys, here. And you're just a girl. And those two are my best friends, and they haven't deserted me, and I'm not about to desert them just because, because," he looks over at Ricky who's still sweeping. "Just because. You don't know them, Lexie. Jesse has a heart o' pure gold. He'd do anything for me. He's like my brother. Both of 'em. Miguel, too. OK, so he's macho, Mr. Big Man, but he's a good guy. He just gets caught up in stuff sometimes. It's not like he goes lookin' for trouble, trouble finds him. I mean, when he buys new jeans, there's trouble in his pocket."

Lexie laughs, looks over Matt's shoulder. "Well, here comes trouble now."

Miguel stumbles along the fence line. The fight's sobering effect seems to have worn off. "Where's Szhesse? Ya see 'im? Yo, Mattyman, where's Szhesse."

Matt hurries over to his pal before he tumbles down into the pile of glass Ricky's just swept up.

"I gotta go. See ya all later." Lexie walks up to Matt, kisses his cheek. "I'm just learning how to be your friend, too, Matt. Be careful."

Ricky lifts the dustpan full of glass and hands Lexie the broom. "I'll walk you out. I wanna go check on Billy the Old Man Kidd anyway." He steals a quick glance at Matt, but for now Matt's attention belongs to his best friend.

Matt takes hold of Miguel's shoulders and guides him toward the fence. "Take a seat, Mig. You're a bit, uh, you need to sit. Have a seat, man."

Miguel laughs, slides down the fence and plops on the dirt. "Yeah, I'm a bit fwasted, man. Thasswhat I am. Shiiit." He grabs his head. "Damn, efrythin's jus spinnin' s'much."

Matt walks over toward the Shack wall to retrieve his Swirl then takes a seat next to his friend. It's the first time the two have been alone since yesterday, since before Ruby and her vomit of secrets. But yesterday feels like a mile away, ten years away from this moment.

It's quiet now at the Shack. Even the birds have flown off and moved further inside the Grove. Their chirping is silent.

"I guess I haffn't been the bes friend lately, huh?"

Matt stretches his legs out straight, bends forward to dust some dirt off his shoes. "You've been the best friend you know how, Mig. That's all. It's OK. I mean, I guess I coulda been a better friend, too, and maybe just told you guys, told you the truth. About me."

"Thin' we woulda reacted inny better?"

The two laugh. "Maybe not? But at least it would've come from me and not from someone's ex-girlfriend." Matt offers the juice to his pal. Miguel sips.

"Shit, firs' Zhesse and Rube, now you and, and, ah, damn, man, iss so weird. I dunno, bro. I mean, we still friends? I mean, can ya be friends. With guys?"

"Are you friends with girls?"

"What? Huh. I guess. I mean, da ugly ones." He laughs, takes another sip, starts returning to earth.

Matt kicks Miguel's leg. "Funny."

"Yeah, well, I mean, I guess. Yeah, I coul' be friends with girls," takes a sip, "if I wasn't such a dick."

"You're not a dick, Mig. You're just, just kinda, you know, you have this way that you see the world. It's kinda old fashioned, or just, like, well, you see it how a lot of people do. Straight. One way. But it's not. There's a lot of twists and turns in the world. That's what makes the world interesting. You never know what's around the bend."

"Not in my house. Damn, if I came home with a guy, like ya know, like Ricky, my dad'd kill me. Shiiit, he'd knock me silly."

"I don't think so, Mig. Your dad loves you. He wants you to be happy. He's a good guy, your dad. Look at all the Manuelisms we've gained over the years."

"Hah! Yeah. He knows some stuff, I guess." He takes another sip, feeling more like himself now.

"Yeah, he does. And he's taught you some good stuff, too."

"Too bad I don't use it. Some friend." Miguel swirls the remaining orange liquid inside the paper cup.

"That ain't true. Don't you see, Mig. If it weren't for you, I might not know who I am. If it weren't for you getting me to play baseball - Hah, kinda funny now, cuz I think you were tryin' to help me be more of a guy, well, your kinda guy, play ball, be macho. Hah, look where that led me." Matt smiles.

Miguel hands the cup to his friend, bends his head and kicks at the dry dusty dirt with the hard heal of his left shoe.

Matt takes the drink. "Mig, in some twisted way you led me to myself, to the courage that I needed to find myself. That's a friend, Mig. You're my friend. When I think about it, there's not a time I didn't believe you had my back, and I hope you've known I had yours. I might not be the guy to back you in a brawl, but I am the guy to back you in life." Matt takes another final sip from the Swirl, wrapping his lips around the plastic straw, gulping down the orange liquid, an elixir of courage, one he hopes will infuse him with the mettle necessary to finish this conversation.

"I guess, maybe," Miguel looks up for the first time in the last ten minutes. He finds his friend's eyes, those unsure circles of green or hazel or brown, the color waivers depending on the lighting, depending on the owner's mood. Right now, they're a steady pool of hazel. He looks away, unable to hold his friend's gaze. "Damn, man, I don't know. It's weird. You're my friend,

I'd do anythin' for you. Anything. Ya know that, but man, this is, I dunno, this is not what I expected."

Of course, Miguel is lying.

This is exactly what he'd expected. He's always had a feeling, always had some inkling deep down inside that there was something more to this friend, something different. He put it off to the awkwardness of the lanky boy, but down inside he knew, felt so sure of something, something that was so unlike him. Another lie; it wasn't so different. Not really. For the first time, Miguel understood something.

We are all on that search, on a path to find comfort, love, familiarity. Call it what you want, paint it any color, French Gray, Mexican Pink, fly a rainbow flag on your front porch or slap a Semper Fi sticker on your Landrover. We all come into this world searching for what makes us whole. We arrive believing we are incomplete. We are not. We simply lack the insight, the conviction, the faith in knowing that who we are is all there is, that what we add to it in this life either accentuates the best in us or brings us down to a level of dirt so low you can't scrape it from the bumper of a rusty red Camaro.

Then Miguel sobers, understands something more. He rises, lifts a small piece of glass and shoots it straight up to the sky. "I'm the hawk, you're the sparrow." He extends his hand to Matt.

Upright, Matt rolls the cool cup along his right cheek. "What? What are you talkin' about?"

"You're the sparrow, the tiny bird that darts around peckin' at the bigger birds, that stays with its own kind. Safety in numbers, or somethin'. And, I'm the hawk, the predator. I could eat little birds like you, but I don't. Predator or protector. I have to choose. Am I gonna kill ev'ry other creature that tries to hurt you, that tries to steal my friend's girl, that thinks he's better than me cuz he drives a car and I drain its greasy oil?"

"Nate, ya mean, huh?"

"Yeah. Well, he's just one." Miguel looks again into the hazel eyes of this quiet sparrow, this little bird that trusts so easily yet fears so much. "There's gonna be other Nate Gibbons. You know that, right? I mean, if you're really gonna own this, if you're gonna be you, ya know, the real you, and like have a, a boy, uh, boyfrien' an' all," Miguel shuts his eyes, inhales deeply, shakes his head, runs his hands around the soft black fuzz that shields the many conflicts within. "Damn, ese, you're really gonna do this? This is you, right? You're sure." The last part, less of a question, more of an offering.

"Yeah, this is me, Mig." Matt can't help but feel the sting of this opt out statement. "It's not a choice, man, this is who I am. It's what I feel. If I'm honest with myself, it's who I've always been." He tries to make eye contact with this friend whose head hides beneath folded arms of uncertainty. "You've known, huh, Mig. You've always known."

Matt chuckles at this, smiles then drains the last drop of juice, smashes the empty cup with his right foot, picks up the crumpled mass and hurls it into the Grove. The incoming object startles a flock of blackbirds whose reflexed departure fills the air with a shutter of flapping wings, the staccato rat-a-tat-tat of machine gun fire.

In this one moment, the two boys share a common experience, staring up at the retreat, two pairs of disparate eyes looking upon the same scene, seeing the same thing but not. For one, it's simply nature's protective impulse that propels the birds as one unit up and out of possible danger. It's natural. It's as things should be. Will be. Must be. For the other, there is nothing natural about the disbursement at all; it's a forced out. They have no choice but to scatter. To flee. To escape. Staying could mean death. They fly then, not toward freedom but away from danger. Victims of a cruel food chain.

Pawn's in life's murky life cycle. They are the prey of the predator. Their wings are small, so they travel as a group. Safety in numbers.

Miguel understands. He has no choice but to choose to stay, to remain the friend who was and will always be part of this flock. He owns the hawk inside himself. He is freed.

"Yeah. I knew."

"I figured. So, uh, so I guess it's kinda weird for you then. I mean, me and Ricky. Well, if there is a me and Ricky." Matt pauses as the blackbirds quietly return to the wire that stretches across the Grove. They settle along the line, sitting, observing. His eyes well, he draws in a deep breath, closes them and tries to absorb the tears so dogged in their escape. As much a relief as they are an uncertainty. "We've been good friends, though, huh, Mig. We've had good times."

Miguel looks up, squints against the late afternoon sun, pulls his hands from his pockets and threads his fingers, pushes his arms up and out, cracks them then rests them upon the crown of his head and looks back at his friend. He shakes his head, grits his teeth. "Dontcha know amigo? *Amigos de por vida. Para toda la vida. Hermanos. Eres mi hermano.*" Then the hawk, the macho fiery one with the wild left foot steps forward, wraps his arms around the sparrow, pulls him toward his chest and offers, "*Te amo, amigo. You're my brother, man, I love ya.*"

The two make their way around to the front of the Shack. It is a ghost town. The crowd long gone, their presence evidenced by the scatterings of chips and fries. Matt peers inside. He sees Ricky wiping down machines but is unable to make out Old Man Connors. Ricky looks up, waits for a sign, puts down his cloth and walks to the side door.

Matt meets him there. "Guess I'm not making much of an

impression on my first shift."

"Don't worry. The old man's gone to the store, muttered something about making signs that we're closed for the night. He left me to close up with you, but don't worry, I'm almost done."

"Thanks. Yeah, I guess it kinda got outta control there, huh?"

"Yeah. It happens."

"He's shot off that pistol before?"

"Once. Twice, maybe. Can't remember. But, yeah, he's had to growl people out before. He says it comes with ownin' a teen joint." The two laugh at this.

"Speakin' of joints, ya seen Jesse?"

"Hmmph. Nah. Well, maybe he was in the bathroom puking awhile ago, but he's not in there now. I know. I just cleaned it."

"Sorry about that."

"You're not his mom. Just part of the job, buddy. You too'll be moppin' up puke before ya know it."

"Great." Matt looks over to Miguel. "So, I guess we need ta find him. Maybe he went into the Grove."

"Ya think? We're not supposed to."

"Yeah, well, we're not *supposed* to do a lot of things, are we?"

Ricky smiles at Matt's gentle flirt. "Finally."

The two walk out front and find Miguel head down on a greasy table top.

"Hey, Mig, not feelin' so good?"

"Ughhh," he moans.

Ricky walks back inside.

"I can't find Jesse. Think maybe he wandered into the Grove? I'm kinda worried; he's not in the best shape and all. We should probably go look for him."

Ricky returns. "Here, Miguel, drink this." He hands the ailing boy a cup of clear bubbly soda. "Sprite. It'll calm your stomach and head some."

Miguel sits up, takes the drink, looks up at Ricky then over to Matt.

"I didn't poison it, if that's what you're thinking?"

"I wasn't," Miguel responds. "But now that you mention it, uh, maybe, here, you go first."

Matt laughs. Miguel, too.

"You'll be OK, drink it."

Miguel takes a few sips, puts the cup down and the three boys make their way through the bent wire and head into the Grove in search of the cuckolded and slightly stoned Jesse Waters.

After less than five minutes inside, the boys locate Jesse. He's slumped over underneath an orange tree. A lit joint teeters between his fingers.

"Damn, ese, what the fuck?!" Miguel swats the small stick from his hand. "You're gonna burn yourself up, man. Yo, Jess, wake up!"

Jesse shudders, squints, open his eyes. "Huh?"

"Dang, Jess, come on. Get up." Matt extends his hand. "Let's go. You needa go home and clean up."

Miguel and Matt take the underside of the queasy boy's arms and hoist him upright.

"Awright, man, I'm up. Leave me." Jesse pushes the two away.

"Come on, Jess. What're ya doin in here, anyway?"

"Jus needed a place to think, and –"

"Smoke?"

"And, get my head together. That's all. Damn. Give a fella some room to grieve. Stupid girlfriends. Stupid me. Stupid,

stupid, stupid."

The boys meander back towards the Shack. The sun is setting; the way out is a maze of trees and paths.

"Yeah, damn straight, fuckin' Nate Gibbons. Big lughead. Let's just find 'im and beat the shit outta 'im."

"Whoa, Mig, settle," Matt turns from one friend to the other. He looks at Ricky.

"Yeah, come on. Let's go back to the Shack. I can whip up some tacos. That'll help ya feel better. Get some food in ya."

"Stop, stop. Stop!" Jesse pounds a narrow tree trunk, kicks its base. He stares out at the three boys, at his two best friends and this third, this stranger. He turns toward Miguel. "That's not it. Nate's not it! He ain't the villain, ain't our villain. Don't ya see, Mig, don't ya see? We're our own villains. We're our own enemies. You and your passion to be the best soccer player on the planet but your fear to really be it, to be so good that you need to leave your family, leave them and live somewhere far away while they stay here in this shithole of a town workin' and sweatin', which is what they do everyday for you so you can have that dream. And you're too afraid to own it, to go for it. That's your villain." He inhales, snorts out his breath like a dragon, turns to Matt.

"And, Matt, you, you're so afraid of life, so afraid that you can't even trust your best friends to tell us who you really are. You think we give a damn that you like guys. Shit, man, at this point, maybe I'm gay too. Maybe girls ain't for me. How the hell am I supposed to know? I'm only 17. I'm a kid. You're a kid. We're just kids. Shit. Nate ain't no God Damn villain."

Jesse grabs a smooth leaf hanging at the end of a low branch. He begins tearing it into tiny pieces, letting them cascade slowly toward the dusty ground. "I bet you're wonderin' about me then, huh? Yeah, I got a villain, his name is Jesse Wayne Waters. He's afraid to put himself out there, to draw anything more than puppy dogs and unicorns for his little sister. He's afraid people will think he's got no talent, so he doesn't even try. Art school? Shit. I ain't goin' to art school cuz I'm too scared of how good everyone else is.

"Those are our villains. Us. Not Nate. Not Ru," he gasps. "Not Ruby, not God Damn little beautiful Ruby Marie Newton. Gawwdd! We don't need to create no God Damn villains and enemies because we've done a pretty good job o' moldin' them inside o' the cowardly shells of ourselves." Jesse stops, looks up at the boys. Their faces are soft, falling, eyes downcast. They know he's right.

"Jess, I'm, I'm sorry," Matt tries to put into words an apology, but he's still not sure why he should apologize. For what, for owning up to who he is, for believing these two friends of his would turn him away when they found out because all their lives all they've ever talked about is meetin' girls, kissin' girls, gettin' girls? He has no more words. He sees something.

His eyes betray his surprise. Jesse turns in the same direction. He sees it. So does Ricky. So does Miguel.

"Shit, no way, shit, man. Are you kiddin me?!" Miguel races toward Nate and Ruby. "No fuckin' way. Pig! Pig!"

Nate, hearing Miguel before he sees him, has to yank up his pants before he can turn around. Ruby, leaning up against the tree, did see Miguel before she heard him, but she was hoping none of them saw her.

They did. Jesse did. He's paralyzed. He doesn't know what to say, cannot move.

Miguel, still feeling the effects of his party, charges toward Nate. "You, ass!" The lithe soccer star with the wild left foot lunges toward Nate; he jumps on top of the mammoth running back. The two boys are now a blur of clothing, legs and dirt. Sounds emit from the tumble on the floor of the Grove, but no one steps in to stop them.

Matt is shouting at them, screaming, turning toward Ruby, yelling at her, 'do something', turning to Jesse who stands frozen, 'make them stop', he is spinning, the world spins around him, the floor beneath him pulls away, and he is standing alone inside this vacuum of space, alone, just a boy, yelling, but there is no sound. There is smoke. He is choking. Someone grabs his arm. He turns. He sees Ricky. He cannot hear him.

"Matt! Come on! Matt! Fire!"

Matt looks out past Ricky and into the Grove from where they'd just come. Flames shoot out over the tree tops, smoke fans its way toward them.

The joint.

Ricky pulls Matt, Matt grabs Jesse. They yell at Ruby. "Come on!" They yell at the scuffling mass on the ground. "Miguel! Come on! Fire! Nate! Fire!"

They run, out toward the exit, away from the flames and smoke. They run, just the three of them.

The fire is alive. It is a thirsty dragon consuming the juicy orange trees in this nightmarish fairy tale. Yet this is no fairy tale. This is real. Jesse, Matt, and Ricky sit along the edge of the dirt driveway entrance to the Shack, nestled deep near the side fence, making room for the wailing fire engines that storm inside the Grove. Knights in Shining Armor.

The boys wait, pray, hope. *When will they come out? Where are they?* Jesse can't take it.

"Oh, god!" he cries. "It's my fault. I killed my best friend! My Ru-, I can't , I-" he gasps for air between sobs. Matt and Ricky flank him, place a comforting arm around this boy who only moments earlier was full of fire himself, scolding them for the errors of their thinking.

"It's gonna be OK, Jess. I feel it." Matt's arm rests across his friend, but he lies. He feels nothing. He stares inside the Grove, feels the heat as it washes in waves over him, prays, hopes. He does not know if it will be OK, but he must believe it.

The firemen have taken their shears and cut open the fence, widening it so much that an entire truck could simply roll right through, but it doesn't. It can't. The trees stand guard, leaving paths only broad enough for a small Chevy, not a wide city fire truck.

Old Man Connors, having returned with poster boards for signs, those now unnecessary signs that would announce *We're Closed*, stands back from the shack, back from the heat, silent within the resurging blaze of memories that sizzle inside his head like a million ants massaging his brain. He cannot move. He will not race in this time, will not be the hero, will choose to sit on the sidelines while the men shielded in fire-retardant attire take the credit – or the fault – for who is saved or not.

Within the smoky haze, Matt sees something, someone coming out through the shear-cut fence. It is a man. No. It is a boy, a boy carrying a boy. It is Miguel and Nate. Matt leaps up.

"Where ya goin?!" Jesse calls after him. Then he sees, too. Jesse leaps up. And Ricky. The boys run toward the exiting duo.

A fireman steps into their path. "Hold on, kids. You can't go in there. You gotta stay clear."

"No!" Matt yells at the burly man. "That's my friend." He points at the soot-faced youths. "Move!"

The man turns, and the three race passed him.

"Mig! Miguel! You OK?"

Nate looks up at Matt. He lays the unconscious boy down on the dirt floor. His clothes are charred and covered in ash. Nate hacks and wheezes. A team of medics races over.

"Move to the side, kids. Let's get this boy to the ambulance. You, too," one motions to Nate. "Come on. You can walk."

Miguel cannot. He does not know that three macho firemen are lifting him, carrying him, placing him gently onto the white polyester sheets of a gurney and wheeling him quickly (gently) into the ambulance. He does not know that his favorite Chucks have melted, that the left one has nearly, completely burned off his foot. But not entirely. Its rubber sole forms a second skin as it cools and melds into one with the sole of this boy's wild left foot.

Matt stares. Jesse cries out, "Rubeee! Rubee!" Quieter, "Where is Ruby?"

The Grove sizzles and cracks.

AFTER

Not all birds migrate The decision to temporarily leave one's birth area depends on the availability of food, the change in weather, the increase in predators, or the need to find a mate. This could mean a short migrate to a higher or lower elevation or a long-distance migrate for warmer weather. However, for the long-distant migrants, the move can take weeks, and at times can even be deadly.

13

FINALLY, ONE BOY TAKES FLIGHT

There is no pot of gold at the end of the rainbow because there is no end to the rainbow. Life bends and twists in an arc of varying colors, blending its purples and pinks and blues into a vast spectrum. Sometimes we climb the bow skyward; sometimes we rest at the top, pausing to take in the scenery and reflect upon our journey; and sometimes we race downward, not at rollercoaster speed but at the gentle glide of a waterpark slide, curving, dipping, spilling into the next level. We move in slow motion. We are not deposited at the bottom in a field of green, dipping our toes inside a pool of gold. The gold itself threads through the color bands; it is our task to find it, see it, appreciate it. It is our choice.

Matt considers the five blackbirds that sit above his head along the stretch of telephone line that swings like a ghost jump rope above the potholes of Eighth Street. Silver moonlight reflecting off their dark wings, they sleep, holding a cautious guard over neighboring nests. Lee is home, and he must walk in the door and find her. He must turn to her, turn her to him and tell her the truth. *The truth.* He laughs.

The truth is like a key, it can lock you in or set you free. Matt's not sure which way this key will turn. Will it open a door to a world full of possibilities, or will it lock the door behind him, trapping him within the walls of fear and self-doubt?

For Matt, there is no other choice, he must turn the key and let fate decide. What is he really afraid of anyway? Why does he fear the truth? It's not really a matter of waiting for others to accept him, he knows this.

Matt West must accept himself.

The only reason he can think of, the only reason he thinks he is unacceptable is because someone got it into his head that it's just not OK. All Matt needs to do is take that thought and remove it. Pick it up like a piece of useless garbage and discard it. All Matt really needs to do is look inside the mirror at a boy who means no harm, at a boy who is kind, at a boy who like all other boys wants only to be loved, wants only to love. Boys do want that. Matt wants that.

He turns his key in the back door. But his news will have to wait. Lee sits at the kitchen table with Jesse.

It has been a long night at the hospital. Francesca and Manuel sit in a nook of the waiting room, the third floor waiting room down the hall from the ICU. Their son lies behind the swinging doors with the blood red sign that barks, *Hospital Personnel Beyond This Point Only*. Tubes enter and leave his body, machines blink and beep, white-coated attendants adjust, monitor, record. They come and go. Miguel remains. He is silent. For once. He is not yelling, joking, teasing. He lies still on the plastic sheets, nearly naked but for a narrow white cloth atop his midsection. His eyes are closed. He is drugged in order to keep him still, in an effort to let his body heal. The machines breathe for him. The doctor tells Francesca and Manuel that they must wait, that his vital signs are low, that they should go home and get some rest, they have their number, they will call if there is a change.

The couple will not go home, so they sit in the small nook at the far right corner of the bright and somber third floor waiting room. Karen Gibbons and her parents sit just feet away. Mrs. Gibbons blots her eyes with a wadded up tissue. Karen rests her head upon her father's broad shoulders. They do not speak to the Alma de Ramóns. They do not even know they are seated in the nook. They live in the grand homes on the other side, across the tracks, away from the Numbers. They do not recognize Francesca who cleans their neighbor's home every Tuesday morning. She is invisible.

Throughout the evening, friends and family come and go. The waste basket in the corner gradually fills with wadded up white tissues, crumpled candy wrappers, chewed up gum, brown-stained coffee cups. A muted loop of symphonic Beatles' tunes plays repeatedly. No one hums along. No one hears these sounds. They are lost inside their own.

"Mom?" Matt enters the kitchen, slides his key back in his pocket. His mother and friend sit at the table sharing a cup of tea. This is not normal, but tonight has been anything but normal. Something else is different.

Lee's hand rests on Jesse's arm. Her eyes are puffy. She sniffles. "Matt, how's Miguel? Any change? His parents? Francesca, how is she?"

He still stands by the back door. He looks at Jesse, but Jesse's head hangs. He rocks his tea mug between his palms.

Jesse doesn't know yet. Matt's sure of this. He inhales, walks toward his mother, and bends to kiss her cheek. She reaches up to hold his. Her warm hand rests gently upon his soft skin. He closes his eyes. He is 7. He is a small boy. His mother is going to bake cookies. He will come home later, hungry from his bike ride, filled with stories about his travels through the Numbers. He and Jesse and Miguel will sit down and Lee will dote on them, ruffle their heads and laugh as the boys indulge in the warm, gooey chocolate chip wonders fresh from the oven. Life is good. Life is simple.

"It's gonna be OK, Matt. It will. Tea?"

Matt opens his eyes, shakes his head, sits down across from his friend, his mother. Lee's hand now rests on Matt's arm.

Jesse looks up, looks at Matt. "What about Ruby? Did you see her? I went by her house, but the lights were out. No one answered. They must be at the hospital with her. I couldn't go. I had to go home. I threw up. I tried calling the hospital but no one could help me. They said I needed to come in with my parents. I couldn't, didn't want to wake them.

"I feel sick."

"Yeah. It's been a long day." Matt looks over at his mom. Tears roll down his pale cheeks. He can no longer hold inside the day. The moments, each one, the library, the Shack, the gunshot, the smoke, Ricky, Miguel, all of it tumbles inside him, but he is frozen. He cannot move, and the tears pour down, dripping onto his shirt, forming dark stains, his nose drips, his eyes leak, he feels like he is simply disintegrating, falling apart. He cannot speak. He gasps, blinks at the pools of salty water that form inside his eyes, waiting to spill out and follow the trail down his cheeks.

"What is it, son?" Lee's hand grips his arm tighter. "Tell me." She looks at Jesse. "It's OK, Matt, tell us. What?"

Matt raises his palms to his eyes and presses against the sockets, trying to push back the tears, push away the pain. He wraps his hands behind his head and presses it down onto the cool table top. "I can't."

"What, Matt? I can't hear you?"

"I can't," he repeats. He sits up, places his hands palms down on the hard surface. "I can't do it."

"Do what?"

Jesse looks at him. "You can, Matt. You can."

But Jesse doesn't know what Matt's talking about. Jesse thinks he knows, but he doesn't, and Matt can't do it, can't say it, can't tell them, tell him.

For a moment, the room is silent but for the quiet ticking of a plastic wall clock and the sound of air sitting inside a chamber, locked in. It's like a pressure cooker. The air has weight, and it sits on Matt's head, his shoulders, and pushes inside his heart. He will explode. He has to relieve it, and so he does. Rips off the band-aid quickly so he doesn't feel the pain.

"She's dead."

The pressure pushes down harder.

"Wh-what?" Lee looks at Jesse, at Matt. "Who? Who's dead, Matt?"

Jesse knows. He doesn't cry. He is raw inside. He knows. He knew all night. He knew the moment Nate carried Miguel out of the Grove. The moment the ambulance sped away, kicking up dust, carrying his best friend. He knew.

"Ruby."

Matt's hands now rest alongside his cheek, palm to palm, he pushes his fingers against his nose and sets his closed hands over his mouth. The pressure eases, and the tears flow again.

"I'm sorry, Jess."

Lee looks at the boy, the boy who she shares a lifetime with, a secret, one she's kept from her son all these years, all his life. To Lee, Jesse is her other son, and she feels the same need to comfort him, the same duty to shield him from harm. But she can do nothing to ease this pain. So she sits at this kitchen table as the evening darkens, so unlike the bright mornings where she sat in the same room, at the same seat and stared across the table just like this at her father, her mother, and prayed for that hope, prayed that things would change, would get better.

They have, and they have not.

"She was pregnant."

"What?"

"Pregnant. She told me this morning, just before math, before the final. She pulled me over in the hall and told me, said she hadn't had her period this month and so she was going to go after school and get one of those kits, a stick or something that you pee on then she'd know for sure."

"Shit," Matt's tears stop falling. "Pregnant? Really? But she wasn't sure?"

"Nah." Jesse pushes out a short laugh. "Maybe she was. Maybe she wasn't'. That didn't stop her from fu-" he pauses, looks over at Lee. "That didn't stop her, though, did it." He looks at Matt.

Matt remembers the Grove. Nate. Miguel and Nate and that blur of clothing, of legs, arms, the sounds, the oomphing and cracking. "So, she probably wasn't, Jess. I mean, well, it seems like maybe she wasn't."

"Doesn't really matter now. She's gone."

A man in a white coat steps into the waiting room on the third floor. "Mr. Gibbons?" he calls out. "Gibbons family?"

The three visitors stand, walk over to the doctor. He speaks in hushed tones. Manuel watches. Francesca sleeps at his shoulder. Mrs. Gibbons hugs her husband, reaches for her daughter's hand. The girl smiles. The doctor escorts the three through the swinging doors with the blood red sign.

Manuel sighs. Francesca stirs. He takes his wide palm and pats her head. "Shh, *no pasa nada, cariño.* Shh."

Downstairs in the first floor emergency room, back in the corner, behind a white curtain, a woman sobs in the arms of her husband as their family stands before the draped white cotton fabric that forms a delicate landscape in the shape of their young daughter. Two small boys hold hands. They look up at their parents. One boy reaches to touch the covered toe of his sister. A tear rolls down his cheek.

Lee starts the rattily engine of the small brown compact, and the three take a short ride up town through the midnight moonlit streets of the Numbers.

She pulls into the concrete structure and finds a spot near the emergency entrance. The trio walk silently through the automatic doors, passed the drawn white curtains and into the narrow hallway of elevators.

Matt presses the up arrow.

Jesse moves to the far right corner of the elevator box, leaning against the cold metal rail, staring into the space that hangs between the three passengers. His mind weighs heavy. Ruby is but one fragment of this hefty pie. There's the thing he talked about with Lee earlier. That thing they were discussing before Matt came home, before Matt told him about Ruby. There was that. And there was Ruby. Miguel.

And then there's the thing about Matt.

He stares at the capacity sign. *Not to exceed 2,000 lbs.* He glances at his lean friend and frail mother. Still, he wonders if the voluminous mass bouncing about inside his head, inside his heart might alone surpass such poundage. He snickers. Lee turns around, turns back.

The 3 illuminates. *Ding.* They exit. Lee first.

It's nearly 2, the Gibbons are gone now, Karen staying by the bedside of her smoky-lunged brother, her parents home to sleep. Out of danger, they will return in the morning. They cannot stay a minute longer inside this building, its sterile lighting and long sad faces, its bitter coffee and closed white curtains. They have gone home to sleep under the soft Egyptian cotton covers of their air-conditioned home. The apple-pie baker's home that once sat behind the temporary *Waters & Sons* sign while a man and his boys lathered French Gray over the stucco walls, whistled, laughed and shared their dreams and hopes.

But that seems so long ago. It was. About ten years. Maybe eleven. Mr. Gibbons considers it's time for a new coat. The paint does not peel, however. Paint usually doesn't on the walls of a stucco home. It sticks. It holds on. But it does fade. Mrs. Gibbons suggests maybe they try a different color. Something livelier. Yellow maybe. Or a light blue. Mr. Gibbons says maybe. Perhaps. In the end, though, he will convince his wife that French Gray is the proper color for a grand home such as theirs.

She will not argue.

Jesse spots Miguel's mother resting in the waiting room nook. She opens an eye. Seeing the boys, she opens the other. She smiles but does not move. Observing the empty coffee cup, Jesse figures her husband has gone to the bathroom.

Lee takes a seat next to this mother. Francesca stares at Matt, remembers, looks over at this boy's mother, back at Matt, reaches out for the pale woman's slender hand, and the two women sit back. They do not speak.

Matt stands there. It's the first time he's seen the two mothers together. He is comforted by such tenderness. His mother smiles at him, and in that moment he knows he can tell her anything. He will. Not now. He will tell her everything after this is over. After Miguel is better. After Ruby's funeral. Maybe he will bring Ricky home after the funeral, and he will sit down in the kitchen, the three of them will sit down, and he will tell

Lee how much he loves her, what a great mom she is, how her belief in him, how all those college pennants hanging on his wall, how everything she's done has forged a strength inside him. He will tell her about his wings.

But not now.

Francesca points to the doors, waves her hand, tilts her head. *They should go in. The sign means nothing.*

The aluminum paneled doors swing shut.

When they find Miguel's room, the door is ajar. A dull light glows in the corner. Voices murmur. Jesse pushes open the door, and Manuel turns his head from his son.

"*Hola, amigos. Bueno, bueno.*" He sits at his son's bedside. His hand rests on the boy's arm. "You come, yes, he is waiting, my boy. He is good. Better."

Matt smiles at the elder Alma de Ramón's broken English. "*Bueno*" is all he can muster, his brain unable to gather anything more. Señora Castañeda would not be impressed.

Manuel stands, wipes his cheek against his shirt sleeve, presses his palms down the fronts of his trousers, extends his right hand. "Gracias, Matt, gracias."

Matt shakes the warm, moist hand, lets go.

"Zhesse, sí, tú también, gracias." Jesse doesn't understand.

"Why are you thanking us? Mr. Alma de Ramón, we didn't do anything. Sir, we should have done something. We –"

"You do everything, Zhesse. Sí. You come. You are friend. Amigo. Hermanos. Sí? Thank you." Manuel looks back at Miguel whose eyes open, whose mouth smiles.

"You can't argue with the man. He's kinda stubborn." His left leg is raised. A white sheet wraps around his thigh and calf. The foot sits in a sling uncovered. Its pus-filled bulbous and red wounds take in the soft air.

Matt forces a smile.

Jesse lets go of Manuel's hand and wraps his arms around him. "I'm so sorry, Sir. I'm so sorry."

Manuel hugs back then pushes himself from the boy. "No. We have our boy. He is OK." He looks at the foot, back at Jesse. "Now, he need to find new dream, but he's OK. Many dreams. Miguel can find new one. Miguel can find many. He's smart boy. You good friends. Miguel's OK."

Manuel looks back at his son, clasps the cross at his neck, touches his chest and chin in the sign, kisses the small piece of metal and quietly utters, "*El bosquecillo está en paz ahora*". He exits the room.

Miguel coughs. Again. He's having a fit. Matt hurries over to the cup and pitcher. Miguel puts up his hand. Matt waits. The coughing subsides. Miguel nods. Matt pours the water and hands over the yellow plastic cup.

"What was that your dad just said? What's at peace?" Matt asks.

"Nothin', he's just mumblin' stuff. You know Manuel."

"Yeah." Matt takes the cup back and sets it down. "So, you're gonna be OK then?" It comes out as a question. Matt meant it to be a statement.

Another cough. "Yeah, ese, I'm gonna be OK. Musta been saved by all the magic fruit." *Cough.* "Doc says the smoke'll clear from my lungs in a day or so. They had me on this breathing thingy." He points at a large white plastic machine with tubes extending out like a sea creature. "But now that I'm awake, they turned it off. Just the cough. And that."

He points at the blistering appendage hanging over his bed.

Jesse sits at the edge, next to his right foot, covered by the orange waffle blanket. "Shit, man. I never shoulda given you that –"

"Stop, man. I ain't gonna hear that. I'm not a baby. I may be stupid, but I make my own choices. So do you. So does Ruby. I made a stupid choice. So now I gotta live with that." He pauses, sips the water. "Can you?"

Jesse heaves a sigh, looks up at Matt who's resting against the breathing machine. "I guess I'll hafta. But, Mig, ya know Ruby. She, uh ... she, uh," he pauses. He can't find the words.

"I know, man. Shit, I know. That's what my dad was talkin' about there. The Grove. It's at peace. Ya know? The curse. The girl. Santa Niña." The boys are silent. "Musta been all that Swirl that saved us. Ruby never liked a Swirl. Remember? Anway, Karen came by. She told us the whole story. Shit, man, I can't remember what happened. I mean, I was diggin' into Nate, felt his fist hit my face," he points to his left eye. "Then it kinda all goes black, blank. I woke up here, and I didn't know what was goin' on. Between my mom, my dad, the nurse, I dunno, it was crazy. Then Karen came in. Told us about Nate, him carrying me, lookin' for Ruby, shoutin' for her, thinkin' she'd already run out. Escaped. Shit, Ruby. Jess, man I'm sorry."

"Yeah. Shit." Jesse runs his finger in and over the waffle ridges. "Guess we all got new dreams to write."

"Yeah." Miguel coughs. "See, damn Manuelisms get ya everytime." He looks up at Matt. "Guess you kinda already started, huh? Leave it to Mr. Smarty Pants to already be one step ahead. You know what you want, and we just get in your way. Well, I do. Me and my stupid macho ideas." He stops again to wait for the coughing to subside.

Matt seizes this interruption. "You're just bein' who you are, Mig. You can only believe in what you know. I get it. I mean, it's all a new world for me, too." He stops, swallows, looks over at Jesse, back to Miguel. "But it is *me*."

"I know," Miguel nods his head. "Don't think I'm dumpin' ya now, though. I'm gonna need some tender hearts to help me out. Look at this fuckin' thing." He points again at the foot.

"Look at it, hangin' there all blistery, laughin' at me, tellin' me this is what happens when you're wild, untamed, when you cling to some stupid narrow dream, when all you dream about is runnin' away. Shit. I ain't runnin' nowhere now."

Jesse releases a nervous laugh. Matt and Miguel hold brief eye contact. "So, you expect us to nurse you then?" Matt smiles.

"Nah, I'll see about Lucy Peña for that." Miguel smiles. "I just need you guys to be there. That's all. Three Musketeers, man. Right? We'll figure it out. It's gonna be different, but, well, it'll just be an adjustment. Right?" *Cough.* "Ain't that what you tell me when I screw up some math problem. You never say, 'dumb-dumb, that's wrong', you just erase my numbers and say, 'gotta make some adjustments here, Mig, it ain't quite right, just a little adjustment'. I mean, there ain't no math formula for this whole scene, here, so we're just gonna hafta make some adjustments."

Miguel extends a closed right fist in the air. First Jess then Matt. *Bump. Bump.*

"Three Musketeers." Jesse stands. "That reminds me. Hungry? Maybe they got some good stuff in the vending machines. I'll go check."

"With what? You broke, ese, remember?"

Jesse digs in his pocket. "Shit, I forgot."

"It's OK," Matt walks around the bed. "I got it. I'll just go raid my mom's purse. She's probably asleep anyway."

Matt makes his way back through the swinging aluminum doors. As expected, his mom sleeps. The Alma de Ramóns have left. Yet he is surprised to see his mother is not alone.

"He's OK?"

"Yeah. His foot's a mess. Soccer's done for him. But, yeah, he's gonna be OK. You?"

"I'm good."

Matt looks over at his mom. "Um, did you, I mean, was she …?"

"Don't worry. She's been asleep. I sat down, figured you were down there with Miguel, so I waited. Now you're back." The smile. The dimple. Matt falls inside. Again. Ricky smiles wider.

What is love anyway? Is the love between two boys that much different than between a boy and a girl? Does the heart of a gay boy beat any differently than that of a straight one? Matt doesn't think so. Matt is banking on this not being true.

Matt West feels his wings press against the hard blades that jut out of his fragile teenage back. He knows it's not confidence he lacks. He just needs time. Confidence threads through his veins masked inside something called humility. Matt West owns humility. It coats his being, clings to those wings. That's why his is less of a holding back, more of a not letting go.

The two are different.

Time sows the seeds of confidence, and faith fertilizes the tender roots so that these wings can flourish, sprout, burst forth into the light of day. There's a reason angel's wings extend behind them. They serve as a propeller toward the future.

This Matt understands. Faith is his family's American Dream. Faith isn't something you cling to in a crisis. Faith must be cultivated, considered with intention, tended to routinely with love and tenderness.

Lee West cultivated her faith every Saturday morning over a plate of bacon as her parents soothed their aching heads. Martin and Cecile Waters tended their faith while they relished their three giggling boys wrestling on a patch of patchy green grass out in the Numbers of Santa Niña. Francesca and Manuel Alma de Ramón sowed the seeds of their faith the day their parents returned to Mexico and left them behind to nurture their own American Dream.

These individuals never stopped, as children, with children of their own. And, perhaps unknowingly, each individual has sown a seed of faith within their offspring. Thus, with this new generation, this faith has matured, allowing a more fluid vine to solidly stretch within the framework of these three young men.

This is surely true for Matt. He pushes back the hospital waiting room blinds, observes the first glow of morning light, and rests his elbows on the dusty wooden sill as he watches the wind pass through the trees; the invisible hand wakes each leaf, gently touching one, then another. The trees bend and sway, their leaves dance and flap.

He considers his mom, how she stepped forward in a moment of uncertainty and made a decision to keep her baby. He thinks of Cecile and Martin Waters who moved on with a life without their youngest son, moved on into a life with those left behind and with the one about to join them. He thinks of Francesca and Manuel Alma de Ramón, how they were left behind, chose to stay behind because what they saw in the future here in America seemed greater than what they saw in their future back home in Mexico. They didn't know for sure, but they cast their faith in what they believed must be true because they needed to make a life for their boy. And they did.

They did everything they needed to for this boy with the wild left foot.

Matt looks back at his mother, now resting against the hard wall of this sterile room. His love expands as this woman, eyes closed, lies still, perhaps praying, dreaming, certainly hoping.

How, Matt wonders, how can you question love's intentions? Love itself is purity and clarity all at once. Love is devoid of judgment. It is a feeling not a thought, an act of giving and in that gift, a return. You love not to be loved but simply to love. You trust, find the courage to step forward, to spread your wings, the wings you always owned that lay hidden beneath your shallow skin, within a thin film of humility, and you find that wind, that invisible force that lifts you and allows you to soar, to glide high above it all, above all of the judgment, expectations, stares and awkward glances. And at once, you are no longer that static bird on a wire frozen with fear, unable to move, stuck in doing what you've always done because it is what you've always done, always known, only known.

You take flight from that wire, and once in flight, you feel that strength in the wind, its motherly arms strong and solid lifting you up, and you fly, higher and higher. You are lost in the ozone, but you are not. You have found yourself. You are the wind. You are the wings. You are everything and nothing. You are one. You are complete. You are home.

Matt turns toward Ricky, extends his hand, threads his fingers in this boy's fingers, swallows one last bit of fear, lets trickle down his dry throat one final line of judgment held within his being, steps closer, turns and places his lips on this boy's lips and feels in this moment how right this is, how perfect, how true, how honest.

And Ricky kisses this boy back.

ABOUT THE AUTHOR

Ellen Plotkin Mulholland grew up in San Bernardino, California. After earning her degree in Journalism and English Literature at the University of Southern California, she moved to London to write. In 2012, she published her first novel, This Girl Climbs Trees. The author is at work on two other tales, including a children's picture book that she plans to bribe her talented son and daughter to illustrate. She lives and teaches in Northern California where she loves to sit and watch the trees sway in the breeze and the birds take flight. You can connect with the author online:

facebook.com/authorellenmulholland
twitter.com/thisgirlclimbs
thisgirlclimbstrees.weebly.com

ABOUT THE COVER ILLUSTRATOR

Tim Sunderman is a graphic designer and illustrator who works in the San Francisco Bay Area. His work includes a number of book designs, magazine work, CD, and DVD covers, as well as commissioned paintings. He lives with his artist wife and two daughters in the great harmony of each day, and looks forward to each new creative project. In his work, he tries to avoid computers until there is no other recourse, doing all his own drawing, painting, photography, calligraphy, and even sculptures. But because there is no other recourse than to finish his projects onscreen, he manages in good spirits. To see more of Tim's work, please visit:

http://www.timsunderman.com
For inquiries or just to say "hi", his email is:
info@timsunderman.com

LOGOS
PUBLISHING
HOUSE

More by this author from
Logos Publishing House

New teenager Eliza Mills ponders life's bigger questions as she sits atop her favorite tree. Once that tree falls to the evils of disease, Eliza wonders how a girl like her can grow roots when the soil of life is so crumbly.

Journey with Eliza as she seeks to understand life, death and boys.

"...a semi-autobiographical narrative with literary leanings." – *Publisher's Weekly*

Second edition reformatted and available direct from the publisher at www.logospublishinghouse.com or from wherever paperbacks are sold.